THE RACE OF LIFE

THE RACE OF LIFE

GUY BOOTHBY

A GUY BOOTHBY BOOK

A GUY BOOTHBY BOOK

Published by Wildside Press LLC.
www.wildsidebooks.com

CHAPTER I

"A BOY'S WILL IS THE WIND'S WILL."

If any man had told me a year ago that I should start out to write a book, I give you my word I should not have believed him. It would have been the very last job I should have thought of undertaking. Somehow I've never been much of a fist with the pen. The branding iron and stockwhip have always been more in my line, and the saddle a much more familiar seat than the author's chair. However, fate is always at hand to arrange matters for us, whether we like it or not, and so it comes about that I find myself at this present moment seated at my table—pen in hand, with a small mountain of virgin foolscap in front of me, waiting to be covered with my sprawling penmanship. What the story will be like when I have finished it, and whether those who do me the honour of reading it will find it worthy of their consideration, is more than I can say. I have made up my mind to tell it, however, and that being so, we'll "chance it," as we say in the Bush. Should it not turn out to be to your taste, well, my advice to you is to put it down at once and turn your attention to the work of somebody else who has had greater experience in this line of business than your humble servant. Give me a three-year old as green as grass, and I'll sit him until the cows come home; let me have a long day's shearing, even when the wool is damp or there's grass seed in the fleece; a hut to be built, or a tank to be sunk, and it's all the same to me; but to sit down in cold blood and try to describe your past life, with all its good deeds (not very many of them in my case) and bad, successes and failures, hopes and fears, requires more cleverness, I'm afraid, than I possess. However, I'll imitate the old single-stick players in the West of England, and toss my hat on the stage as a sign that, no matter whether I'm successful or not, I intend doing my best, and I can't say more than that. Here goes then.

To begin with, I must tell you who I am, and whence I hail. First and foremost, my name is George Tregaskis—my father was also a George Tregaskis, as, I believe, was his father before him. The old dad used to say that we came of good Cornish stock, and I'm not quite sure that I did not once hear him tell somebody that there was a title in the family. But that did not interest me; for the reason, I suppose, that I was too young to understand the meaning of such things. My father was born in England, but my mother was Colonial, Ballarat being her native place. As for me, their only child, I first saw the light of day at a small station on the Murray River, which my father managed for a gentleman who lived in Melbourne, and whom I regarded as the greatest man in all the world, not even my own paternal parent excepted. Fortunately he did not trouble us much with visits, but when he did I trembled before him like a gum leaf in a storm. Even the fact that on one occasion he gave me half-a-crown on his departure could not altogether convince me that he was a creature of flesh and blood like my own father or the hands upon the run. I can see him now, tall, burly, and the possessor of an enormous beard that reached almost to his waist. His face was broad and red and his voice deep and sonorous as a bell. When he laughed he seemed to shake all over like a jelly; taken all round, he was a jovial, good-natured man, and proved a good friend to my mother and myself when my poor father was thrown from his horse and killed while out mustering in our back country. How well I remember that day! It seems to me as if I can even smell the hot earth, and hear the chirrup of the cicadas in the gum trees by the river bank. Then came the arrival of Dick Bennet, the overseer, with a grave face, and as nervous as a plain turkey when you're after him on foot. His horse was all in a lather and so played out that I doubt if he could have travelled another couple of miles.

"Georgie, boy," Dick began, as he got out of his saddle and threw his reins on the ground, "where's your mother? Hurry up and tell me, for I've got something to say to her."

"She's in the house," I answered, and asked him to put me up in the saddle. He paid no attention to me, however, but was making for the house door when my mother made her appearance on the verandah. Little chap though I was, I can well recall the look on her face as her eyes fell upon him. She became deadly pale, and for a moment neither of them spoke, but stood looking at each other for all the world as if they were struck dumb. My mother was the first to speak.

"What has happened?" she asked, and her voice seemed to come from deep down in her throat, while her hands were holding tight on to the rail before her as if to prevent herself from falling. "I can see there is something wrong, Mr. Bennet."

Dick turned half round and looked at me. I suppose he did not want me to overhear what he had to say. My mother bade him come inside, and they went into the house together. It was nearly ten minutes before he came out again, and, though I had to look more than once to make sure of it, there were big tears rolling down his cheeks. I could scarcely believe the evidence of my eyes, for Dick was not a man given to the display of emotion, and I had always been told that it was unworthy of a man to cry. I admired Dick from the bottom of my heart, and this unexpected weakness on his part came to me as somewhat of a shock. He left the verandah and came over to where I was standing by poor old Bronzewing, whose wide-spread nostrils and heaving flanks were good evidence as to the pace at which he had lately been compelled to travel.

"Georgie, my poor little laddie," he said, laying his hand upon my shoulder in a kindly way as he spoke, "run along into the house and find your mother. She'll be wanting you badly, if I'm not mistaken, poor soul. Try and cheer her up, there's a good boy, but don't talk about your father unless she begins it." And then, more to himself I fancy than to me, he added, "Poor little man, I wonder what will happen to you now that he's gone? You'll have to hoe your row for yourself, and that's a fact."

Having seen me depart, he slipped his rein over his arm and went off in the direction of his own quarters, Bronzewing trailing after him looking more like a worn-out working bullock than the smart animal that had left the station for the mustering camp three days before. I found my mother in her room, sitting beside her bed and looking straight before her as if she were turned to stone. Her eyes, in which there was no sign of a tear, were fixed upon a large photograph of my father hanging on the wall beside the window, and though I did not enter the room, I fear, any too quietly, she seemed quite unconscious of my presence.

"Mother," I began, "Dick said you wanted me." And then I added anxiously, "You don't feel ill, do you, mother?"

"No, my boy, I'm not ill," she answered. "No! not ill. Though, were it not for you, I could wish that I might die. Oh, God, why could You not have taken my life instead of his?" Then drawing me to her, she pressed me to her heart and kissed me again and again. Later she found relief in tears, and between her sobs I learnt all there was to know. My father was dead; his horse that morning had put his foot in a hole and had thrown his rider—breaking his neck and killing him upon the spot. Dick had immediately set off to acquaint my mother with the terrible tidings, with the result I have already described. The men who had accompanied him to the muster were now bringing the body into the head station, and it was necessary that preparations should be made to receive it. Never, if I live to be a hundred, shall I forget the dreariness, the utter and entire hopelessness of that day. Little boy though I was, and though I scarcely realised what my loss meant to me, I was deeply affected by the prevailing gloom. As for my mother, she entered upon her preparations and went about her housework like one in a dream. She and my father had been a devoted couple, and her loss was a wound that only that great healer Time could cure. Indeed, it has always been my firm belief that she never did really recover from the shock—at any rate, she was never again the same cheery, merry woman that she had once been. Poor mother, looking back on all I have gone through myself since then, I can sympathise with you from the bottom of my heart.

It was nearly nightfall when that melancholy little party made their appearance at the head station. Dick, with great foresight, had sent the ration cart out some miles to meet them, so that my mother was spared the pain of seeing the body of her husband brought in upon his horse. Rough and rude as he was, Dick was a thoughtful fellow, and I firmly believe he would have gone through fire and water to serve my mother, for whom he had a boundless admiration. Poor fellow, he died of thirst many years after when looking for new country out on the far western border of Queensland. God rest him, for he was a good fellow, and did his duty as far as he could see it, which is more than most of us do, though, to be sure, we make a very fair pretence of it. However, I haven't taken up my pen to moralise, so I'll get along with my story and leave my reader to draw his or her own conclusions from what I have to set down, good, bad, or indifferent as the case may be.

As I have said, it was towards evening when my father's body reached the homestead. My mother met it at the gate of the horse paddock and walked beside it up to the house, as she had so often done when what was now but poor, cold clay was vigorous, active flesh and blood. It had been her custom to meet him there on his return from inspecting the run, when he would dismount, and placing his arm around her waist, stroll back with her to the house, myself as often as not occupying his place in the saddle. On reaching his old home he was carried reverently to his own room and placed upon the bed there. Then, for the first time, my mother looked upon her dead husband's face. I stole in behind her and slipped my hand into hers. Together we stood and gazed at the pale, yet placid face of the man we had both loved so well. It was the first time I had met that grim sovereign, Death, and as yet I was unable to realise how great his power was. I could not understand that my father, the big, strong man, so fearless, so masterful, was gone from us beyond recall—that I should never hear his kindly voice again, or sit upon his knee while he told me tales of Bunyips and mysterious long-maned brumbies, who galloped across the moonlit plains, and of exploration journeys he had undertaken as a young man in the wilder and less known regions of the North and West. Even then I could not realise my loss. I asked my mother if he were asleep.

"Yes, dear," she answered, very softly, "he is asleep—asleep with God!" Then she led me from the room and put me to bed as quietly and composedly as she had always done. Her grief was too deep, too thorough, to find vent in the omission of even the most trivial details. I learnt afterwards that when she left me, after kissing me and bidding me "good-night," she returned to the death chamber and spent the night there, kneeling and praying beside the bed on which lay the body of the man she loved, and to whom she had always been so good and true a wife.

Realising how overwrought she was, Dick Bennet made all the necessary arrangements for the funeral, which took place two days later on a little knoll that over-looked the river, some two miles below the station house. There he was quietly laid to rest by the hands, who one and all mourned the loss they had sustained in him. Dick it was who read the service over him, and he, poor fellow, broke down in the middle of it. Then, after one final glance into the open grave, we, my mother and myself, took our places in the cart beside him and returned to the house that was destined to be our home for only a short time longer. As a matter of fact, a month later we had bade the old place "good-bye," and were installed in a small house in the neighbourhood of Melbourne, where I was immediately put to school. My father had all his life been a saving, thrifty man, so that, with what he left her, my mother was able not only to live in a fairly comfortable way, but to give me an education by which, I can see now, I should have profited a great deal more than I did. I am afraid, however, that I had not the gift of application, as the schoolmasters express it. I could play cricket and football; in fact, I was fond of all outdoor sports—but book-learning, Euclid, Algebra, Latin, and Greek, interested me not at all. Among my many other faults I unfortunately possessed that of an exceedingly hot temper, but from whom I inherited it I am quite unable to say. At the least provocation I was wont to fly into fits of ungovernable rage, during which I would listen to no reason, and be pacified by nothing short of obtaining my own way. It was in vain that my mother argued with me and strove to make me conquer myself; I would promise to try, but the next time I was upset I was as bad as ever. To punish me was useless, it only strengthened my determination not to give in. I have often thought since, on looking back on it all, that it must have been a sad and anxious period of my poor mother's life, for, after all, I was all she had left in the world to think of and to love. What would I not give now to be able to tell her that I was sorry for the many heartaches I must have caused her by my wilfulness and folly?

It was not until something like nine years after my father's death, and when I was a tall, lanky youth of close upon eighteen, that I was called upon to make up my mind as to what profession I should adopt. My mother would have preferred me to enter the Government service, but a Civil Service clerkship was far from being to my taste. The promotion was slow and the life monotonous to the last degree. My own fancy was divided between the bush and the sea, both of which choices my mother opposed with all the strength and firmness of which she was capable. In either case she knew that she would lose me, and the thought cut her to the heart. Eventually it was decided that for the time being, at least, I should enter the office of an excellent firm of stock and station agents to whom my father had been well—known. Should I later on determine to go into the Bush, the training I should have received there would prove of real value to me. This compromise I accepted, and accordingly the next two years found me gracing a stool in the firm's office in Collins Street, growing taller every day, and laying the flattering unction to my soul that since I could play a moderate game of billiards and had developed a taste for tobacco, I was every day becoming more and more a man of the world. All this time my mother looked on and waited to see what the end would be How many mothers have done the same! Alas, poor mothers, how little we understand you!

As I have said, I endured the agent's office for two years, and during that time learnt more than I was really conscious of. There was but small chance of advancement, however, and in addition to that I was heartily sick and tired of the monotony. Bills of lading, the rise and decline in the price of wool and fat stock, the cost of wire netting and of station stores, interested me only in so far as they suggested, and formed part and parcel of, the life of the Bush. For me there was a curious fascination in the very names of the stations for which my employers transacted business. The names of the districts and the rivers rang in my ears like so much music—Murrumbidgee, Deniliquin, Riverina, Warrego, Snowy River, Gundagai, and half a hundred others, all spoke of that mysterious land, the Bush, which was as unlike the Metropolis of the South as chalk is unlike cheese. At last, so great did my craving become, I could wait no longer. Being perfectly well aware that my mother would endeavour to dissuade me from adopting such a course, I resolved to act on my own initiative. Accordingly, I took the bull by the horns and sent in my letter of resignation, which, needless to say, was accepted. Almost wondering at my own audacity, I left the office that evening and went home to break the news to my mother. On that score I am prepared to admit that I felt a little nervous. I knew her well enough to feel sure that in the end she would surrender, but I dreaded the arguments and attempts at persuasion that would lead up to it. I found her in our little garden at the back of the house, sitting in her cane chair, darning a pair of my socks. Nearly fifty though she was, it struck me that she scarcely looked more than forty. Her hair, it was true, was streaked with grey, but this was more the handiwork of sorrow than of time. On hearing my step upon the path, she looked up and greeted me with a smile of welcome.

"Come and sit down, dear boy," she said, pushing a chair forward for me as she spoke. "You look tired and hot after your walk."

I took a chair beside her and sat down. For some time we talked on common-place subjects, while I stroked our old cat and tried to make up my mind to broach the matter that was uppermost in my mind. How to do it I did not quite know. She seemed so happy that it looked almost like a cowardly action to tell her what I knew only too well would cause her the keenest pain she had known since my father died. And yet there was nothing to be gained by beating about the bush or by putting off the evil moment. The news had to be told sooner or later, and I knew that it would be better in every way that she should hear it from my lips rather than from those of a stranger. That would only have the effect of increasing her pain.

"Mother," I blurted out at last, "I've got something to say to you which I am very much afraid you will not be pleased to hear. I have been thinking it over for a long time, and have at last made up my mind. Can you guess what I mean?"

The happy light at once died out of her eyes, as I knew only too well it would do.

"Yes, dear," she replied very slowly and deliberately, as if she were trying to force herself to be calm. "I think I can guess what you are going to say to me. I have seen it coming for some time past, though you may not have noticed it. George, dear. You are tired of your present employment and you want to go into the Bush. Is that not so?"

"It is," I said. "Mother, I can stand this drudgery no longer. It is worse than what I should imagine prison life must be. The same sort of work day after day without any change, the same dreary old ledgers and books, the never-ending acknowledgment of the 'receipt of your esteemed favour of such and such a date'—it is enough to drive any man mad who has a love for the open air, for the sunshine and the doing of man's work. Why, any girl could carry out my duties at the office, and probably better than I do. And what do I get for it? A paltry salary of thirty shillings a week, upon which I have to live and dress like a gentleman and fritter the best years of my life away on the top of a high stool with next to nothing to look forward to. No, mother, I have been convinced in my own mind for a long time that it cannot go on. I must go into the Bush, as my father did before me. Like him, I must work my way up the ladder, and you may be sure, if only for your sake, I shall do my best to succeed."

I paused, not knowing what else to say. For the moment I had forgotten to explain the important fact that I had sent in my resignation to the firm, and that they had accepted it. My mother shook her head sadly. She had seen so many start out filled with ambition and the desire to carry off the prize in the Race of Life—only to succumb before the contest was completed under the crushing weight of competition, which in the Bush is perhaps keener than anywhere else.

"Ah, my dear boy," she said, laying her hand upon my arm, "you are young, and, like most young folk, you imagine you have only to go forth armed with the strength of youth and ambition to carry all before you. Do you think you realise that if your life in this wonderful city is monotonous, it will be doubly so in the solitude of the Bush? Who knows that better than I, who have spent so many years of my life there? You see it through the rosy spectacles of romance. I am afraid, however, you will find it very different in reality. It is both a rough and a hard calling, and, unhappily, it as often as not unfits a man for any other, so that when he tires of it, he is apt to discover, as so many have done before him, that he must continue in his servitude, for the simple and sufficient reason that there is nothing else that he can do. At the best it is a wearing, soul-tiring profession, and even if a man is lucky the profit can only be a small one in these days."

"You are not very encouraging, mother," I remarked, with what was, I fear, but a forced laugh. "After all is said and done, it is a life fit for a man, and as such must surely be better than that of a miserable, ink-slinging, quill-driver, such as I have been for too long."

"Think it carefully over," was her reply; "do not act too hastily. Look at it from every point of view. Remember the old saying, 'A bird in hand is worth two in the bush.'"

"Yes," I answered, "that is so. At the same time, in my opinion, twenty clerks in town are not worth five good men in the Bush—which is another side of the question. No, dear, my mind is made up, and—" here I hesitated, and I noticed that she looked at me in a startled way. "Well, the long and the short of it is, my resignation has gone in."

"Oh, George, George," she said, "I am afraid you have been very ill-advised to take such a step. I only pray you may not live to regret it. Oh, my boy, you must not be angry with me, your mother, for you don't know what you are to me. I have only you to look to, only you to think of. When you leave me I shall be quite alone."

"But only for a time, mother," I answered. "I will work hard to make a home for you so that we may be together again. That will make me anxious to get on, if nothing else does. Who knows but that some day I may get the management of the old station where I was born and where you were so happy. Think of that!"

But she only shook her head; she was not to be comforted merely by speculation as to what the future might or might not bring forth. While I was dreaming my day—dreams, she was standing face to face with the reality.

"Then in a month's time you will be wanting to go off," she said after a long pause. "Have you any idea where you are going? The Bush is a big place, and since you have set your heart on going, I should like you to start well. My experience has taught me that so much depends on that. Could not the firm advise you on the matter? They know that you have served them well, and, doubtless, they would be willing to lend you a helping hand. Try them, dear lad."

But, as I have already said, I was an obstinate young beggar, and to use a strong expression, I was anxious to start my new life off my own bat. Besides, the managing partner had rather taken me to task on the matter of my resignation, and had prophesied that it would not be long before I should find reason to regret my "hasty and ill-considered determination," as he was pleased in his wisdom to term it. For this reason alone I did not feel disposed to solicit a favour at his hands, however trivial it might be. I argued that before very long I would be in a position to prove to them that the change I had made in my life was not for the worse, but for the better. Who knew but that the time might come when I should be enrolled upon their list of clients—a client before whom they would bow and scrape, as I had so often seen them do during the time I had been with them? That, I flattered myself, would be a triumph big enough to compensate one for any amount of privation and hard work. How sanguine I was of success you will be able to estimate for yourself. After all this time, I can look back on it with a smile of compassion for the poor deluded youth, who not only thought his own wisdom infinitely superior to that of anyone else, but was foolish enough to act upon it. How he fared you will be able to see for yourself, if you can find sufficient patience to read on.

After that memorable conversation on the lawn, when I had told her of my resolution, and of the action I had taken, my mother raised no further objection. Probably she realised that it would have been of no use if she did.

During the month's grace that was allowed me, I did not permit the grass to grow under my feet. I made enquiries in all directions, and brought to bear every influence I could think of. But like every new player of the game, I was too much inclined to be fastidious. I made the mistake of settling in my mind the sort of station I wanted, without pausing to reflect that it was within the bounds of possibility that that station might not want me. For this reason I threw aside more than one fair offer, which later on I should have been glad to jump at. But one has to learn by experience in the Bush as well as elsewhere, and I was only doing what many another deluded youngster had done before me.

Slowly the month wore on, and each day found me nearer the end of my clerkly service and closer to the new life which I had assured myself was to bring me both wealth and happiness. So far I had not succeeded in hearing of anything I liked, and was, in consequence, beginning to fear that to avoid being laughed at it would eventually be necessary for me to end by taking whatever I could get. The position was humiliating, but the moral was obvious.

At last the day arrived on which I was to bid farewell to the firm and my old associates. I am not going to pretend that I felt any great sorrow at severing my connection with them; it was unlikely under the circumstances that I should. Nevertheless it is scarcely possible to discard a life to which one has been long accustomed without some small feeling of regret. The grey-haired chief clerk hoped, but not too confidently, that I might be successful; the junior partner wished me good luck in his best society manner; while the senior, before whom we were all supposed to tremble, sincerely trusted I might never have occasion to reproach myself for the course of action I had thought fit to pursue. It did not strike any of them to ask me whither I was going. Had they done so, I should have found it difficult to tell them.

CHAPTER II

"A BIT OF A 'SCRAP.'"

On the Thursday following the termination of my connection with the company who had taught me all they could of business, I left the suburb in which my mother's house was situated and went into the city in the hope that I might meet someone who would be in a position to put me in the way of obtaining employment. By this time I had learned not only a useful, but at the same time a humiliating lesson. This was to the effect that it is not so easy to obtain a situation in the Bush as folk are apt to imagine, particularly when the seeker is, as in my case, young and entirely devoid of experience. However, I was determined to succeed one way or another, and the greater the difficulties at the beginning, the greater, I told myself, the honours would be when I had surmounted them. By reason of my business training, I was familiar with the haunts of squatters when they visited the city, and I tried each of these in turn. I was entirely unsuccessful, however, in obtaining an engagement. Driven into a corner, I was compelled to admit that I knew nothing of stock, save the question of sales in town and the travelling announcements in the newspapers. I had never shorn a sheep in my life, and should not have known how to set about it had one been placed in my hands. My humiliation was complete when I had to confess that my horsemanship was of the most rudimentary description possible, that I had never had a branding iron in my hand, and that I no more knew how to tell the age of a sheep than I did of Arabic. In point of fact, as one man, more candid perhaps than polite, found occasion to point out to me, it would take as long and as much trouble to show me the way to do a thing as it would for him to do it himself. Another looked me over with a supercilious sneer that made my blood boil, and, noticing my fashionably cut clothes, enquired if I had ever slept in the Stranger's Hut, and whether on this occasion I proposed taking my valet with me? The roar of laughter which followed this witticism drove me from the place in a whirlwind of rage. I had been insulted, I told myself, and, worse than all, I knew that I was powerless to retaliate. But though I was considerably cast down by these repeated rebuffs, I was in nowise dismayed. On the contrary, I was more determined than ever that I would succeed. It was late in the evening when I returned home, thoroughly tired out. Being skilled in the somewhat difficult art of managing me, my mother did not enquire what success I had met with; indeed, there would have been no need for her to do so. She had but to look at my face to see the result plainly written there. Next day I determined to have another try, so after breakfast I set off for the city once more, to begin the round of which I was heartily sick and tired. Fate, however, for some time was still against me, and though I tried in every direction, and questioned all sorts and conditions of people, no success rewarded me. Later in the day, however, my luck changed, and I changed to hear of a man, a drover, who was going into Queensland for a mob of cattle to bring down to a station on the Lower Darling. He was short of hands, so I was informed, and I determined to apply for the job. Having obtained his address, I set off in search of him, and eventually discovered him in a small public-house in the neighbourhood of Little Bourke Street.

It was not a nice part of the town, being situated in close proximity to the Chinese quarter. The house itself more than matched its surroundings, and the customers who frequented it were in excellent keeping with both. The front bar, when I entered it, was crowded to its utmost capacity, and I don't think I should be overstepping the mark if I were to say that more than half the men it contained were decidedly the worse for the liquor they had taken. The reek of the place was enough to choke one; bad cigars, the strongest blackstick tobacco, spirits and stale beer, onions from the kitchen at the end of the passage, and the intolerable odour of packed humanity of the roughest description, were all united in an endeavour to see what really could be achieved in the way of a really nauseating stench. I had never to my knowledge smelt anything like it before, and I sincerely trust I may never do so again.

Pushing my way up to the counter, I enquired for Mr. Septimus Dorkin, and was informed by the highly-painted damsel in attendance that I should probably find him in the private bar if I looked there. I departed in search of the room in question, and discovered it without much difficulty. Why it should have been dignified with its name I could not for the life of me understand. It was in no sense "private," seeing that anyone was at liberty to use it; while if the name had been given it on account of its selectness, as distinguished from the ordinary or common bar, it was an equally unhappy choice, inasmuch as its patrons were for the most part of the same class and, in nine cases out of ten, partook of the same refreshment.

I pushed open the door and entered the room. In comparison with its size, it was as well filled as that I had just left. In this case, however, the majority of its occupants were seated in faded velvet armchairs, secured to the walls, a precaution probably taken in order that they might not be used as weapons of offence and defence in times of stress, which, I learned later on, not infrequently occurred. Scattered about the room were a number of small tables, littered with glasses of all shapes and sizes, pewter pots, and upwards of half-a-dozen champagne bottles. The majority of the men were, to put it mildly, in a state of semi-inebriation, while some had crossed the borderland altogether and now lolled in their chairs, sleeping heavily and adding to the best of their ability to the general uproar that prevailed. The picture of one elderly individual remains in my memory to this day. He might have been from fifty to fifty-five years of age, and was the possessor of an extremely bald pate. His chin rested upon his breast, so that the top of his head, with its fringe of faded hair, looked directly at the company. Some wag, with an eye to a humorous effect, and sketched with burnt cork the features of a face—nose, eyes, and mouth—upon it, and the result, if lacking in taste, was exceedingly ludicrous. The artist had just finished his work when I entered, and was standing back to see the effect. I was informed that he had once been a famous scene painter, but was now a common bar-room loafer, who would do anything if he were well paid for it. He was, I believe, found drowned in the Yarra some few years later, poor wretch.

Turning to a tall, soldierly-looking man seated near the door, I enquired in an undertone if he could inform me where I should find Mr. Dorkin, the well-known drover, who I had been informed was staying in this house. As I have just said, the man from his appearance might have been taken for a soldier, a cavalry officer for preference, but when he spoke the illusion vanished like breath upon a razor blade. The change was almost bewildering.

"Dorky, my boy," he cried in a voice like that of our old friend Punch, "here's somebody wants to see Mr. Septimus Dorkin, Esq., Member of Parliament for Mud Flats. There you are, my boy, go and 'ave a look at 'im. He won't eat you, though he do somehow look as if he'd like to try a bite."

The man to whom he referred, and for whom I was searching, was standing before the fireplace, smoking an enormous cigar and puffing the smoke through his nose. He must have stood a couple of inches over six feet, was slimly built, particularly with regard to his legs, which were those of a man who had spent his life in the saddle. His face might have been good-looking in a rough fashion, had it not been for an enormous scar that reached from his right temple to the corner of his mouth—the result of a kick from his horse. His nose had also been broken at the bridge. His eyes were his best features, well shaped and at times by no means unkindly. He wore a large moustache and a short beard, dressed simply, and, unlike so many of his class when in town, wore no jewellery of any sort or description. A plain leather watch-chain was the only adornment he permitted himself. When I came to know him better I discovered him to be a past master of his profession, a shrewd man of business, a superb judge of stock, a fearless rider, and the most foulmouthed ruffian, I firmly believe, that it has ever been my luck to become acquainted with. Wondering how I should be received, I approached him, a silence falling upon the room as I did so. This did not strike me as looking well for the success of what was to follow. Mr. Dorkin looked me over as I approached him, and I thought I detected a sneer upon his lips as he did so. As it seemed evident that I was about to be insulted, I began to regret that I had been foolish enough to come in search of him. Indeed, had it been possible I would have backed out of it even then; that, however, was out of the question. My blood was up, and I was determined to go through with it at any cost to myself. Whatever else they might call me, it should not be a coward.

"Mr. Dorkin, I believe," I said, looking him full and fair in the face as I did so. "I was told I should find you here."

"And whoever told you that, young fellow, told you the—truth" (I do not repeat the adjectives with which he garnished his speech. They were too comprehensive for repetition.) "What do you want with me? Got a letter for me from the Prince of Wales to say that he's goin' to leave me a fortune, eh? Break the news to me gently, for I'm not so strong as I used to be."

This banter did not promise well for what was to come. Such of the assembled company as were awake evidently regarded the situation with satisfaction, and I have no doubt were looking forward to seeing what promised to be some excellent fooling at my expense. If so, they were destined to be disappointed, for I had by this time got myself well in hand, and in consequence was ready for any emergency.

"I believe you are acquainted with Mr. Gerald Williamson," I said, feeling sure that he would know my friend's name. For a few moments he did not reply, but stood stolidly pulling at his cigar and looking me up and down while he did so, as if he were thinking deeply. I could feel that every eye in the room was steadfastly fixed upon us. At last he withdrew the cigar from between his lips and addressed me as follows:—

"Mr. Gerald Williamson," he drawled. "And who the—may he be when he's at home? Is he a shearer from the Billabong, who never called for tar—or what is he? Know the cuss, how should I know him—think I carry the visitin' card of every dog—rotted, swivel-eyed, herring-stomached son of a mud turtle in my waistcoat pocket? I guess not. Now out with it, young fellar, what is it you want with me? I've got my business to attend to, and can't afford the time to go moosin' around here listening to talk about Mr. Gerald Williamsons and folk of his kidney. Mr.—Gerald—Williamson—the infernal skunk—I don't believe there ever was such a person."

This was more than I could stand. It was bad enough to be addressed as he had addressed me, but it was a thousand times worse to have it insinuated that I was endeavouring to cultivate his acquaintance through the medium of a person who had no existence. My temper was rising by leaps and bounds.

"I saw Mr. Williamson this morning," I said. "He is the managing clerk for Messrs. Applethwaite and Grimes, whose offices are in Swanston Street, and with whom, I believe, you have done business from time to time. He told me that you are about to leave for Queensland to bring down a mob of cattle."

"He told you all that, did he?" drawled Dorkin, replacing his cigar in his mouth. "Well, I don't say he's wrong, nor do I say that he's right, mark you. What I want to know is, what the—you've come to me about."

"To be straight with you, I want work," I replied, looking him in the face as stoutly as I knew how. "I want to go with you."

"Suffering Daniel," he returned, and accompanied it with an oath of such magnificent atrocity that I dare not attempt to recall it. "Did I understand you to say that you want to go with me? With me, Sep. Dorkin? Well, well, I'm—I'm—" He stopped and shook his head; the situation had got beyond him. Then, looking round the room, he continued, "Boys, what do you think of this for a sprightly bull calf? Wants to come with me. Now if it was Bill Kearney, or Tod Griffiths, I could have understood it; but for him to want to come with me!" Words again failed him, and he lapsed into a moody silence that lasted for upwards of a couple of minutes. Then, placing his hand on my shoulder, he said, very much as a father might address a small child, "Run along home, bub, and tell your mammie to give you a Johnny—cake. When you're a man come to me again, and if I've got time I'll teach you the difference between a 'possum and a Jackeroo-Savee. Now run along to mother, dear."

I flushed up to the roots of my hair as I heard the laugh that followed. I had never been treated in such a way in my life before, and I felt my heart thumping inside me like a sledge-hammer. Seated between the two windows that looked out on the street was a middle-sized horsey-looking man in a loud check suit and wearing a sham diamond horseshoe pin in his tie. He was by no means sober, and I had noticed also that he had always been amongst the loudest laughers at my expense. He had now an opportunity of showing his own wit, and he hastened to take advantage of it. Rising from his chair, he came slowly forward to the fireplace, before which we were standing.

"I say, Dorky, my boy," he began, "you're a bit too 'ard on the gentleman, it appears to me. Take 'im along with you, and be proud of 'is company. Don't you be afraid of him, young man. Have a drink along with us, and we'll talk it all over quiet and sociable like. There's nothin' to be gained by quarrelin', as the bantam said to the Shanghai rooster, when the rooster had pecked 'is heye hout. What's your particular poison, Dorky, Esquire? Give it a name. A glass of rum! Good! Mine's a brandy. And yours, Mr. Williamson—I mean Mr. Williamson's friend. Do me the honour of takin' a glass with me—now do! Don't be bashful."

Feeling that it might only have the effect of adding to the unpleasantness of my position if I were to refuse his invitation, I expressed my willingness to drink a glass of beer with him, upon hearing which he professed to be much delighted. He struck the bell on the table, and presently the barmaid appeared in answer to it. The look of eager expectation on the faces of the company should have warned me that some trick was about to be played on me, but I was thinking about something else and gave no heed to it.

"What's the order, gentlemen?" inquired the girl, balancing her tray upon its edge and spinning it as she spoke, to the imminent danger of the glasses on the board. Then she added flippantly, "Don't all speak at once or you'll deafen me. Oh! it's you, is it, Conky Jim? Fancy you doing a shout after all these years. Money must be very plentiful just now."

A roar of laughter followed this playful badinage, which did not seem to affect my host in the least. He looked round the room and winked at the company as if to warn them that a joke was coming.

"Now, Polly, my dear," he said with a patronising air, "don't waste the precious moments in idle conversation. I'm standing treat to-day, and don't you forget it. A nobbler of rum for Mr. Dorkin, a ditto of brandy, out of the right bottle mind, for me, and what was it? Let me see. Ah, yes, a glass of Nestlé's milk for the baby. It was milk you said, was it not, my little man?"

When the laughter died down, I told him that a glass of milk would serve my purpose as well as anything else, and though he thought I was joking I can assure you I meant it. He was not going to have it all his own way, whatever he might think. Of that I was determined! When the laughing maid had withdrawn, there was a short silence, during which I noticed that Mr. Dorkin watched me with an expression that was half curious, half sneering, upon his face. Meanwhile my host was explaining his theory of raising infants and training them in the way they should go to those about him. Then the maid reappeared upon the scene, and with the help of the looking-glass behind Mr. Dorkin I could see that she carried the rum and brandy and also the glass of milk that was the cause of all the merriment. She handed the spirits first, and then held out the tray with the milk upon it to me, saying as she did so, in a low voice, "It's a shame. Don't you take it if you don't want to." To which I replied by asking her to remain in the room for a moment. Again I noticed that Dorkin was watching my face. Whether he despised me or not for swallowing the insult so meekly I could not say. At any rate he said nothing on the subject.

"Well, here's good health and good fortune, Dorky, old boy." Then to me, "I looks towards you, younker, and take care that milk doesn't get into your head, or you'll be put to bed when you get home."

This sally was exactly to the taste of the company, with the exception of Mr. Dorkin, who seemed to be deeply occupied in thinking of something else. Now was the time for me to act, and I lost no time in doing so. Without raising my voice above its usual level, I turned and addressed myself to the man who had gone out of his way to play the trick upon me.

"I don't know what your name may be," I observed, endeavouring to speak as calmly as possible, "and I'm very sure I don't want to. There is one thing, however, that I do know, and that is the fact that you have laid yourself out deliberately to insult me. Very good. You have warned me not to let this milk affect my head. I am willing to take your advice, as doubtless the friends who surround you would do under the circumstances. I must get rid of the milk, since it is dangerous, and this is how I do it." So saying, I tossed the contents of the glass full and fair into his face. Such an object as he looked when I had done so I cannot hope to make you understand. Before he could recover himself I had placed the glass upon the table and had prepared myself for what I knew full well would follow. Fortunately I am a fairly good boxer, though of course I ought not to sing my own praises. Even then, in spite of my youth, I was also fairly strong. To crown it all, my blood was up, and I was ready for anything he might attempt.

"You—" he cried furiously, as he mopped the milk from his face and clothes; "you shall pay for this. See if he don't, boys. Throws his dirty milk in a gentleman's face, does he? All right."

Two or three of his friends rose as if to take his part, and then for the first time for nearly ten minutes Mr. Dorkin spoke. What he said was short, but to the point. "The man who interferes has to fight me," he remarked. "The young 'un is a good plucked 'un, and, by the Lord Harry, he shall have fair play. You, Jim Baker, down on your hunks again or I'll give you what will help you. Now, Conky, what have you got to say? Take care you haven't bit off more than you can chew. It does happen so sometimes."

The redoubtable Conky's only reply to this was a curse. Then turning to me, he continued, "As for you, I'll learn you to chuck your cow juice in a man's face. Take that." As he spoke, and almost before I had time to get up my guard, he had launched a vicious blow at my head. If I had not been quick it would have made me see stars for some time to come. As it happened, however, I was able, more by good luck than good management, to ward it off, and with a left hander, straight from the shoulder, landed him on the jaw and sent him down like a ninepin.

"A fair knock out," said Mr. Dorkin critically. "If I know Conky, he won't come up to time. Shake hands on it, my lad, and though it's not my way as a general rule to sing small, I'll ask your pardon. It was me that put it on you first, and by rights I ought to be where Conky is now." He went across the room to where the fallen warrior lay and gave him a hearty kick. "Get up," he said, "get up and beg pardon. You're only shamming, and you know it."

After a short interval the gentleman addressed struggled to his feet, explaining as he did so that he had been struck unfairly and that he would have his revenge later on. Again Mr. Dorkin spoke.

"Stow that rubbish," he observed. "You know as well as I do that you haven't a chance against the youngster. He could double you up, you turnip, with one hand, and he'll do it again if you don't take precious good care. Now say you beg pardon, unless you want to go down again."

The other thought first of endeavouring to carry matters off with a high hand, but a look on Dorkin's face induced him to change his mind. I thereupon came to his assistance, and in an unexpected manner.

"I don't want him to apologise," I said. "I am afraid it would not be sincere. If I may offer a suggestion, I would rather drink with him. You must remember that on the last occasion he did not give the order quite correctly," Then I called the girl to me. "I think, Mr. Dorkin," I began, "you ordered a glass of rum; I will have a glass of beer; and our friend here will, I hope, join us in a glass of milk."

The girl left the room, smiling all over her face. She and my late antagonist had never been friends, and she was by no means displeased at seeing him receive a thrashing. Presently, amid breathless silence, she returned with the drinks I had ordered. One was handed as before to Dorkin, while I myself held out the milk to my late antagonist. "Take it and drink it," I said, "or I promise you I'll do what I did before. You will find it an excellent drink, better for you than brandy and less likely to go to your head. Come, drink it up, if you don't want further trouble."

Amid the jeers of his former admirers who, according to their wont, were quite ready to drop him now that he had fallen from his high estate, he took up the glass and, with the remark that he hoped my next drink would choke me, tossed off the contents. Having done so, he took his departure from the room, more like a whipped puppy than any other animal I could liken him to.

"Young 'un, you're a good plucked 'un, and I'll do you that credit or my name's not Sep. Dorkin," remarked the individual of that name. "We've got to have a bit of a talk together before we've done, and if it comes out satisfactory, as the lawyers say, I don't know but what I won't give you the chance of coming with me when I start out. What's your name, anyway?"

"George Tregaskis," I answered. "My father was once manager of Warraboona Station on the Murray. He was killed when I was only a little chap of nine."

An elderly man who had entered the room a few moments before the Conky Jim episode rose hastily from his seat and came forward to where we were standing. He looked very hard at me, and somehow his face seemed to recall old associations, though I could not for the life of me remember where I had seen him.

"Did I understand you to say that your name was Tregaskis?" he said, looking closely into my face. "Son of George Tregaskis, who was thrown from his horse out mustering when the clumsy brute put his foot in a hole?"

"Yes," I replied, "I am his son, but though I feel sure I know your face, I can't recall where I last saw you. Give me a helping hand. It wasn't in Melbourne, I'm certain of that."

"No, it wasn't in Melbourne. It was out on the Murray at Warraboona. That's where it was. I remember the day you were born and the day you were breeched. I gave you your first riding lesson, and I'm not quite sure that I didn't do most of the work in teaching you to walk. Many's the mile I've carried you on my back, for your mother would trust you with me when she wouldn't with anybody else. Now think for a minute, and see if you can give me my name."

In a flash it occurred to me. How I could ever have forgotten it I could not understand. This old and grizzled man, who knew so much about me, could be no other than my father's faithful henchman and friend, Dick Bennet. I said as much, and as I did so, I saw tears rise in his eyes.

"Yes, it is Dick Bennet, sure enough," he said. "Old Dick Bennet, and to think that you are Master Georgie. Well, well, how you have grown up, to be sure."

Mr. Septimus Dorkin here placed his hand on my arm.

"If you want to kick me, you can do it and welcome," he said. "I give you my word I won't hit back. If I'd a' known you were George Tregaskis's boy I'd have licked your boots before I'd have said what I did to you. Law bless my cabbage tree, I knew your father afore he married your mother, and many's the droving trip we did together when he was a grown man and I was only a sprig of a boy, scarcely big enough to do up his own girths. He was a first-class bushman and an A1 man, and glory be with him. What say you, Dick Bennet, old pal?"

"Amen to it, and many of them," Dick replied, and then he brought his conversation back to me. "And to think of your being little Georgie. Well, well, I never thought to see this day—may I drop dead in my tracks if I did. And your mother, I hope she's hale and hearty?"

"Perfectly," I answered. "You must come out and see her. We're living at Caulfield, and I know how glad she'd be to have a talk with you about old times. Why not come with me now? It's no use my staying in town, for I don't seem to be able to hear of anything that would be likely to suit me. Goodness only knows I've tried hard enough."

"Not quite so fast, my young fellow," remarked my whilom enemy Dorkin. "Things have changed a bit since last we talked it over. You're George Tregaskis's boy, and you're a friend of my friend Dick here. That's good enough for me, and makes all the difference. You don't know much of Bush life, you say, and you've only learnt what you do know behind a desk, in this dod-ratted city that's not fit for a man what calls himself a man to live in. Well, I'm the chap who's got to teach you, and you may put your bottom dollar down on that. I leave here for Sydney next Friday, then go on by rail to Bourke. After that, it's all plain sailing for the Diamintina. Make it right with the old lady, and come and see me here to-morrow morning about this time. We'll square up matters then, and if I don't turn you into as proper a bushman as there is on this 'ere old Continent inside of six months, well, may I never be able to tell the difference between a kangaroo rat and a rock wallaby again. Are you game?"

I certainly was, and I said so. Then, wishing him good-bye, I left the hotel in company with Dick and set off for the railway station, where we were to catch our train for Caulfield.

CHAPTER III

LOSES A MOTHER: GAINS A FRIEND.

It would take too long to follow my career in detail for the next four and a half years. Indeed, it would necessitate some effort of memory on my part to recall all that befell me during that eventful period of my life. Let it suffice, therefore, that after the memorable scene recorded in the last chapter, which heralded, or perhaps I should say preceded, my engagement with Septimus Dorkin, I left for Queensland with that worthy, but, if the truth must be confessed, somewhat headstrong gentleman. We made our way up to Bourke, crossed by way of Hungerford and the Paroo River, thence to the Barcoo, and so on by easy stages to our destination. This proved to be a station of some importance on the Diamintina, that sometime mighty river which, augmented by the Western, the Wokingham, and the Mayne, to say nothing of numerous other smaller streams, runs half across the Continent to find at length an ignominious end in the Great Stoney Desert of South Australia.

That journey taught me more of the Bush, its charms and its vicissitudes, than I have ever learnt since. I was young, my brain was receptive, I had a natural liking for the calling I had chosen, and what was perhaps better than all else, I had inherited a considerable proportion of my poor father's intuitive knowledge of live stock. With my employer and mates I think I may say without boasting that I got on well, though of course there was trouble at times, as there always must be when several men are compelled to put up with each other's society for several months at a time. On the whole, however, we contrived to hit it off together, and I, for my part, have nothing but pleasant memories of that, my first experience of over landing. After a couple of brief holidays I made two more trips with Dorkin, one almost up into Cape Yorke Peninsula, and a hard time we had of it, for it was a bad season; the other from a station near Cobar, in New South Wales, to another on the Lower Murray in South Australia. During the latter journey we passed through Warraboona, my birth-place and early home. As we were camped there for two days, I managed to make time enough to ride over and have a look at the old place. It was no longer the house I remembered; the homestead had been added to, and what had been the sitting-room in my father's time was now the back portion of the edifice. The shearing shed, which in our time was nothing more pretentious than a bough-shade, was now superseded by a costly iron erection, with yards and drafting pens ad libitum. They had introduced machine shears, scoured their own wool, and dumped by means of the latest improved hydraulic press. An American windmill raised water from the river for irrigating purposes, while the overseer's and men's quarters were equal to anything I had ever seen in either of the four Colonies. On my way back to camp I rode down the river bank to have a look at my father's grave. To the credit of the present manager be it said, it was well taken care of. A neat but strong fence had been erected round it to protect it from the cattle, and what more could I expect? How the memory of the day on which we had laid him there came back to me as I sat on my horse looking down at it! I could seem to see the pale, sweet face of my mother as she watched them lowering into its last resting—place all that was mortal of the man she had loved so tenderly and whom she had followed so willingly into the exile of the Bush. I could see old Dick, with his honest, sunburnt face, reading the Burial Service over the man who had been his friend and master for more than twenty years. What was more, I could remember a little boy, scarcely up to his mother's elbow, with a round and chubby face and curly hair, who only half realised the importance to him of what was then taking place. How different was he to the long, gawky, sunburnt youth now seated on the horse beside the selfsame grave! It seemed difficult to believe that they could be one and the same person.

As things turned out, that proved to be my last journey with Dorkin, not because we had any fault to find with each other, but because he had discovered that he had amassed a competency sufficient for his modest wants, and felt an inclination to settle down. This he did, marrying at the same time a buxom widow in the public—house line of business in the town of Bourke, where, as may be supposed, he had many opportunities of renewing acquaintance with old friends, and now and again of showing that he had not altogether laid aside his business capabilities when he exchanged the pig-skin for a seat in his own bar-parlour. I have heard since that his wife led him a pretty life, and that they would doubtless have been compelled to part company had he not made a mistake one dark night and walked off the wharf into the river instead of into his own front door. He had many faults, doubtless; which of us has not? But I never heard of his having done an unjust action (horse dealing always excepted), nor do I think he ever went back on a man whom he had once admitted to his friendship. It's a pity more of us can't say as much.

When I parted company with the man whose virtues I have just described and whose vices are no concern of mine, I was in Melbourne. It was my intention to spend a month with my mother, and then to take up a job I had heard of on the Bogan in the vicinity of Nyngan. It was to be my first experience of an overseer's billet, and I was eagerly looking forward to the experience, having some idea of starting for myself in a few years, if all went well. I had managed already to save a fair sum, and hoped to have a nice little amount at my back by the time I felt equal to launching out as an owner on a small scale. A thousand-acre block would do very well for a start, and with the usual confidence of youth, I felt that I could make it pay. As of old, I told my mother of my ambition, prophesying that before very long I should want her to venture into the wilds once more in order to keep house for me. But she only shook her head, a trifle sorrowfully I thought, and declared that she could never go into the Bush again. Of late her spirits had not been of the brightest description, and the knowledge had distressed me more than I could say. That there was nothing radically wrong with her she constantly assured me, and yet she was by no means her old bright self. Among other things I noticed that she left more of the management of her small household to the girl who had acted as her companion since I had left home, which in itself was by no means a reassuring sign. In the old days she would as soon have thought of turning me out of house and home as of doing that. I suggested a change of air, a voyage to Tasmania and New Zealand, but she would not hear of it. She was perfectly content to remain where she was, she said, provided she could see me at not too long intervals. I then endeavoured to enlist the doctor on my side and to induce him to order her away, but much to my chagrin he declared that he could not discover any adequate reason for so doing. Thus foiled in every direction, nothing remained for me but to submit with the best grace I could put upon it. It did not tend, however, to send me off to my new duties in any too happy a frame of mind. Despite everyone's endeavour to convince me that I was frightening myself about her unnecessarily, I knew her too well to be easy in my mind about her. You will presently be able to see for yourself which of us was right and which was wrong.

At the expiration of my holiday, I left for Sydney, and journeyed thence by rail to Nyngan, by way of Bathurst and Dubbo. Mount Gondobon, as the station was called, is a fine property on the Macquarrie River, and at that time was up-to-date in every respect. Its area, number of sheep carried, description of grass, and other details, would in all probability not interest you. I will, therefore, content myself with saying that I should have remained there longer than I did had I not received alarming news of my mother's condition, and been compelled to hasten back to Melbourne in the middle of my second year, and just as we were beginning shearing. My return being uncertain, the owner could not, of course, wait, so there was nothing for it but for me to take my cheque and sever my connection with one of the most pleasant stations it has ever been my good luck to work upon. The manager and I parted with mutual regret, and two and a half days later found me once more at Caulfield.

To my sorrow I discovered that the report I had received as to my mother's condition had been by no means exaggerated, indeed I could only feel that they had not made me realise sufficiently how ill she was. I sought the doctor as soon as possible, and implored him to tell me exactly what the position was. I had had enough of uncertainty and was anxious to know the worst.

"Well, Mr. Tregaskis," he said, stabbing his blotting pad with his pen as he spoke, "since you wish it so much I will be explicit with you. Mrs. Tregaskis has for some time past been suffering from a malignant growth, which should have received treatment long ere this. Like most of her sex, she bore it until she could do so no longer, but only to find that to all intents and purposes she had left it until it was too late for an operation to be performed with any degree of certainty. Every effort has been made to relieve her of pain, but the trouble is increasing daily, while the drugs we are compelled to employ are slowly but surely losing their effect."

I had no idea it was as serious as this, and it shocked me more than I can express.

"But is it impossible that anything can be done?" I asked, half afraid to put the question to him.

"If you mean in the way of an operation, I am reluctantly compelled to admit that it is," he replied. "There is the chance that it might be successful, but I think it only fair to you to state it as my honest opinion, and I have taken the precaution of consulting one of our most eminent surgeons on the point, that the risk would be too great. In all probability it could only have the effect of hastening the end. I am more than sorry to have to tell you this, but, as you have yourself asked me to do so, I think it better to let you know the plain, unvarnished truth, so that you may be prepared for the worst. Your mother is a noble woman, and I would do anything in my power for her, but beyond relieving her of acute suffering, I fear I am powerless."

"Poor mother!" I groaned. "And how long do you think it will be—before—before the end is likely to come?"

He shook his head. "It is impossible for me to say," he replied. "In cases like this they not unfrequently linger for a long time. It may be only a question of weeks, it may even be of months. I regret for your sake that I cannot be more explicit. You will remain with her for the present at least, I presume?"

"You may be sure of that," was my reply. "I shall stay with her and comfort her until the end. It is the least I can do for her, and my conscience tells me I have neglected her too long. I am more obliged to you than I can say for having told me everything. The uncertainty was more than I could bear. Now I can see the track clear ahead of me, I know what I have to do."

I bade him good-bye and set off on my homeward walk. What my feelings were like you will doubtless be able to imagine, particularly if you have ever been called upon to face such an ordeal as lay before me then. God knows I would willingly have taken her place had such a thing been possible. But that, alas, was denied me. It was to be my portion, and perhaps a part of my punishment for having been selfish enough to quit my home, to have to watch her day by day suffering intolerable agony, and to know that I was powerless to afford her relief. Yet never once, even in her direst moments, did I hear her complain. For my sake she made heroic efforts to be cheerful, and I am not sure that this did not hurt me even more than the knowledge of the actual suffering she was undergoing. Between the paroxysms of pain she would talk to me of my Bush life and of the old days when she and my father were so happy together and so full of pride in me, their only child.

"Well, I ought to be thankful," she said once to me as I sat beside her, holding her dear thin hand that even now bore traces of the hard and loving life of toil she had once known, "I have had my days of happiness; I have known a good husband and a good son, so I have been blessed beyond most women. Now my time has come to join him, and, if God wills, we shall be permitted to watch our boy together making his way bravely in the world as his father did before him."

This was the first time she had spoken to me concerning her end, and as I listened, I felt as if life could never have any happiness for me again. I bent over her, and kissed her tenderly upon her forehead, such a kiss as I had never given her before. Now that I was about to lose her I was beginning to realise what a queen among women she was; an earthly saint if ever there was one. Read my story, and learn how I profited by the lesson I might and should have learnt from her. She may forgive me in her infinite compassion, but God knows I can never forgive myself. Mine was the cruelty, and mine will be the eternity of repentance.

Nearly two months elapsed before the end came, and her suffering during that terrible time I could not make you understand, even if I tried to do so. At last her bodily and mental strength began to wane, and the doctor gave me his assurance that the end was very near. Heaven knows I could not, dearly as I loved her, and lonely as I should be without her, find it in my heart to wish that it might be delayed. It would not have been human to desire such a thing. It came in the night. I had been with her until ten o'clock, and had then allowed myself to be persuaded by the doctor and nurse to go to my room and lie down, but I did so only on the express condition that they should rouse me should any change occur. That change came towards midnight, and they immediately fulfilled their promise.

"She cannot last many minutes," said the doctor in a whisper; "I fear she will not regain consciousness." He was right, for she passed quietly away a few minutes after twelve o'clock, and when I rose from my knees and stooped over her to kiss her, I knew that I was alone in the world—she who had loved me so fondly, who had watched over me so tenderly, who had borne with my many faults and weaknesses, was gone to her long rest, where who knows whether I shall be permitted to follow her?

This was the first time I had ever been brought face to face with Death since I was old enough to be able to understand what it meant. Strange to say, I was not so awed by it as I had imagined I should be. Possibly the long period of waiting, knowing all the time that the end was slowly but surely approaching, may have been responsible for this; be that as it may, however, the fact remains that it was as I have said. When I had bade the doctor good-night, I went to my own room and to bed. Worn out by watching I fell asleep almost immediately, and did not wake until nearly nine o'clock.

Not to dwell too long on what is to me even now a painful subject, I might say that my mother was laid to rest next to her father and mother in Ballarat Cemetery, and that when all the legal formalities had been complied with, the house and furniture sold, and all the other necessary legal arrangements made, I found myself my own master, without a relation that I could lay claim to, and the respectable sum of fifteen thousand pounds standing to the credit of my name at the bank. I can well remember what a large sum it seemed to me, but though it opened up a vista of such dazzling possibilities, I would only too thankfully have exchanged it to have had my mother back with me once more.

No one knows better than I do now, that the most profound grief does not last for ever, that there comes a time when the first violent shock of the loss sustained becomes less severe, when the acute agony becomes a half-numbed pain. Then as the weeks and months go by the spirits revive, hope and ambition return, and the dead, dear as their memory may be, become part and portion of the past, and henceforth are looked upon only as such.

Now, for the second time in my life, it became necessary for me to decide what I was going to do in the future. I detested a town life, and I loved the Bush: the latter was the only one that suited me, so much was certain. My capital was more than I had expected to have; at the same time it was not sufficient to warrant my going in for anything on a large scale. In other words, while it was ample to enable me to work a thousand-acre block, it would not go far towards running anything on a more ambitious scale. After my mother's death, Melbourne became so distasteful to me that I determined to leave it as soon as possible. I therefore packed my traps and departed to Sydney, where I hoped to be able to solve the problem that was of such vital importance to me. I made enquiries in every direction, sought advice from the men who were most competent to give it, and at the end of a fortnight found myself as far off a decision as I had been at the beginning. The most attractive offers were made me. Some folk wanted me to fit out trading schooners for the South Seas, and were not polite when they found that I declined to invest my money in concerns of which I had not the very slightest knowledge. Others again had gold mines they wished me to exploit, pearl beds in the neighbourhood of the Arifura Sea, that could be profitably worked with the help of bribery and Dutch corruption. There were men with patents to sell, company promoters, dealers in land, shares, and varieties of business, and, indeed, every sort of commodity under the sun, each of which was guaranteed to make my fortune quicker than any other I could adopt. But though I listened to them I gave them no cause for hope, whereupon they left me, cursing me, I have no doubt, in their hearts, though invariably outwardly polite. So far I was as much advanced as I was at the beginning. At last I determined to bank my money and go back into the Bush, and trust to time and my luck to show me what to do. I accordingly settled my hotel bill, and took the train on the day following to my old station near Nyngan, where I remained as the manager's guest for nearly a fortnight. Then, having purchased a couple of serviceable horses, one for pack work and one for riding, I set off up the Macquarrie, and thence across the Tableland, until I struck my familiar and much esteemed acquaintance, Bourke town. For upwards of a week I remained with Dorkin, fighting our battles o'er again, and both of us devoutly wishing we could be on the road together once more. More than once I had told him of my wish to find a suitable place and settle down as my own master, but though he was always prodigal of his advice, he brought me no nearer the accomplishment of my desire. But my luck was destined to triumph in the end, and as is so often the way in such cases, quite by chance. I had been down to the post—office to despatch some letters, and was returning to Dorkin's abode when I nearly stumbled over a man who was lying senseless in the gutter. At first I thought he was drunk, but when I bent over him I discovered that I was mistaken. He was unconscious, as the result of a blow on the head, evidently inflicted by some blunt instrument, and was lying in a pool of blood. I carried him into the circle of light from the oil lamp at the corner, and then set to work as well as I could to restore him to consciousness.

At first glance he appeared to be a Bushman of the ordinary type, but on closer inspection he proved to be somewhat superior to the general run of men with whom I had been brought in contact. His age could not have been more than forty-five or forty-six at the highest computation, possibly it was not so much. His face, despite its pallor, was by no means unhandsome, while his features, though thin, were regular, and had what I suppose would be called an aristocratic air about them. His dress was that of the ordinary dweller in the Bush, that is to say, it consisted of a pair of white moleskin trousers, kept in position by a leather belt, a Crimean shirt, a white cotton coat, and a soft felt hat. His hands were small, and it did not look to me as if they had done very much rough work. At any rate, they were not like mine, scored all over with cuts and the markings of old sores. Taken altogether, I was decidedly prepossessed in his favour.

I had just arrived at this conclusion and was wondering what I should do with him, when he opened his eyes and looked about him.

"Hullo," he said, very faintly, "what's the matter?" Then before I could answer, he continued, "I feel as if my head is coming off; what on earth has happened, and who are you?"

I satisfied his curiosity as well as I was able, and then asked him if he felt well enough to get on to his feet. He replied by making the attempt, and eventually, with my assistance, he managed to scramble up. I thereupon propped him against a verandah post and endeavoured to discover the extent of the injury he had received. The light, however, was so bad that beyond convincing myself that he had lost a lot of blood, there was little more to be ascertained.

"How did you get into this plight?" I enquired at last. "It looks as if you've had a bad time of it."

"I don't remember very much about it," he answered. "I believe a man came up to me and asked me the time, then something hit me on the back of my head, and I can recall no more." He slipped his right hand into the breast pocket of his coat. "The brutes," he said a moment later, "they've taken my cheque for a hundred pounds. What on earth shall I do?"

"We'll soon settle that," was my rejoinder. "What you've got to do is to get to bed as quick as you can and have that head attended to. If you feel equal to walking, come along with me to my place, and I'll put you up for the night. In the morning we can talk matters over and see what can be done to find the beasts who robbed you. Do you think you can manage the walk; it is not more than a hundred yards or so down the street? Put your right arm round my neck and hold on to me."

I placed my left arm round his waist, and in this apparently affectionate style we proceeded in the direction of Dorkin's hostelry. My companion was certainly as weak as a kitten, which, after all, was scarcely to be wondered at considering the blow he had received and the amount of blood he had lost. However, he bore up bravely, and in due course we reached my abode. I took him in by the side door, for I had no desire that the folk in the bar should see him. It was within the bounds of possibility that the very men who had assaulted and robbed him might be in there drinking their ill-gotten gains. It would be time enough to look for them when I had got him to bed.

Leading him quietly along the passage, I at last reached my room. A candle was soon lighted, and in something less than five minutes I had him safely in bed and was on my way to the bar in search of Dorkin, who had had more experience in the matter of wounds than I had had. Getting him out of the bar into his little snuggery behind I told him my tale. He listened attentively. Then an idea seemed to strike him, and he returned to the bar for his pipe, which he had left upon the shelf. There were about half a dozen customers present, three of them residents in the town, one a drover well-known to Sep., and two extremely unprepossessing strangers, one of whom, a muscular fellow enough, carried a formidable looking stick in his hand. It was evident that both had had as much whisky as was good for them; in point of fact, one who stood at the end of the counter was compelled to support himself by its edge in order to remain upright. His companion, the man with the stick, was stolidly smoking with his elbows on the counter. If ever the word "lag" was written on a human countenance, it was on his. I have met some tough customers in my time, but I don't remember in my experience to have come across a more repulsive face; it was more like that of an animal, a bulldog for instance, than that of a man. Here was just the scoundrel to commit an assault such as the occupant of my bed had suffered from that evening.

"Well, matey, have you done that for me?" he asked of the barman, as Dorkin joined me in the parlour once more. "Look sharp about it, lad, for I want to get along to camp, and it's close on closing time. You're as slow as my old skewbald mare, that's what you are. Hurry up and ask the guv'nor to oblige a good customer what'll spend the money in 'is 'ouse."

"Hand it over then, and I'll see him about it," replied the other, "but I don't know that he's got enough in the house. It's a good 'un, I suppose, 'cause we don't want any fly-paper here."

"It's as good as any you ever set eyes on, my bloke," answered the fellow with an oath. "But I only show it to the boss. If Richard James Wilberforce's name to a cheque ain't worth something, I don't know whose is, and so you may take it from me. Cut your lucky now, and bring me back the cash. Look sharp."

"I thought as much," said Dorkin in an undertone to me. "If I'm not very much out in my reckoning, we've got the men who played the game on your pal in yonder. Hurry along to the room and ask him his name, and whether it was a cheque he lost, and, if so, whose signature was at the foot of it. Then slip back here. If he says Wilberforce, walk into the bar as if you didn't suspect anything. Sing out that it looks like rain, and leave the rest to me. We'll have a bit of fun out of this, or my name's not Dorkin."

I did as I was ordered, and learnt that my protége's name was Flaxman, and that he had worked for Mr. Wilberforce of Carrandara Station, one of the largest properties on the New South Wales side of the Queensland border, for upwards of three years as storekeeper, and that four days previous he had taken his cheque for close on a hundred pounds, and had come south with the idea of having a holiday. Primed with this information I returned to the bar.

CHAPTER IV

OLD FRIENDS MEET.

Pushing open the swing door I entered the bar and approached the counter. The two men were still there; Dorkin, however, was not present. I could, however, hear him moving about in the little parlour at the back, whistling softly to himself over something he was doing. The barman nodded to me good-humouredly, and in return I invited him to join me in a drink, remarking at the same time, and in a voice loud enough to be heard in the adjoining room, that in my opinion we were going to have rain before the night was out.

A significant cough from Dorkin gave me to understand that my signal had reached him. I then took stock of my neighbours. One of the townsmen had departed, and it was easy to see that the man with the stick was growing every moment more and more impatient.

"If the boss don't soon 'urry up, I'll have to go without it," he said. "What's he doin' of? This ain't the way to treat good customers. I can't say that I think much of it myself."

"He won't be long," the barman replied. "I expect he's looking to see how much he's got in the cash box."

The man ordered whisky for himself and some rum for his companion. The suspense was evidently telling on their nerves. At last Dorkin made his appearance.

"Who is it wants a cheque cashed?" he asked, looking about him for the individual in question. "If he's after an advance he'd better look sharp and see about it, for it's well up to closing time."

"I'm the man, boss," said the rascal with the stick. "It's got Mr. Wilberforce of Carrandara's name on it, so I reckon it's good enough for you, and for me, too. What do you think?"

"Never mind what I think," returned the other; "all I know is that I wish I had his money. What have you been doing up there? Stayin' with the family, I should say, by the look of your hands and face."

"Never mind my face," growled the man. "I've been shearin' up there, that's what I've been doin'. We cut out last Friday, and next day he give me the cheque for my vallyble services. Now what I want you to do is to cash it for me straight out, or as near as you can get to it. If you can't manage it all, I'll come in for the rest to—morrow. I can trust you I reckon. Sep. Dorkin's word is as good as bank notes, so I've heard folks say."

"Folks is mighty civil all of a sudden," remarked Dorkin contemptuously. "Howsomever, that's neither here nor there. Just hand over the cheque and let me have a look at it. Then I'll tell you what I'll do for you. I banked up this afternoon, but I may be able to manage it."

Never suspecting anything, the fellow produced an envelope from his pocket and from it a slip of paper, which he passed across the counter to the landlord. Then he waited to see what would happen next. In spite of his bravado, I noticed that his hand trembled as it took up the glass of whisky and put it to his lips. Dorkin turned it over and over before he put it down.

"What's your name?" he asked at last. "I don't mean any offence, but a man has to protect himself."

"What do you think it is?" enquired the other angrily. "Ain't it writ there as plain as this glass that's in my 'and? Don't it say Robert Flaxman? If it don't, then I'm a Rooshian."

"That's what it does say," was Dorkin's rejoinder, "but how am I to know that you're the man? Your name may be Bill Jones for all I know. A nice thing it would be for me if I was to give you the money for this—what is it? ninety-eight pounds, fourteen shillings and sixpence—and find out afterwards that I'd been spoofed. Is there anybody in the town that can speak for you? Fetch 'em along, and if it's all right I'll do it straight off, I give you my word."

This was a new way of looking at the matter, and the ruffian by no means approved of it. What was worse, Dorkin had possession of the cheque, and, owing to the width of the counter and the fact that the other was standing with his back against the bottle-rack, it was impossible for him to take it from him.

"You seem mighty distrustful all of a sudden, boss," he remarked. "I don't know as how I altogether like the way you're talkin'. Anybody to 'ear you would go and say you thought I'd stole it."

"Well, find somebody to speak for you," said Dorkin, folding and unfolding the little blue slip as he spoke. "That's all I want. If you've been up at Carrandara, there must be somebody here who knows you. You can't blame me for takin' care of myself, can you? I'd be a fool if I didn't."

Suddenly an idea occurred to the man, and he was quick to act upon it.

"There's my mate here," he said. "As nice and sociable a feller as you'd meet between Bourke and Sydney. He was rouseabouting up there along of me. He'll tell yer that I'm quite respectable, and speak for me anywhere, won't you, Bill? Talk up like a man to the gentleman."

Unfortunately for the success of his scheme, the genial William was by this time sound asleep, with his head on the counter and his legs spread out like a pair of dividers. His friend did his best to rouse him, and at length succeeded. But even then his great intellect proved unequal to the strain of thinking. He began by flatly and firmly declaring that he had never seen the other before, then that he would not be seen in his company for all the money in the world, and concluded his remarks by observing that he was like the Prophet Daniel, inasmuch as he had "fallen into a burning fiery den of thieves." With this assertion on his lips he slid quietly down to the floor, where he resumed his slumbers as contentedly as a little child. To say that his friend was disgusted at such behaviour would not be to express his feelings at all. He kicked him viciously and called him by certain names which I will not pollute my pen by recording. Meanwhile, Dorkin watched him like a cat does a mouse.

"Drop that," he cried in a voice of thunder, as the other was about to raise his foot for a second kick. "I'll have none of that here, so you'd better stop it or you'll hear from me."

"I'd knock your head off for a nobbler of whisky," growled the man, and then added somewhat inconsequently, "Call this 'ere a civilised country? There's a nice mate for you—eats your tucker, sleeps in your blankets, cadges your money, and when you want 'is word to speak for you, ups and says he don't know anything about you. Wait till I get 'im outside. If I don't give 'im what for, well, my name ain't Johnny Walker. You mark me. I'll learn him to miscall me, if I do time for it."

"So your name's Johnny Walker, is it?" asked Dorkin. "I had a sort of an idea you said it was Flaxman?"

"Well, and isn't it?" asked the man, and then added with a cunning that deceived nobody, "Haven't you never 'eard the sayin' about Johnny Walker? You didn't surely think that was my name, did you? That's a good joke, if ever there was one. Lord, how my mate would laugh if he could hear it. Never mind about that there cheque, boss. Hand it over here, and if you won't cash it, I make no doubt but that I shall find somebody else as will."

But Dorkin refused to return the draft, and there was a look on his face that boded ill for the man who might try to force him to do so. Johnny Walker, if that were his real name, had met his match at last, and it's my belief that he knew it. To feel that one has made a vital mistake and is absolutely powerless to retrieve it is by no means a pleasant sensation, particularly where the appropriation of other people's money is concerned. Dorkin, while he had been meditating, had folded up the paper and placed it in his waistcoat pocket. Then he came forward and leant over the counter.

"Look you here, Mr. Robert Flaxman, Johnny Walker, Bill Jones, or whatever else you may call yourself, for the present that 'ere cheque stays with me, Sep. Dorkin. Later on I'll send it back to the party who it rightfully belongs to. If you kept it, it might get you into a power of trouble, so I'm going to take care of it for you just for a while. It isn't any use your getting wild about it, for you know me and I know you, though you pretend to let on you don't."

Here a violent oath escaped from the rascal on the other side of the counter, which he capped with another to the effect that he had never set eyes on the landlord before.

"Then you're a bit more forgetful than I took you to be," replied Dorkin, who was not in the least put out by the other's language. "I reckon it'll be necessary for me under the circumstances to tell you where and when I first had the honour of clappin' eyes on that lovely face of yours. It may come as a bit of a surprise, like, to know how I've treasured your memory all these years, like the girl in the song Sailor Joe used to sing. Bless me, how does it go now? Ah! I have it." Here he commenced to lift up his voice in melody.

" 'Tis in the silence of the night
Your dear face comes to me; I linger long on that fond sight.
And sweetly dream—and sweetly dream of thee!"

"Pretty ain't it? Well, that's how I feel about that face of yours, though I haven't dropped into poetry yet."

"Oh, stow this rot and 'and over that cheque," said the object of his admiration. "I'm not going to be kept 'ere all night, not for you nor anybody else. Fetch it out and let me get my mate back to camp. As he gets sober, he gets that quarrelsome you'd be ashamed to 'ave 'im round the place."

But Dorkin still showed no sign of relinquishing possession of what the other declared to be his property. On the contrary he put it in his coat pocket and buttoned it up. Then there ensued an ominous pause, during which each man steadily regarded the other. The man on the wrong side of the counter was the first to break it.

"This is a nice sort of game you're playin' on me," he said. "If you won't 'and it over, I'll 'ave to see what the law will say to you. You won't like that, you know."

Dorkin laughed good-humouredly. He knew perfectly well that the other was only playing a game of bluff. To employ a Bush expression, he had now got him roped into a corner and was going to finish him off in proper style. The man looked more and more uncomfortable the longer he regarded his tormentor's face. More than once he glanced over his shoulder at the door, as if to make sure that it was ready in case he might want to make his escape by it. Noticing this, I edged my way towards it with the idea of frustrating his intention. The critical moment had arrived.

"Just one moment," said the landlord, speaking very slowly and with unusual impressiveness; "there's just two little questions I should like to ask you before we go any further, and for the simple reason, as the lawyers say, that they 'ave a bearin' on the point at issue. First and foremost—no, you needn't look round at that door, it's just where it was five minutes ago, and my friend is takin' all sorts of care that it don't run away. As I was sayin', first and foremost, who was Bill Bailey? Perhaps you'll be good enough to answer me that."

"Never 'eard tell of 'im," answered the other sullenly, looking everywhere but at his questioner. "What do I know about yer Bill Baileys?"

"More than you're game to stand up to, I reckon," was the quiet rejoinder. "Well, if you won't tell me, I suppose I'll have to tell you. Bill Bailey, sometimes called Roarin' Bill, sometimes called Bill the Liar, was a gent as gave his best attention to raisin' horseflesh, and he did that same rearin' in a mighty curious sort of fashion—that is to say, with a saddle and bridle when the owner wasn't round handy to notice him. One day he sold a friend of mine a likely sort of nag out on the Upper Barcoo, and—well, to make a long story short, poor Bill went up for five years' hard. He was terrible surprised, was Bill, I could see that, when the beak sentenced him. Then close on four and a half years went by and most folk had given up thinkin' of him and didn't want to remember him when they did, till one day there was a pretty little bit of cattle duffin' done out Cunnamulla way, and the police were soon on the track, and Michael White, alias Bill Bailey, alias Roarin' Bill, alias Bill the Liar, had to face the judge's chin-music once more. It was seven years this time. Well, allowin' for good conduct marks, we might say, therefore, and this is my point, that he ought to have been out a matter of a month ago. He was a rare one to gammon the chaplain they tell me, was Bill, so perhaps he's come to be a reformed character, perhaps he ain't. What would you say, Mr.—Johnny Walker? I believe you said that was your name?"

Again I regret to say that it is impossible for me to give that gentleman's reply in his own picturesque language. I may remark, however, that while it was terse and to the point, it did not paint a very hopeful picture of my friend's hereafter.

"Just one more point, and then I'm done with you," continued the inexorable Dorkin, calmly lighting his pipe and speaking between the puffs of smoke. "It so happens, and I want your attention, gentlemen all, if you please; it so happens, I say again, that an individual fresh from Carrandara Station arrived in town to-night. He had in his pocket a cheque signed by Mr. Wilber-force for ninety-eight pounds, fourteen shillings and sixpence. It was made out in the name of John Flax-man, not Bill Bailey or Johnny Walker, only plain John Flaxman. Now a couple of forties—you know the term, gentlemen—happened to get hold of Mr. Flaxman and laid him out with a club. By the way, I like your stick, Mr. Walker, it's a pretty weapon any way you look at it. When my friend over there discovered the individual to whom I refer, he was lying insensible in the gutter, with a big bump on the back of his head, bleeding like a stuck pig; his cheque was gone. What is more, that gentleman is now under my roof, where he will stay until he has recovered himself a bit. What I want to ask you, gentlemen all, is this—what you would do with a couple of dead-brokes like that, who first try murder and robbery, and then do their best to drag an innocent publican into their dirty business? If it hadn't been for Mr. Tregaskis there, they would probably have done me brown—this very night. Shall I hand them over to the police, or what shall I do with them? If I lock them up, it's certain we'll all have to give evidence against them, and this time, Mr. Walker, it will as like not be fifteen instead of seven years."

At this point the latter forgot himself and was imprudent enough to declare that Dorkin had invented the whole story, and that, so far as he was concerned, he was prepared to prove his innocence. It was an unfortunate statement for him to have made, as he immediately discovered, for the words were scarcely out of his mouth before Dorkin had vaulted over the counter, elderly man though he was, and had given the other such a blow in the face that he shot across the room and fell headlong upon the prostrate body of his snoring companion, thereby waking him up most effectually. The latter, imagining himself to be assaulted, hit out wildly, right and left, and continued to do so long after I had dragged his fellow villain out into the middle of the room by the heels.

"Get up, you dog," cried Dorkin, standing over him with clenched fists. "Get up, or I'll kick you into a jelly. Don't you lie shamming there. Get up, I say, or I'll give you something to remember me by that will last you till your dying day. I'll teach you to try and palm your robberies off on me, you skunk. What you want is the cat to make you jump, and if you're not a bit more careful it won't be long before you get it. Up with you now!"

Mr. Walker looked at the tall figure standing over him and realised that the game was played out so far as he was concerned. He thereupon scrambled to his feet, and began, more for form's sake than for any other reason, to brush his clothes, which were covered with sawdust from the floor. An excellent lump was steadily rising on his left cheekbone. It promised to achieve decent proportions before many hours were past.

"Now then, out you go," cried Dorkin, pointing to the door. "Get out of my house, and if ever you dare to show as much as your nose in it again I'll man-haul you till your own best friend wouldn't know you. Git!"

Someday, perhaps, Mr. Walker will learn, probably he has done so by this time, if he has not already been hanged, that instant obedience is a virtue to be assiduously cultivated. Had he done so earlier in life he might have come off better on this occasion. The woman who hesitates is lost, we are told. In this case it was the man. That moment's hesitation cost him another painful bruise, to say nothing of his lacerated feelings—the seat of his trousers and a torn coat collar. It came about in this fashion. Observing that the other did not quit quite as soon as he might have done, Dorkin seized him by the two last-named portions of his attire and ran him to the door, which I threw open. Then, with one mighty swing, he hurled him forth into the night, to ricochet from a verandah post and finally to lie prone in the inch—deep dust of the road. The landlord then returned for his companion, who followed his leader's ignominious flight. Personally, I have never tried it, but I should say that there are few things in life more humiliating than to be ejected so summarily and violently from a place of popular resort. It not only does not look well for one's self—respect, but the after effects are apt to be as unpleasant as they are lingering.

Later the other guests of the house departed, and, while my friend was locking up, I went off to ascertain how my protegé was prospering. Mrs. Dorkin had bathed and plaistered his head, and when I entered the room I found him sound asleep. Next morning he was almost himself once more, and absurdly grateful to me for having rescued him. I may here, perhaps, confess that the more I saw of the man the more I liked him. In spite of his Bush clothes, the veriest tyro could have told that he was a gentleman. He was tall, but not well built, with a curious stoop, the result of round shoulders. At first glance, you would doubtless have inclined, as I did, to the belief that he was consumptive, but he certainly was not. Among other things, he possessed an exceedingly pleasant voice and a charm of manner that I have never known equalled. He was also the possessor of one of the most equable tempers a man could possibly be blessed with. Nothing ever disturbed it. Indeed, throughout our long and more than intimate friendship I am quite sure I only once saw him in anything remotely approaching what might be termed a rage. He was, I believe, though I could not test him, an excellent linguist; I knew him for an expert musician; his small library, consisting of some half-dozen authors, proved him a Latin and Greek scholar, while one or two little slips he made on various occasions gave me good reason to suppose that he had once been a University man of some importance, or, at any rate, one from whom greater things than a Bush life had been expected. That he had not fulfilled them was evident from the mere fact of his presence in Australia. As I found out later, he had one serious fault—that is to say, so far as I was capable of judging—and that was the fact that, blessed with the gift of accumulating knowledge, he was, like myself with my own studies, totally lacking in that of application. It was in itself perhaps a weakness rather than a fault, but it had been sufficient to spoil his entire life.

For upwards of a week he remained in Dorkin's house, and it was not until the end of that time that he and I came to the resolution that was destined to change the course of both our lives. We were equally tired of New South Wales, and we were also anxious to make a bid for fortune on our own account. The unfortunate part of it was that we neither of us knew how or where to begin. However, we had taken a great liking to each other, and were ready to throw in our lots together so soon as we should hear of something we fancied might suit us. To my delight I discovered that Flaxman had an amount almost equivalent to my own lying to his credit in a Sydney bank, so that as far as money went we were more than ordinarily well equipped. Day by day we had long discussions with Dorkin, whom we both regarded as a standard authority on anything connected with the Bush. The vexed question as to whether cattle paid better than sheep was debated, the different markets were taken into consideration, the varying descriptions of country had to be thought of, with half a hundred other matters, at first sight comparatively unimportant, but apt to become little short of gigantic when focussed against the magnitude of the stake at issue. We were neither of us millionaires, and one big loss, the result of hasty judgment, might spell irretrievable ruin for both of us. Small wonder therefore, that we made up our minds to exercise the greatest caution, and not to put our feet down until we were certain that the ground on which we were treading was likely to prove a sure foothold. Personally, I was strong for cattle, and though I fancy Flaxman would have preferred sheep, he was easy going enough to give in to me. That was always his way; rather than have trouble, he would throw aside his own wishes in favour of anything proposed by a person he liked. It would have been better for him, and, Heaven knows, a great deal better for me, had he always spoken his mind as he felt, and not have taken any notice of my likes and dislikes. But what had to be, had to be. It was Kismet, and who shall try to avert his fate?

At last, and when we were almost tired of the subject, we resolved to set out on what might have been termed a tour of inspection through the two Colonies. It was not without regret that we bade Septimus Dorkin "good-bye," little dreaming that neither of us was destined ever to see him in the flesh again. I have already told you what his end was. Heaven rest him, he was a kind friend to me, though when I first met him I did not anticipate it.

It was on a bright sunny morning at the commencement of winter that we said farewell to Bourke. Our horses were far too fat after their long rest, and Flaxman and myself were but little better. However, we hoped by careful riding to knock them and ourselves into shape before we crossed the border into Queensland. It is wonderful how quickly a Bush horse hardens himself if only he be judiciously managed.

We had not been long upon the road before I began to discover that my companion, good fellow as he was, could by no means be considered a first-class Bushman. Seeing that he had spent most of his time in the store at Carrandara—the only station on which he had been employed since his arrival in Australia—this was scarcely to be wondered at. Yet I could not help marvelling that with all his cleverness in picking up other things, he had not managed to acquire the insight into matters, which, without boasting, I might say had come to me intuitively. Without meaning any sort of disparagement to him, I ought, for the sake of what is to come, to remark that he could not leave the camp to put the horses on to water half a mile away without getting bushed; while his cooking, when I allowed him to try his hand at it, was bad enough to have made the very poorest lodging-house slavey weep for shame of the human race. His damper was invariably brick-like; his Johnny-cakes would have made excellent fishing-line sinkers had they been used as such, while to trust him in any way with the cooking of meat was only to court inevitable disaster. Yet with it all he was never anything but cheerful, ready at all hours to do more than his fair share of work, never grumbled if short commons became necessary, and was always sanguine as to the success we should meet with in the future. A better companion in that way no man could possibly wish to have.

Having crossed the border, we made our way up the Bulloo River, then in full flood, crossing the Cheviot Range three days after leaving Adavale. Horse feed was abundant, water plentiful, and we ourselves were in the very best of spirits. Were we not like modern Don Quixotes, going forth in search of adventure? From the Cheviots, we crossed on to the Barcoo, and then headed away for the Diamintina and the Great Plains that stretch thence beyond the Herbert River into the vast Unknown. Ye gods! what magnificent country it is, and what great things might be done with it were it but better watered. For hundreds of miles we rode through it, keeping our eyes open continually for any place that might suit us. So far, however, our search had been entirely unsuccessful.

"We must try further north," I told Flaxman one evening when we were discussing it round the camp fire. "This country's too big for us—a place the size we want would be lost in it. What's more, we couldn't afford to lay out the money necessary to conserve the water."

"It seems a pity, too," my companion replied, "for, as you say, it is wonderful country, and if we could only master the water difficulty a fortune would be standing waiting for us to pick it up. Why don't we possess a few thousands more capital?"

But it was no good our wishing for what we had not got, so we were perforce compelled to make the best of it. Leaving the Far West behind us, we struck out towards the North-East, in the direction of the Flinders River.

After a long and wearisome journey across hundreds of miles of almost treeless plains, we at length reached the township of Hughenden, a quaint little place on the banks of the Flinders. Here we remained to rest and refit, and here it was that we made the discovery that was ultimately destined to play such an important part in both our lives. Chance had brought us together, and fate was now arranging to bring to perfection the work that chance had begun.

CHAPTER V

MAKING A HOME.

It was a steaming hot night, such as few places can produce in greater perfection than Northern Queensland. To give you an adequate description of it is, I fear, beyond my limited powers, but if you will try to imagine a steaming wash-house, a Turkish bath, and a hot kitchen all rolled into one, a smell of kerosene, stale tobacco, and ardent spirits, with millions of mosquitoes thrown in to keep one both interested and amused, you will have arrived at some faint understanding of it. The hotel at which we had taken up our abode was located in the main street, and was a long low wooden building that drove a roaring trade both by day and night. Its bedrooms were full continually. Bearded, lonely-eyed men made their appearance from stations situated away at the back of Beyond, transacted their business or their pleasure after their own peculiar fashion, drank deep as a rule, as often as not more for the sake of custom than because they cared for it, and later on disappeared as quietly and as unostentatiously as they had arrived. There were squatters, who were almost kings in their own right; managers and overseers, who shone in their reflected glory; drovers; dealers; commercial travellers; labour agitators; bullock drivers, or teamsters as they are more usually called; Chinese storekeepers; bakers and laundrymen; Hindoo and Afghan hawkers; black fellows more or less degraded, according to the length of time they had been resident in the township; and a certain white population, fallen beyond the hope of redemption. It was a motley assemblage such as could only be met with in a frontier town, and one which I was never tired of watching.

On this particular evening I could see that the weather had made up its mind to be thundery, indeed it had been working up for it all day. The air was so close that it seemed as if one could scarcely breathe. Inside the hotel the atmosphere was so thick that, to use a common expression, one could almost cut it with a knife. Feeling as if I could not bear it, I went on to the verandah and threw myself down in a long cane chair near the water bag. Lightning was playing continually away to the west, accompanied at intervals by the low rumble of distant thunder. As a rule, mosquitoes do not trouble me very much, but on this particular night they would not leave me alone, smoke as I would. Flaxman had gone to his room with a bad headache, the result, no doubt, of the peculiar condition of the atmosphere. Personally, I was not in the best of spirits. Our long journeying and our inability to discover what we wanted, weighed on such nerves as I possessed. I wanted to be settled down and to feel that I had once more a place that I could look upon as a home. I was tired of wandering in this aimless fashion, and longed to be at work once more. From the bar behind me came the raucous voices of its patrons, while under a verandah across the street a drunken man was challenging another and more sober comrade to fight him for a bottle of whisky. Heavy clouds were rising in the sky, and anyone might have been forgiven for supposing that rain was imminent. I knew Queensland too well, however, by this time to place much faith in such manifestations. It would be time enough to believe when we actually saw the rain falling. Thunder and lightning and dark sullen clouds did not by any means foretell a deluge. I have known it, away on the Great Plains, look like a storm every night for weeks on end, so like it indeed that one waited almost breathlessly for the clouds to burst and the welcome roar of rain to sound upon the roof, but nothing resulted save disappointment, and in the morning every vestige of a cloud would have passed away, leaving behind a sky of dazzling, pitiless blue.

I had been seated on the verandah upwards of a quarter of an hour, and was halfway through my second pipe, when an old man, whose personality had interested me a great deal during the last few days, made his appearance from the bar, and, after stepping on to the pavement to examine the sky, returned and dropped into a chair beside me. He was an old man, as I have just said, possibly close upon seventy years of age, with snowy hair, a clean shaven, not unhandsome face, and an air of being out of keeping with his rough surroundings. Only that afternoon I had commented to Flaxman on his likeness to the typical aged nobleman of conventional drama. He was possessed of one or two peculiarities; he took snuff, but did not smoke; he wore a black silk stock, after the fashion of our great grandfathers; he always looked spruce and neat, which is not the invariable rule with Bushmen; moreover, he used no oaths, but talked with the air of a cultured gentleman. From the first moment I set eyes upon him I took a fancy to the man, and was very glad now to be permitted an opportunity of talking to him. His voice was refined, and I noticed also that he occasionally employed little phrases that are to-day but seldom used. While talking to him one almost felt as if one were conversing with a character in a book, though I cannot liken him to any personage in fiction with whom I am acquainted, unless it might be dear old Colonel Newcome.

"I believe I am addressing Mr. Tregaskis," he began, when he had been seated in his chair some moments. "I had your name from our landlord, who tells me you have come in from the West."

"Yes, my name is Tregaskis," I answered, "and the landlord was quite correct in saying that my friend and I have been out in the Far West. We managed to get as far as the other side of the Herbert River. Do you happen to be acquainted with that district, may I ask?"

"No," he replied, "I have never travelled so far, and now I do not think that I ever shall. There was a time when I knew no greater happiness than roving about the world, and this Continent in particular; but when one finds oneself on the borderland of seventy one does not contemplate doing much more of that sort of thing. Forgive my impertinence, but you are perhaps native born?"

"I am," I observed. "My companion, however, is an Englishman, but has been out here some few years."

"I thought as much. I also fancy I should not be very far from the mark if I were to hazard the guess that he is an Oxford man. May I ask if I happen to be right? It is merely a supposition on my part."

"Yes, you are quite right," I answered. "His college was Christ Church, and I believe he did rather well there. At any rate, he certainly should have done so, for he is an undeniably clever man."

"He has a clever head—a distinctly clever head," continued the old fellow. "I commented on it to myself the first moment that I saw him. I am delighted to hear you speak so well of your friend, and, with your permission, I will add that I should much enjoy making his acquaintance."

"I am quite sure the pleasure would be reciprocated," I replied politely. "I must find an opportunity of making you known to each other. He has gone to bed now, I am sorry to say, with a severe headache, otherwise I know he would be delighted."

He was silent for a few minutes, while the thunder rumbled in the distance and the lightning played above the housetops opposite. I was wondering, for my part, what it was that had brought this charming old man out to Australia and had induced him to take up a life for which one might have been excused had one deemed him quite unfitted. If Flaxman's past were a mystery, here was evidently a greater one, and though I am not as a rule curious in such matters, I must confess that I should much have liked to have known his secret. When he next spoke it was as if he had been turning some important matter over in his mind. It struck me that he was a little nervous as to what he was about to say, and not knowing, of course, his reason I was unable to help him.

"Am I right in supposing, Mr. Tregaskis," he said at last, taking snuff as he spoke and tapping the lid of the box afterwards, "that you and your companion are out in this part of the country on the look-out for a pastoral property of moderate dimensions? At least, that was the information which was communicated to me."

"Your informant was quite right," I answered. "That is our reason for being here. Unfortunately, however, we have so far been entirely unsuccessful; the particular description of place we require seems to exist nowhere save in our imaginations. It is disheartening, to say the least of it. The more so as it is impossible to say how long these good seasons may last."

"Perhaps you would not mind letting me know what it is you are so anxious to secure," he continued. "It is within the bounds of possibility that I may be in a position to help you. I have a very fair knowledge of this country from the Gulf as far down as Boulia. Will you not confide in me?"

His manner was so genial, and his offer was evidently so kindly meant, that I told him everything. He heard me out in silence, and then promised to sleep on it, after which he bade me good-night, promising to let me know the result of his cogitations in the morning. For upwards of an hour I continued to smoke in the verandah, to the growling accompaniment of the thunder, after which I too sought my couch and was soon in the arms of Morpheus.

Next morning I was standing on the verandah once more, waiting for Flaxman, who had gone out to the hotel paddock to look at our horses, when Mr. Densford, my old friend of the previous night, made his appearance and accosted me. He was as neat as ever, and, as usual, looked better fitted to play the host in some ancestral hall than to waste his good looks on the barren desert of a Bush hotel.

"Good morning," he said, giving me his hand. "I see our storm of last night has blown itself away without leaving any rain behind for our benefit, as usual. Are you at liberty to spare me a few minutes?"

I replied to the effect that I would do so with much pleasure, and we accordingly seated ourselves in the chairs we had occupied on the previous evening. He took a pinch of snuff with all the elegance of a Beau Brummel, and then prepared himself for conversation.

"I have been thinking over what you said to me last evening," he began. "It has afforded me considerable pleasure to think that I may be of service to you, my dear sir. There is nothing more delightful in this world than the knowledge that one is in a position to prove of use to one's fellowman. I take it your desire is to obtain a property not too large and not too small, compact, well grassed and watered, sheltered, and capable of carrying a fair number of sheep or cattle, as the case may be. You would require as comfortable a house as could be obtained under the circumstances, with hut accommodation for, shall we say, six men?"

"You have described our need exactly," I answered. "But where are we to find such a place?"

"I am delighted to inform you that I have the exact place in my mind's eye," he declared. "Your description tallies with it most admirably. I know that the owner is anxious to dispose of it, having determined to return at an early date to the Mother Country, where, please God, he will end his days. It is a most attractive property from a picturesque point of view; the house is old-fashioned, but comfortable, while the run itself possesses the various advantages you are so anxious to secure.

What is more, it is to be sold at a sacrifice and for what is probably less than half its real value."

"You make my mouth water," I said. "And where is this wonderful place? Is it far from here?"

"Not more than thirty-five miles," he answered. "If you would care to inspect it, I would guide you to it myself, for I shall be starting in that direction to-morrow, all being well. What do you say to my proposition?"

"I will consult my partner as soon as he returns," I answered. "The prospect seems such a glowing one that I am sure he will agree with me we ought not to allow the opportunity of inspecting it to slip through our fingers. Would you mind my asking the name of the place and of its owner?"

"There is no objection to your knowing both," he replied. "The name of the station is Montalta, and its owner is—well, its owner is none other than myself. Pray do not think I am attempting to take advantage of you. It is a charming little place in every sense of the word, chosen with great care, and it has the merit, not a small one as you will admit, of having helped me to amass a very fair competency, which I intend to enjoy on my return to my native land."

"But forgive my saying so, is it not possible that we may not be in a position to pay the price you are asking for such a desirable property? Neither my partner nor I are wealthy enough to afford a big figure."

He smiled indulgently. "I don't think we shall be likely to quarrel on that score," he remarked. "If I were going to stay in Australia I should not sell it at all, but surely if I am compelled by the exigencies of circumstances to do so, an old man may be permitted to indulge his fancy. I have ever been a man of moods. Since I took possession of it I have made the place my hobby, and it would cut me to the heart to allow it to pass into the hands of people who perhaps might not appreciate it. Perhaps it may not have struck you, or you may not have noticed, how few people there are who have any real affection for the work of their own hands; who, that is to say, when they have built up a place and the time comes for them to leave it, would rather demolish it altogether than permit another to enjoy the fruit of their handiwork. This is not my way, believe me. My sole desire is to feel sure that my place will be well cared for when I have left it, and that all I have done will not have been in vain. I will pay you the compliment of telling you that I have received many offers for it, but, as you can see for yourself, I have not accepted one of them. If I wished to dispose of it, I intended that it should be to someone whom I could trust to carry on the good work I had begun."

I thanked him for the compliment he was paying us, and assured him that should we take the place we would endeavour to deserve it. Then he left me to think over what he had said. Fortunately, Flaxman put in an appearance just in the nick of time, so that we were able to halve the labour. I told him the news, and with his usual impetuosity he jumped at it. He affirmed that we could not have been luckier. Everything sounded most propitious, and if I were willing he was quite prepared to stake all he possessed upon the experiment.

So much pleased were we with our new-made friend's description of the place, that we were not only willing, but anxious to set out for it without delay. Accordingly, next morning, shortly after daybreak, we had our horses brought in from the paddock outside the township, saddled and packed them, and then, accompanied by our venerable friend, left Hughenden for Montalta Station. The track, for it was little more than a track, ran first beside the Flinders River, and then, at a distance of some ten or twelve miles from the township, commenced to ascend almost abruptly. Thereafter it became picturesque in the extreme, threading its way sometimes through deep ravines, later over the bold faces of hills, diving deep down into valleys where tiny torrents brawled unceasingly. So far it certainly did not belie the good account we had received of it. Flaxman was enraptured. I'm afraid, however, he was thinking more of the pictures he would paint than of the cattle we should there breed. But there! I suppose it would be impossible for us all to look at matters in the same light. We should probably quarrel if we did.

At mid-day we halted for a couple of hours to give our horses a rest, and then pushed on again, the scenery, as we progressed, becoming more and more romantic. Suddenly, on turning a corner, we found ourselves confronted with a gate.

"This," said our conductor, "is the boundary of Montalta. I offer you a hearty welcome, gentlemen. We shall catch a glimpse of the homestead very shortly."

True enough, we did so half a mile or so further on, and a pretty picture it made. The house itself was situated on a natural plateau on the hillside, and commanded a magnificent view down the valley. It was not a large building, but was compact, old-fashioned, and capable of accommodating more people than one would have at first supposed. It possessed a broad verandah on three sides, while the men's hut and the stockyard were situated some hundred and fifty yards further to the right. In front of the house was a small garden, enclosed with a white fence, from which the track led down to the valley below. Both Flaxman and I expressed our appreciation of the excellent judgment which had been displayed in the selection of such a spot for a residence.

That the old gentleman was proud of it I could tell by the way he received this compliment. "Yes," he observed, "time has proved to me that I did not make a mistake when I chose this site. It was my first camping place when I came out here to take the country up. The place is hallowed by many associations. Here my son was born, here in my absence he was killed by blacks, and there he lies beside his mother in that little graveyard you can see across the valley. For fifteen years I have been alone, and at one time had made up my mind to live and die here. But man proposes and God disposes, and now in my old age I am returning to the land of my birth, to end my days among such as remain of my own kindred. But enough of that, let us push on to the house."

We accordingly urged our horses forward and ascended the somewhat steep track that wound its way round the hillside up to the plateau on which the house was built. At last we reached the garden gate, where we found a couple of black boys waiting to take our horses. That they entertained a great affection for their master it was easy to see by the way they grinned all over their ugly faces when he spoke to them. It would have been strange had they not done so, for a more kindly old fellow I never met. Having unstrapped our valises, we walked up the garden path under the spreading banana fronds towards the house. On closer inspection, it looked even more comfortable than it had done from a distance. The creeper-covered verandah was broad and cool, just the place for a comfortable lounge with one's pipe and a book on a hot Sunday afternoon. On either side of the front door were French windows, admitting to two rooms. That on the right was the living room, that on the left a bedroom. There were two other bedrooms behind, with a smaller room, which was used as an office. The kitchen and Chinese cook's room were on the further side of a small yard. Behind all rose the hill, covered with fine timber to its very summit. From the front verandah one could look down the valley for miles and see the river gliding along like a silver snake until it disappeared round the elbow of the hill, at the foot of which we had camped at mid-day. If cattle would not do well here, I told myself, they would not do so anywhere. There was food, water, and shelter in abundance.

The house itself was plainly but comfortably furnished. It could not be said that its owner had permitted himself many luxuries, but all that he had was good and substantial of its kind. What was more, from front door to back it was as clean and tidy as a new pin. On learning from our host that the Chinaman was responsible for this perfection, I registered a mental vow that if we took over the place, Ah Chow should be induced to remain with us.

The day following was devoted to a tour of inspection of the property. We started early in the morning, and by the middle of the afternoon had seen enough to enable us to judge of its worth and its capabilities. Our host had certainly underrated rather than over-rated its capabilities. It was, however, evident to anyone with eyes in his head that for some years past he had been allowing the working of the run to go very much as it pleased. A large proportion of the stock might very well have been got rid of with advantage to his pocket instead of having been allowed to remain eating their bovine heads off to the detriment of themselves and his profit. However, those were matters which could very easily be remedied.

When we returned to the homestead and were alone together, Flaxman and I exchanged ideas. On one thing we were both determined, and that was that by hook or crook Montalta must become our property, and as soon as possible. Next morning we accordingly broached the subject to our host, and a business discussion commenced. Never was a property disposed of with less haggling, and seldom, if ever, have two men discovered so good a bargain. At the very moment we were beginning to believe that we should be compelled to give up the search in despair, we had alighted on our feet. By mid-day we were, to all intents and purposes, the owners of Montalta.

"God bless you, dear old George," said Flaxman, as we shook hands upon our partnership. "This is just about the happiest day of my life. Let us hope it is the beginning of real prosperity for both of us."

"Amen," I answered to that.

Yet if we had only been able to pierce the veil of the future, what should we both have seen? I think we should have fled the place and never have gone near it again. Though a long time has elapsed since the things I am telling you of happened, I can never look back upon my life at Montalta without a shudder. Small wonder, you will doubtless observe when you know everything.

The next fortnight was a busy one for us all. The stock had to be mustered and examined, and arrangements made for sending away for sale such as were not to be kept. We had agreed to purchase the furniture of the house, so that the worry and expense of procuring any other was obviated. At last everything was completed, and on one memorable Monday morning our old friend, who had spent so many years of his life there, bade us farewell, looked his last at the home that had been the theatre of his happiness, as well as of his sorrow, and, with a wave of his hand, rode off down the track. We stood on the verandah and watched him depart; we saw him cross the river at the ford and vanish from our sight among the trees, only to reappear later within a hundred yards or so of the little burial ground where his wife and son lay at rest. Without the aid of a glass we could see him dismount and kneel beside the stone that marked the double grave. Presently he rose, remounted his horse, and in less time almost than it takes to tell had vanished completely from our gaze for ever. Since that moment I have neither seen nor heard of him. I do not even know whether he is alive or dead, nor have I ever been able to learn his history. That it was a strange one, and would be worth hearing, I have not the least doubt. The Australian Bush is the home of many strange pasts.

Being now formally settled in at the station, you may be sure we were not allowed to remain idle. Our work was divided as follows: while Flaxman looked after the store, kept the books and attended to the victualling of the men and our own immediate domestic affairs, interviewed such strangers as called, and generally controlled the correspondence and banking part of the firm's business, I, on my side, managed the run proper and gave my whole attention to the cattle and their needs. A healthy and a jolly life I found it. The possibilities of the place were comparatively boundless, and every month that went by found me more and more contented with my lot. By the time we had been there a year, and I had got matters fixed up according to my liking, I would not have changed places with anyone. To add to my satisfaction, the season proved an excellent one, and when I handed over our first mob to the drover who was to take them south for sale, I can assure you I was a proud man. They were as prime a lot of beasts as any lover of cattle could desire to run his eye over, and I flattered myself they would come upon the market just in the very nick of time. And sure enough they did so, and a nice price it was that they brought us in.

"This is better than clerking in a Melbourne office, George, my lad," said Flaxman, when we had read our agent's congratulatory letter. "Old Brownlow, the banker, will open his eyes when he sees this draft."

"I hope he'll see a good many more like it, before we've done with him," I answered. "We're only just beginning, my boy! Given two or three more good seasons like the last and we'll be thinking of buying our next-door neighbour out. Then we'll show them what we can do."

Our next-door neighbour, as we called him, owned the property to the north of us, a run somewhat larger than our own, which, had it been properly managed, would have paid equally well. The owner, however, was a wild, dissipated Irishman, who neglected everything but the whisky keg. In consequence, his affairs were trembling in the balance, and, not for the first time, he found himself hovering on the verge of ruin. His stock had deteriorated for want of fresh blood, his home life was as unhappy as it could well be, while his children, the descendants of Irish kings as he was wont to describe them when in his cups, were well nigh as savage as their pagan ancestors. Ever since we had come to Montalta I had cast envious eyes on the place, and Flaxman and I were thoroughly determined to acquire it as soon as an opportunity should present itself. But close as he often ventured to the edge of the precipice, O'Donoghue never actually lost his balance. Where others would have toppled over and have been lost to sight for ever, he invariably managed by some cunning trick to wriggle back into a position of safety once more. Fortunately for us we saw but little of him, and what little we did see usually had the effect of making us less and less desirous of developing a more intimate acquaintance. Flaxman and I found we were quite good enough company for each other, and, therefore, we could dispense with his companionship. That was perhaps the reason that gained us the reputation for unsociability in the little township thirty miles away to the north-east.

"Never mind what they say," remarked my partner one day some two years after we had taken over the station, when something had reached my ears and made me angry. "What does it matter? We can afford to laugh at them. We're happy enough, and they're miserable because they can't sponge on us, as they'd like to do. That's the long and the short of it, you may take my word for it."

"It's Mr. O'Donoghue who's at the bottom of it," I growled. "He hates us like poison, because he knows we want his run. But, by Jove, we'll have it sooner or later, just see if we don't. If he wants to show his teeth, he shall have good reason to do so."

"Live and let live, old man," replied my partner soothingly. "He's his own enemy, so let him go his way in peace. It is no business of ours."

"It's all very well to say let him go in peace," I retorted hotly, for somehow Flaxman's equable temper always added fuel to my rage. "I decidedly object to having it said that we jewed the old man out of this place and that our heads are now so swollen by success that we cannot put our hats on. If O'Donoghue says that in such a way that I can bring it home to him, I'll give him something that will induce him to mind his own business for the future, and chance the upshot."

"You'll do no good, my dear fellow," replied my partner. "He'd like to quarrel with you, if only to get himself talked about. Besides, it is in his blood; he cannot help a liking for what he would probably call 'the devil's own cousin of a row.' Don't worry about him. Give him rope enough and he'll hang himself in his own good time."

"Yes, and then we'll step into his shoes," I answered; "we'll unite the two places and run sheep on one, and cattle on the other. Forgive me, old boy, for losing my temper just now. But you know how easily offended I am, and what rages I get into about things you would not trouble a snap of the fingers about. However, we won't quarrel, will we?"

He laid his hand gently on my shoulder and looked me in the face.

"It would take a great deal to make me quarrel with you, George," he said.

I shall remember that speech to my dying day, and perhaps afterwards—that is to say, if the dead can remember anything.

CHAPTER VI

A FATEFUL MEETING.

Four years had elapsed since we had become the owners of Montalta, and never once throughout that time had either Flaxman or I found occasion to regret either our bargain or our partnership. Our good luck, which had brought us the place, continued to abide with us, and in consequence we were making money fast. If I had a grievance at all it was that we could not become the owners of the adjoining station, for O'Donoghue, to everyone's surprise, was still playing his old game—that is to say, one month tottering on the brink of insolvency, and the next spending money like water in the nearest township. Where it came from was a riddle which everyone asked, and none could answer. His wife, who was of the same extraction as himself, dressed like a peeress of the realm; his daughters rode the best horses in the district; while he himself was in a state of hopeless inebriation for weeks at a time. On the occasion of one of these outbursts he came within an ace of burning himself out of house and home, and doubtless would quite have done so, but that a man, camped in the scrub behind his house, saw the flames in time and sounded the alarm. Even then the miserable owner had to be carried out by the overseer and one of his own daughters, singing "Lannigan's Wake" at the top of his voice, and hitting out wildly at everyone who came near him. The fire had originated in his office, where he had been drinking alone. Strange though it may appear, this near thing did not induce him to mend his ways; on the contrary, he became worse than ever, until the whole district made up its mind that the end must shortly come. And come it surely did. His eldest daughter, Kate, a wild, brazen hussy of five and twenty, who spent the best part of her time flirting with the men about the place and quarrelling with her mother and sisters, took it into her head to run away from home with the ne'er-do-well son of the township's chief publican. O'Donoghue perceiving a chance of a row, and bent upon making a fool of himself, immediately he discovered it, rode off to interview the youth's father, taking enough liquor with him to make sure that he should be in proper fighting trim by the time he arrived there. The owner of the hotel (save the mark!) had been similarly occupying himself, and a battle royal ensued. The greater part of the population turned out to witness it, and the story of the encounter is told to this day. Fortunately, but small damage was done, mainly by reason of the fact that neither man was in a condition to control his own movements, much less to direct them against his adversary. Eventually they were separated by their respective friends, induced to allow bygones to be bygones, and three hours later parted company so affectionately that some people found it difficult to believe that they had ever quarrelled. The result was inevitable. Mrs. O'Donoghue, never too amiable, upbraided her husband in no measured terms for his behaviour, attributed her daughter's flight to his disgraceful conduct as a parent, commented on the fact that they were ruined, that the bank had called up the mortgage on the property, and then left him to reflect upon the situation. He did so, with the assistance of that devil's agent, the demi-John, and to such good purpose that by midnight he was ripe for anything. Accustomed though he was to heavy drinking, he had reached the limit at last. He took a gun from a corner and loaded it with ostentatious care, muttering to himself as he did so. It was an ancient muzzle-loader, and perhaps for the reason that he had not used it for some considerable time, he made the mistake of giving each barrel a double charge. It took him some time to find caps for the nipples; after which he opened the door and went out into the passage. A flood of light streamed from the sitting-room, the door of which was open. He crept towards it to find his wife there, sitting at the table staring straight before her out into the dark verandah.

"Ellen, my honey," he said, in a wheedling tone, "here's your loving husband come to see ye, with a pretty little toy in his hand which ye'll be after admirin', when ye know the use of it."

She looked round, saw what he carried, and took in the position at a glance. Whatever else she may have been, she was as brave as a lioness. She did not scream or beg him to put it down. She merely remarked that he'd get no ducks on the lagoon if he did go out, and then rose and walked quietly towards him. He was afraid of her as a rule, and even now he might have succumbed to her influence, but for the devil that was inside him.

"And shootin' ducks on the lagoon is it ye'd have me be afther?" he cried, flourishing the weapon as he spoke. "Sure, I've got me own duck at home, an', by the Merry Piper, I'll make her dance to me tune—so hark to that, my darlin'. None of your tantrums for me, ye Jezebel. Who put me children on to hate me? Who drove me gurl into runnin' away from home and her lovin' father? Look at this now, and say your prayers, for ye'll be wantin' 'em all before I've finished with ye. If ye but make a sound I'll shoot ye that minute."

The wretched woman must have realised by this time in what a terrible position she stood. He was mad with the drink and crazy with the hatred he had long felt for her.

"Dennis," she said, "ye would not shoot your own wife, the girl ye used to say ye loved?"

"Isn't it shoot ye, ye mean?" he answered. "And why not? We're ruined, are we? Then ye're better dead; 'tis a pity, for sure, that we have not Father Callaghan with us now to give ye a kindly partin', but there was no time to arrange it, seein' the way these little divils wid the green eyes has been followin' me about. Never mind, I'll beat them yet, or my name's not Dennis O'Donoghue."

As he said this he looked wildly round, and immediately gave a spring backwards as if to escape from something that was pursuing him. His eyes were nearly out of his head with terror and the perspiration was streaming down his face. A death watch was ticking in the woodwork of the wall, and in the silence that followed, the blood curdling howl of a wild dog reached them from the darkness outside.

"Look, look," he cried. "Holy St. Pathrick, look at thim. Thousands of them, all twisting and curling and curling and twisting like divils of the pit. Oh, save me, save me, they're crawlin' all over me. Down, down ye divils or I'll fire. Ye won't, won't ye, thin here goes."

Whether he really meant to fire or not, I cannot of course say, but the fact remains that he did so, either by accident or design. The result, seeing the way in which the rusty old weapon was loaded could scarcely have been otherwise. Both barrels burst, the man was killed instantly, while his wife fell to the floor with half her left side blown away. So Dennis O'Donoghue came by his end.

The noise of the explosion roused the house and brought the overseer flying in from his quarters, which were close by. There was nothing to be done for the man, but between them they carried the dying woman to her bedroom and laid her on the bed. A messenger was despatched post haste for the doctor, who lived in the township twenty miles away, but they might have spared themselves the trouble, for the case was hopeless, and an hour or so before daylight she, too, had said good-bye to the troubles and misfortunes of this mortal life. A month later the children were sent South to relatives, the bank had taken possession of the station, and it and the stock were for sale. Unfeeling though it may seem to say so, our opportunity had come at last. We immediately placed ourselves in communication with the bank, made the necessary enquiries, and looked forward to the time when we should be able to turn the two properties into one.

Winter was just commencing when we commenced our negotiations with the bank, and I was anxious, if possible, to get matters in proper trim before the rainy season properly set in. Times out of number did we anathematise the delay; banks, like the law, will not be hurried. Everything must be done according to precedent, and as slowly and with as much red tape as possible. However, like most other things, it came to an end at last, and the firm of Tregaskis and Flaxman were registered as the proprietors of the Stations Montalta and Condalba. It was a proud day for us, as you may suppose, more especially for your humble servant, whose ambition it had ever been to unite the two properties. The next thing to be done was to dispose of the cattle that remained and to stock it in their place with sheep. Then there would be a woolshed to build in readiness for the next season, a large amount of fencing to be done, boundary riders' huts to be built, and an efficient staff to be engaged, under the direction of a head overseer, who would reside at the homestead which had seen the tragic end of the O'Donoghues, man and wife. At first we had thought of dividing our time between the two places, but Flaxman had put his veto on the arrangement. Nothing, he declared, would ever induce him to pass the night in that melancholy house; and from this attitude I could not get him to budge. I have not hitherto mentioned that among his other peculiarities he was strangely superstitious—believed implicitly in visitants from the other world, and even carried his fancy to such extremes that it made him uncomfortable to go into a dark room; saw winding sheets in the candle, mysterious faces in the fire, and would no more have thought of sitting down thirteen at table than he would have thought of smoking a cigar in a powder magazine. In all my experience I do not think I have ever met a man so thoroughly saturated with superstition. At one time I used to chaff him on the subject, but finding that he took it to heart, I abandoned it and permitted him to continue undisturbed in his belief in spirits, wraiths, portents, and other mysterious denizens of the other world.

One morning in early spring I returned from a long ride that I had been obliged to undertake into the back country to find that a black boy from Condalba had ridden over with a note from Ellicott, the overseer, for which he required an answer. It appeared that he was anxious to see me concerning a tank we were about to commence, and which was to be used for conserving the water on the western boundary of the run. He had discovered, it appeared, what he considered to be a better spot for it, and was desirous of consulting with me about it. In reply, I scribbled a note to the effect that I would come as early as possible on the following day without fail, and sent the boy back with it. According to my promise I set off next morning soon after daylight, intending, if possible, to return the same night. Ellicott received me, and we inspected the new site together. I agreed with him that it was an improvement on the old, and bade him set to work on it as soon as possible. The afternoon was spent in visiting the wool-shed, then in course of erection, planning some new drafting yards, and trying to induce a fencing contractor to realise the fact that spending half his time in the township was not only bad for his health, but also detrimental to his business, so far as I was concerned. So quickly did the time pass, that it was four o'clock before I was ready to start for home. Ellicott endeavoured to persuade me to remain for the night, but this I did not wish to do, for the reason that I had arranged a meeting with a drover for the following morning, and wanted to have a look at some of the stock before he should put in an appearance.

"I think you would be well advised to stay," said Ellicott. "I fancy we're in for a heavy storm. Those clouds look very threatening, and you'll be pretty sure to find it dark in the scrub."

But I would not listen. Having made up my mind I was determined to stick to it. I accordingly mounted my horse, bade him good-bye, and rode off, devoutly hoping it would not rain before I reached home. My hopes, however, were not destined to be realised, for I had not gone five miles before it began to descend upon me. I prayed that it might soon stop, but instead of doing so it became steadily worse, until at last it came down a veritable deluge. Worse than all, it was growing so dark that it was only with difficulty I could see my way ahead of me. The track, if by that name it could be dignified, had not been used for many years until we came into possession of the station, and for that reason was barely decipherable at the best of times. In the dim light by which I was now travelling it was every moment becoming more and more a matter of pure guess work. Indeed, at last I came to the conclusion that I had lost it altogether. I dismounted and looked about me, only to have my supposition confirmed. There was no sign of it to be discovered, look where I would. The rain was pelting down in true tropical fashion, and as I had not come out prepared for it I was soon in that pleasant condition generally described as being "wet to the skin." A pretty plight I was in, to be sure—a thick scrub, pouring rain, almost total darkness, wet through, unable to light a fire, no blankets, and not a mouthful of food to eat. What a fool I was not to have accepted Ellicott's advice. Had I done so I should have spent a warm, comfortable evening; instead of which I was to wait in misery and utter discomfort as best I might until it should be light enough for me to continue my journey. I was experiencing one of the most uncomfortable phases of Bush life, and anyone who has ever done so will corroborate me when I say that there is nothing more miserable than a wet camp, even when one is provided with the most approved coverings. But, as the saying has it, "what can't be cured must be endured," so I unsaddled my horse, hobbled him with a stirrup leather, and prepared to put in the night as best I could. Fortunately I had my pipe to comfort me, which was better than nothing; otherwise I don't know how I should have beguiled the tedious hours.

Towards midnight the rain ceased for a time and a heavy thunder storm set in, the lightning was almost incessant, while the thunder boomed and rattled overhead as I had never heard it do before and hope I never may again. How devoutly I wished I were out from among the timber, I must leave for you to imagine. I never knew from minute to minute what might happen. In the intervals between the flashes the darkness was so dense that it was quite impossible to see one's hand before one's face. Then for a second all would be lit up with a blue glare and I could see the trunks of the trees around me, the rocky side of the hill round which the track ran, or should have run, and, occasionally, my horse, standing head up, ears pricked, amazed at the wildness of the night. Then all would be Cimmerian darkness once more. During one of these brief periods of light I caught a glimpse of a large rock some fifty or sixty feet distant from where I was standing. I waited for the next flash to come and then started for it, groping my way over the rough ground to the accompaniment of the thunder. At last I found it and sat myself down on the warmest side of it, if either of them could by any stretch of imagination be so described. Would the night never pass, I continually asked myself. Every minute seemed an hour, and every hour an eternity. To amuse myself I repeated every word of poetry I could recall, not once, but dozens of times; tried to sing, but gave up the effort when I discovered that it only added to the misery of the night. Once during a lightning flash I saw a dingo slinking by not a dozen paces from my shelter. Whether he saw me or not I cannot say, but he went his way up the hillside, and a quarter of an hour or so later, during a temporary lull, I heard him raising his melancholy voice in lamentation a quarter of a mile or so away. If you have never heard a dingo howl, pray that you never may. It is the most blood-curdling sound with which I am acquainted—the cry of a screech-owl, or of a dog baying the moon, is as nothing compared with it.

Another hour went by, and yet another, and still the storm did not abate one jot of its violence, nor did there seem to be any prospect of its doing so. It would not be daylight for at least another three hours, and how I was to put in the time I could not, for the life of me, imagine. I dared not move about among the timber, for more than once a heavy crash had told me that some giant of the forest had succumbed to the fury of the tempest, and bad as my present condition was I had not the least desire to make it worse to the extent of a broken arm or leg, or possibly a severe crushing from a falling tree. I accordingly remained where I was and thought of my warm bed at home and the fool I was not to have started a couple of hours earlier from Condalba.

After what seemed an eternity I struck a match, and screening it with my hand examined my watch. The time was just ten minutes to three. As I replaced it in my pocket a vivid flash of lightning lit up the little open space in which the rocks stood. Startled by it I looked up and saw a sight I shall never forget as long as I can remember anything. I had only time to see it and it was gone again, but not the impression it had produced upon me. I don't mind confessing that my first feeling was one of complete surprise; my second of absolute terror; and I would defy you, my reader, to have felt otherwise than I did under the circumstances. Let me tell you why, and you can judge for yourself.

In the first place I knew, or at any rate felt positive, that I was alone as far as human beings were concerned on that part of the run, the nearest boundary rider's hut being some eight miles distant to the east, with no one at all to the west. Yet, standing not a dozen paces from me the lightning now showed me the figure of a woman, dressed in some dark fabric. I was as sure as I could be of anything that it was not a creation of my imagination, and, as if to prove it, another flash came swiftly after the other and showed her to me again. She was looking directly at me, and now her arms were stretched out to me as if in supplication. Recovering from my surprise I sprang to my feet, but the light had gone again and I could see nothing of her.

"Who are you?" I cried at the top of my voice, for the howling of the wind would otherwise have rendered me inaudible. "And what is the matter?" As I spoke, I took a step or two forward in the hope of finding her. She did not answer, so I called again. Then there was another flash, and I found myself within two or three yards of her. This time I saw her quite distinctly. Her hat was gone, if she had ever possessed one, and her long hair was streaming in the gale. She looked more like some strange spirit of the night than a human being. Again darkness closed down upon us, and again I called. This time she answered by imploring me to save her. A moment later I felt her touch me, and, cold as I was myself, her hand on mine was like a lump of ice.

"Help me, help me," she shrieked. "I am terrified. For God's sake, help me. If you leave me, I shall die."

Without answering I seized her by the arm and dragged her, rather than led her, in the direction of the rock, where I had been sheltering myself up to that time. Once there I shouted to her to seat herself, and took my place beside her. She was trembling violently, and cried out at intervals like a mad woman. What had produced it all—I mean, of course, apart from the storm—I could not imagine, and it was some time before she could tell me. Side by side we sat waiting for the violence of the storm to abate and for day to break—two things which I felt inclined to believe would never come to pass. More than once she tried to rise, and struggled fiercely with me when I sought to detain her, which struck me at the time as being in perfect keeping with the whole extraordinary affair. If I had been told when I bade Flaxman good-bye at Montalta on the previous morning that I should be sitting beside a rock in the middle of the next night, in a raging tempest, with a woman of whom I knew nothing, driven crazy with fear, beside me, I should have laughed my informant to scorn. Yet it was quite true. It was more than that; it was most disagreeably and abominably true.

At last, thank Heaven, the darkness began to lift and a faint grey light to appear in the sky. The wind was as fierce as ever, but the thunder and lightning had ceased with the rain. Presently I was able to distinguish objects about me. My mysterious companion I could not see very plainly, and for the reason that she had found a shelter in a hollow between the two rocks in which the shadow still lingered. It was not long, however, before I was able to make her out, and to note the piteous picture of dumb despair her attitude suggested. She was seated with her back against the nearer rock, in a huddled up position, her head bent forward as if she were studying some object before her on the ground, and her hands dropped upon her knees. Her long black hair lay thick upon her shoulders, and so covered her that I could not see her face. At first I thought she was asleep, but while I looked she turned towards me, and for the first time I realised what she was like. How to describe her to you I do not know. To do justice to the subject I should require a greater skill than I possess, or am ever likely to possess. Yet, having in view what is to come, I must make an attempt to enable you to see her as I saw her then.

I am able now to state that at the time of our first meeting she was exactly twenty years of age; but had I judged from her appearance as I saw her then, I should have added to it at least another ten or possibly more. That, under happier circumstances, she would be beautiful admitted of no doubt, but at present she was too haggard and terrified to appear to any advantage. Her pallor, whether natural or the result of her night's exposure, was certainly unusual, and contrasted strangely with her dark eyes and raven hair. Her hands and feet were small and shapely, and I noticed that she wore no ring. Her dress was old and much torn. Possibly it might once have boasted some pretence to style, but I am not sufficiently well up in such matters to be able to form an opinion upon that point.

For a moment we looked at each other, then I rose, and she hastened to follow my example. It was then that I discovered how tall she was. At a rough guess, she could not have stood much under five foot eleven. Her figure was lithe, and properly dressed would doubtless be graceful. As it was it did not show to the best advantage. What her nationality was I could only conjecture from her English, but that she had some foreign blood in her veins struck me as being more than probable. Her dark eyes and raven locks said as much, as did the graceful way in which she carried herself, the like of which I had never seen before.

"You saved my life," she cried impulsively, holding out her hand to me as she did so. "I shall never forget it. My God! what should I have done had I not met you. I was mad with fear. Oh, this awful night, I shall never be able to rid myself of the memory of it!"

She covered her face with her hands as she spoke, as if to shut out the picture from her mind.

"Time will do that," I answered. "I am thankful, indeed, that we came across each other. Had you been wandering long before we met?"

"An eternity," she replied, clenching her fists and looking straight before her as she spoke, though why she did so I could not understand. "I believe I must have gone mad for the time being. I can only remember running on and on, striking against trees, falling over large stones, and shrieking with terror at the lightning, which, I believed was chasing me like an evil spirit to slay me. Then I saw you, seated beside this rock. At first I thought it was only my madness come back again. Then I heard your voice and believed that I was saved. Who are you, sir, and how is it that you happen to be here? I thought there was not a human being within miles."

"I might ask the same question of you," I replied. "A lady was the last person I expected to find out here. As for myself, my name is Tregaskis, and I am one of the owners, of this and the next station. I lost my way in the dark, and not being able to proceed, was perforce compelled to remain where I was and to await the coming of daylight before continuing my journey. Hence my good fortune in being able to render you this small service. Surely you are not alone out here? You must have friends somewhere whom you have lost. Is that not so? This is a wild part of the world for a girl to be alone in. I wonder whether I could manage to find your party while you wait here in the shelter of this rock. If you can give me any idea of the direction, I would find my horse and set out in search of them at once. Doubtless they are not very far away."

"I am alone," she answered, and I cannot hope to give you any idea of the way she said it. "I had a companion, but he is dead. God knew him for the villain he was, and sent the lightning to kill him. I hated him so that I was glad at first, but I grew frightened later and ran through the forest for my life."

"Do you mean that your companion was struck by lightning and killed?" I cried, looking at her in amazement. "Surely you don't mean that? Your terror must have made you believe it."

"It is true," she cried, stamping her foot as if in anger at my contradicting her. "It's as true as that I am speaking to you now. The devil sent him into the world to wreck my life, but God was on my side and killed him to save me. I can see that you do not believe what I say. Come with me, then, and see for yourself. I ran in the dark, knowing nothing of where I went, yet I will take you straight to the spot where he lies. Call it magic—call it what you will, but you will find that I am telling you the truth. Come."

By this time I was becoming more and more convinced that the terror of the night had deprived her of her reason. She saw what was passing in my mind and laughed scornfully.

"Have no fear," she cried, "I am as sane as yourself. But you must see him. You are a man, I challenge you to accompany me."

After that there was nothing for it but for me to go with her on what I felt sure could only prove to be a wild goose chase.

CHAPTER VII

WHEN EVE ENTERS EDEN.

In the previous chapter I described to you at some length the strange challenge offered by the still stranger girl to whom I had played the part of a protector during the previous night. I have also told you the belief I felt bound to entertain concerning her mental balance. She had declared to me most positively that her companion, a man, had been struck by lightning and killed, and it was his body she desired that I should accompany her to see. In itself this would have been a rational enough wish, but, when taken in conjunction with her tirade against him and the curious language she had employed, I think I may be excused if I felt some little doubt as to her sanity. However, as she seemed so bent on my going with her, I saw nothing for it but to acquiesce in her proposal. Tired though she must have been after all she had gone through during the night, she nevertheless sped along before me at such a pace that, active man as I am, I found some difficulty in keeping up with her. I have already remarked on her graceful carriage. I may say that I was now permitted an opportunity of observing it to greater advantage. Her step was as light and sure as that of a fawn, and, rough as the walking was, she never once stopped or appeared to experience the least inconvenience. Her glorious hair she had brought into something approaching order, though for lack of the necessary toilet appliances she was unable to make a very artistic affair of it.

For more than a mile she hurried me on, never once looking behind, but taking it for granted, I suppose, that I was following her. How she knew what course to steer, seeing that by her own confession she had only come through it once before, and then in the dark, I could not for the life of me understand. We left the hillside at last, and descended the plain, crossed a small stream by means of a fallen tree, which acted as an impromptu bridge—how had she crossed it during the storm, when she could not have seen her own hand before her face?—and then continued our march over a stretch of open ground towards some thick timber on the further side. Still she did not look round. Personally, I felt as if I were engaged in a walking tour in which I took but little or no interest. We entered the timber and began to climb a slight rise; then it was that I noticed that her speed was slackening. What, I asked myself, was going to happen next? Could her curious statement have been true after all?

Having reached a curiously-shaped little plateau, she stopped suddenly, and facing round on me bade me look. I followed the direction in which she was pointing with outstretched arm and saw, lying on the ground some ten yards away, what at first I took to be a bundle of clothes carelessly thrown down. Another look, however, was sufficient to convince me that it was a human body. Realising this I hastened to her side, and together we approached it. It was the body of a man, and a white man, there could be no doubt on that point. Reaching his side I knelt down to examine him, and as I did so uttered a cry of horror. Never before had I seen anything so repulsive as his face. It was convulsed into the most hideous grimace that the most imaginative mind of man could conceive. It was for all the world as if he had known that he was about to die and was caught by death in the act of laughing at his terrors. There was one other peculiarity I noticed. One side of his head was burnt almost to a cinder, as was his left side and leg. Since then I have seen the body of a man who had perished in a Bush fire, and I can liken it to nothing so much as that. That he had perished instantly was quite certain; so terrible were his injuries that he wouldn't have had time to suffer any pain. There was some consolation in that knowledge.

In age he might have been anything between forty and fifty. It was impossible to tell with any degree of certainty for obvious reasons. His hair on the right side of the head was tinged with grey; the face, which would probably have been by no means unhandsome under other circumstances, was decorated with a short grey beard and moustache. His clothes were those of a townsman and not of a Bushman; like the girl's they were well cut, but had seen much wear. I examined his pockets, to see if I could discover any clue as to his identity, but could discover nothing save a pipe, a broken penknife, a broken lead pencil, and an empty tobacco pouch—which last is a thing seldom to be found in the possession of a Bushman, preferring, as he does, to carry his smoking mixture in the solid plug. Having convinced myself that nothing else remained, I rose from my knees and turned to the girl. She looked at me with what I thought was almost a contemptuous expression on her face.

"You see I told you the truth," she said, as calmly as if she were stating a self—evident fact "There is the man I spoke to you of; the man who has spoilt my life, and whom I hated as I never thought it possible one human being could hate another. Times out of number I would have killed him without compunction, but something always prevented me; now, however, he has received his deserts."

"Hush, hush," I said, for though I am far from being as straightlaced as I might be, it seemed infinitely shocking to hear such vindictive sentiments fall from a woman's lips. "However he may have treated you, the man is dead, therefore let him rest in peace."

"Bah!" she answered, with a scorn that it would be futile for me to attempt to reproduce with any likelihood of success. "Why should you pity him because he is dead? If you knew him alive, you would hate him as I do. But simply because he no longer lives you try to make me believe that I must play the hypocrite, and pretend to feel towards him as no saint could ever bring herself to do. Why should I pity him, who showed no pity to man, woman, or child? Why should I forgive him, who did not know the meaning of the word—save as a gibe? Were I lying where he lies now, and he stood looking down at me, do you think he would have had anything for me better than a sneer? No! I knew him better than that. But I see that it gives you pain to hear me talking like this. Forgive me, I pray. Since you do not wish it I will say no more. You have proved yourself my friend, and I must do something to show my gratitude. Alas! it is all I can do, for I do not know what is to become of me. I have not a living being in the world to whom I can turn for help, and I have nothing wherewith to support life. What will become of me?"

Here the spirit which had carried her so impetuously forward hitherto gave way altogether, and she seated herself upon a boulder and fell to weeping bitterly.

Feeling that it would do her good, I allowed her to have her cry out, and occupied myself meanwhile in building a cairn of large stones above the dead man. I had nothing where-with to dig a grave, so that this was all I could do for the poor body until I could send men out to give it proper sepulture. By the time my task was finished my companion had dried her eyes and was watching me from her seat upon the rock. From her expression I could see that she was not taking the slightest interest in my labour, and still less in the subject that had occasioned it. She must have suffered greatly, I argued, to have come to this, poor girl. Though I would have given much to know, I could not ascertain, without putting the question too bluntly to her, in what sort of relationship the dead man had stood to her. At any rate, she did not volunteer the information, while I, of course, could not ask her for it. And now I found myself face to face with a curious situation. The girl had herself told me that there was not a being in the world to whom she could appeal for help, she was both friendless and penniless. What, therefore, was to be done with her? She could not be allowed to wander about the Bush alone and unprotected, that was out of the question. I knew all the managers' wives of the district, and felt sure that she would be unable to find a home with them. She could not go on to Condolba, that was out of the question; and what would Flaxman, who was a pronounced woman—hater, say if I took her home with me to Montalta, for that seemed the only course open to me? Though this would appear, by reason of the length of time it has taken me to write it, to have occupied my thoughts for a considerable period, it was not so. A couple of minutes, probably, decided the whole matter and brought me to the conclusion that I would retrace my steps, endeavour to find my horse, and then carry her back with me to the head station, and brave the upshot of my partner's wrath. I knew his kind heart too well to think for a moment that he would raise any objection. The mere fact that I had deemed it the right thing to do would be sufficient to settle everything.

"I think, if you have no objection, we will now set off in search of my horse," I remarked, as I placed a last stone upon the cairn. "If you will accept our hospitality at the head station, which is about ten miles distant, I am sure my partner will join with me in doing all we can to make you comfortable. You will need a rest after all you have been through."

She gave a little shudder as I said this, and I noticed that her eyes turned instinctively towards the heap of stones I had just erected.

"You are more than good to me," she answered, with what was for her unusual humility. "I thankfully accept your offer. If I do not I must perish of hunger, I suppose, and yet I would not be a burden to you for anything. If you will give me food enough to carry me on, I could doubtless make my way to some town where I might obtain employment. I can teach music and singing—there must be many ways in which I could make a living for myself."

"We will talk of that later," I said. "In the meantime, do you feel equal to walking back as far as the place where I left my horse and saddle last night? If you do, I could leave you somewhere and pick you up when I have collected my things. I should not be gone very long if the animal has not strayed far."

"No! no! let me go with you," she cried vehemently. "I could not bear to be left alone. I believe it would kill me, I do indeed. Mr. Tregaskis, you hate me, I know, for my behaviour just now, but that is because you do not know—wait, and when the opportunity offers you will find that I can be as grateful as I seem to be vindictive. I owe you my reason, if not my life, for had I not found you last night I should have been a mad woman by this time."

"You must not allow your mind to dwell on such things," I said soothingly. Then, descending to the practical, I continued, "I wish I had some breakfast to offer you, I am afraid you must be very hungry."

"I believe I could eat an elephant," she laughed, with a sudden change to levity, which I later on discovered was one of her strangest characteristics. "However, you are in just as bad a plight, so that the sooner we move from here, the sooner we shall be able to satisfy our hunger."

As she spoke she rose from the rock on which she had hitherto been sitting, and thus gave me to understand that she was ready to proceed. I gave one last look at the cairn, and then, side by side, we set off down the hillside to go in search of my horse.

Now there was a curious thing that afterwards afforded me food for considerable reflection. As you will remember, she had on the previous night found her way to me across the plain, the stream, and through the thick scrub on the other side; after daylight she had led me without stop or hesitation by the same route back to the spot where her companion, the man, had been struck dead by the lightning. Yet now, she appeared to have no notion of the direction we should take in order to reach the friendly rocks beside which we had met some hours before. I asked her if she could remember the way, but she only shook her head. It had all gone from her, she said. She could not find her way if she tried. She was as hopelessly bushed as a new chum would have been. Now what had brought this about? Had her terror endowed her with a sense of which she knew nothing, for guesswork it certainly could not have been? But again the question, what was it? And why had this strange faculty departed from her now? I determined to put the question to Flaxman later on and to find out what explanation he could give for it. That he would have one pat for the occasion, I could easily believe.

Whether she had been frightened by the storm, I cannot say; but the fact remains that my horse had gone a-wandering despite her hobbles. Nearly two hours elapsed before I found her, and by that time my companion was well-nigh worn out. Her thin boots were torn by the rough walking, and she was faint from fatigue and want of food. Yet she plodded steadily on by my side, trying, I believe, to make up by her cheerfulness for the bad impression she believed that she had made upon me on that little plateau where I had built the cairn. At last we came upon the horse, calmly feeding beside the same small creek which we had crossed and recrossed that morning some miles lower down. She looked none the worse for the storm of the past night, but submitted to be caught and saddled with all the patient equanimity of a trained camp-horse. This work done, I turned to my companion, who was standing behind me watching me. It then struck me for the first time that while I had told her my name, she had not, as yet, given me hers. I informed her of the fact, where-upon she stood for a moment confused, as if she did not know what answer to give me.

"Please do not tell me if you would rather not," I said, I am afraid a little coldly, for I must confess her hesitation did not please me. "I have no right to ask the question. Why should you, therefore, tell me?"

"It was not because I would not tell you that I hesitated," she flashed out, with something of her old fire. "It is because I am ashamed of it. My name is

Moira Pendragon, so now you know it. Once, I believe, we were a noble family—now—" she stopped and threw her hands apart with an expressive gesture. Both were strange names—the Christian name was, I believed, Irish; the surname Cornish, without a doubt.

"It would seem, then, that by our names we both hail from the same part of the world," I observed, "You remember the old rhyme—'By Tre—Pol—and Pen, You may know the Cornishmen!'"

"I am a Tregaskis, you are a Pendragon, we only require someone with the prefix Pol to make our number complete. And, by Jove, now I come to think, we are complete, for my old mare's name here is Polly, which divested of the 'ly' would come to the same thing. It looks like an omen, does it not?"

"An omen of what?" she asked, with her dark eyes fixed upon me. "I distrust such things."

"An omen of friendship," I replied. "Unless you would prefer not to look upon me as a friend."

She laughed scornfully, just as she had done earlier in the morning when I had asked her to remember that the man was dead. "I never had a friend worthy of the name in my life," she answered. "Why should you offer to be kinder to me than the rest of the world has been? Ever since my childhood I have stood alone—the world against me. But what would I not give to know that there was someone whom I could trust implicitly, as sometimes men trust their comrades, but as women never trust a woman."

"Let us try to be such friends then," I replied, fired with unusual enthusiasm, not so much by what she said as by the way she said it. "When you know me better you will discover that I am not one who gives his friendship lightly, but having once given it, it takes more than a little to break it. Will you trust me?"

"I will," she answered, and held out her hand to me as she did so. "I will trust you as I have never trusted anyone before."

And so our compact—surely one of the strangest, as you will afterwards see for yourself, that was ever made by man and woman—was sealed between us.

"Now," I said, when mere formalities were at an end, "I am going to put you upon my mare, and we will proceed to the station as quickly as possible. I am afraid you will not be very comfortable, but, at least, it will not hurt you or tire you as much as walking."

At first she declared that she was quite able to walk, but eventually I persuaded her to do as I wished. Without further demur she placed her foot in my hand and allowed me to swing her up into the saddle. I next arranged the stirrup in such a fashion as to give her some sort of support, and then we commenced our march for Montalta, which I hoped, all being well, to reach by mid-day. It was a long and tiring walk, for the ground was heavy after the rain we had had during the night. However, I plodded steadily on, talking to my companion on almost every subject I could think of, in order to divert her thoughts from her own unenviable position and all she had been through in the last twenty-four hours. So far as I was able to judge, I found her a clever conversationalist, and whatever else she may have lacked, her education had certainly not been neglected.

At last, when, I must confess, I was beginning to feel a little tired myself, I saw the boundary fence of Montalta come into sight, and pointed it out to her. Ten minutes later we had reached it, and I was lifting her down at the foot of the steps. Just as I did so, Flaxman appeared on the verandah, and I noticed the look of astonishment upon his face as he saw my companion. He did not remark upon it, of course, but I knew as well as possible that he was wondering what it all might mean. Having given my horse to one of the boys, I turned to Miss Moira and bade her welcome to Montalta, after which I conducted her up the steps to the verandah and introduced her to my partner. In a few brief words I told him of our meeting during the storm of the previous night, and added that I had persuaded her to accept our hospitality for the time being. Whatever he may have thought, and woman-hater though he was, Flaxman was too true a gentleman to permit her to see that her presence was unwelcome. On the contrary, he escorted her into the house as if she were a princess honouring us with a visit. I remained behind for a minute in the verandah to give some instructions to the boy and then rejoined them in our sitting—room, where I found them conversing together in a most satisfactory manner. Needless to say, my mind was considerably relieved.

Remembering all she had been through, and how tired she must be, I persuaded her after a while to go to the room which had been prepared for her, and whither I had seen a substantial meal conveyed. I escorted her myself as far as the door, where she stood facing me.

"How can I thank you?" she began, and doubtless would have said more had she not broken down. Thereupon I hastened to inform her that if she desired to prove her gratitude for such small service as I had rendered her, she could best do so by making a good meal and afterwards sleeping soundly for several hours to come. She gave me a faint little smile and then retired, when I returned to the sitting-room, where I found Flaxman awaiting me.

"My dear fellow," he began, "what on earth does this mean? I did not like to ask any questions before the girl, but where did you pick her up? She's the most extraordinary looking young woman I ever set eyes on. You could have knocked me down with the proverbial feather when I saw you two coming up the track. Tell me all about it!"

I did so, commencing with my losing myself in the dark, and finishing with their introduction to each other in the verandah a short time before.

"But who can she be?" he asked. "And who was the man who was struck by lightning? What relation was he to her?" I shook my head. "She will not tell me," I replied. "All I know about their relationship is that she declares he had treated her badly and that she hated him for it."

"And she told you nothing of where she came from, nor where she was going?"

"Nothing at all. And I did not like to ask her. She was too distressed to stand much questioning. You're not angry with me for bringing her here, are you?"

"Angry, my dear fellow," he said. "Why should I be? I hope I'm not such a cur as to be angry with a man because he does the right thing by a woman in distress. But I confess I don't understand the young lady. I don't think I've ever met anyone quite like her before. To use a word I detest, it seems to me as if there is something uncanny about her. Had we been in England I should have inclined to the belief that there is gipsy blood in her veins. Those dark eyes and black hair would be quite in keeping with the Romany race. Cornish I should certainly not have taken her to be."

"And yet the name? Does not that suggest association with the Duchy? You remember the distich, 'Tre, Pol, and Pen'? Arthur and Uther were both Pendragons."

"And to you belongs the honour of having rescued a descendant of the ancient leaders from imminent peril in the Australian Bush. It is quite a romance."

"I can assure you it did not seem so to me in the middle of the night," I answered; "I don't think I was ever more miserable in my life. When I saw her standing before me in that lightning flash I felt sure I was looking upon an inhabitant of another world. You cannot imagine anything more ghostly than the picture she presented."

"You won't be so ready to laugh at me for the future," he said, with a smile.

"I would not laugh at you at all," I hastened to say, "if I thought it gave you pain. Put it down to my stupidity that I am unable to believe in all that you do. Sometimes I almost wish that I could. And now I must be off about my work. I'm behind-hand enough as it is."

So busily occupied was I kept that the afternoon was well advanced before I reached the homestead again. One of my first acts was to despatch a couple of men to bury the unfortunate man who had been killed by lightning; that done I felt easier in my mind, though for the life of me I could not have said why.

As I rode up to the house I became conscious of a tall dark figure standing on the verandah. On closer inspection, it proved to be Miss Moira, but so transformed that I might well have been excused had I not recognised her at first glance. Her glorious hair was now brought into order, she had also done something to her dress, what I cannot say, that to my mind made it appear like a different costume altogether. Though the hunted look was still to be seen in her eyes, it was not as marked as it had been when I had first brought her to the homestead. And to think that, had it not been for her accidental meeting with me, this girl might even now be wandering in the scrub, mad, starving, and homeless! Under such circumstances in all probability it would not have been long before death claimed her for his own. Now, for the time being at least, she was safe.

On hearing my horse's step she turned and saw me. There was a smile of welcome on her face. It was wonderful the difference it made in her, one would scarcely have believed it to be the same countenance, certainly not that which I had seen staring wildly at me in the lightning flashes of the previous night.

"You have rested, I can see," I called to her. "You look better already."

"It is you whom I have to thank for it," she answered; and then continued, in a lower voice, "I scarcely dare to think of last night. It seems as if it must all have been an evil dream from which I have only just awoke."

"Why think of it at all?" I continued. "Try to forget it if you can. You are safe now, nothing can harm you here. The best thing you can do is to let the dead past bury its dead."

I realised that I had said a foolish thing, so to divert her attention, I called up a boy and gave him my horse, after which I ascended the steps and joined her on the verandah. The change in her appearance was, to say the least of it, remarkable. She was more womanly, more ladylike I ought perhaps to say, than I had thought it possible for her to become in so short a time. There was, it is true, the same curious litheness of movement, the same air of unconventionality, the same panther-like grace that I had noticed before, but it was now controlled, like a would-be masterful horse which, while it obeys its driver, is none the less conscious of its power to kick over the traces at any moment should occasion present itself.

One way and another we had seen some curious things at Montalta since we had taken the station over, but I do not fancy we had ever spent so strange an evening as we did on this particular occasion. Had anyone told us a few days before that we should be acting as hosts to a young girl, of whose antecedents, by the way, we knew nothing, I doubt very much if we should have believed it. Yet not only were we doing so, but it was evident that we were deriving considerable satisfaction from the fact. Never before had I seen Flaxman lay himself out to be amiable as he did on this occasion. Hitherto I had always found him reserved, I might almost be excused if I said "bearish," in the presence of the opposite sex. On this occasion, however, he came out of his shell completely and talked as I had never heard him do before. Among other things, we had some months before indulged ourselves in the luxury of a piano, my partner being a musician of more than average ability.

During the evening he sat down to it and began to play. I watched the girl's face as he did so, and noticed the eager look that took possession of it. I forget now what he played, but I remember as distinctly as if it were but yesterday the way in which she appeared to hang upon every note. When he stopped, he turned on his chair and looked at her. Her hands were clasped upon her knees and she was looking straight before her, as if she were watching something that we could not see. Then Flaxman rose, and, after a short pause, during which none of us spoke, she left her chair, almost involuntarily, and took his place. After a moment's hesitation, she struck a few chords and began to sing. What her voice was I could not tell you, a mezzosoprano would, I fancy, be the proper description; I only know that it thrilled me to the very centre of my being. The song she sang was one of Schubert's, a sad little melody that was destined to haunt me for many a long day to come. On Flaxman her music produced an effect as extraordinary as hers on him. He lay back in his chair, with closed eyes, drinking in every note that fell from her lips, as if he were afraid of losing a single one. When the last chords died away and she rose from the instrument, we almost forgot to thank her, so completely had she held us in her thrall.

Later, when she had retired for the night, I went to the office to look up some information I required for the next day's work. Having obtained it, I strolled out on to the verandah, according to custom, for a smoke before turning in. It was a beautiful moonlight night, and the view down the valley was like a glimpse of fairyland. Flaxman was at the further end, leaning upon the rails, pipe in mouth. Apparently he did not hear me approaching him. Assuming a cheerfulness I certainly did not feel, I offered him a penny for his thoughts. He gave a start of surprise, and, without turning answered bitterly:—

"My thoughts! Bah! They are not worth even a penny. They are only ghosts, such as you affect not to believe in. Ghosts of what was once, can never be again, yet must always be remembered. Do you understand? I think you do, but should you not, listen to Themistocles, 'Memini etiam quae nolo: oblivisci non possum quae volo,' and you have it in a nutshell. But when you've finished your pipe, let's to bed, old friend, it must be nearly midnight, and you are probably tired out."

My partner always thought of others before himself.

So ended the first day of Miss Moira's stay at Montalta.

CHAPTER VIII

"OH! BEWARE OF JEALOUSY."

More than three months had elapsed since that eventful day on which I had brought Miss Moira to Montalta. It is very possible that it may strike some people as peculiar that she should have remained so long with us. For my own part, and I think I may speak for my partner, Flaxman, I can safely say that we did not look at it in the same light; at least, let me be strictly accurate, we did not do so at that time. Under such circumstances I cannot imagine what the consequences would have been; it is quite certain, however, that they could not have proved more disastrous than they did. I think you will be of the same opinion when you have read all I have to tell.

As I have already said, I had started with the belief that Flaxman would not approve my action in bringing her to the station at all. In this I very soon discovered that I was mistaken. The first feeling of antagonism having departed, he not only reconciled himself to her presence, but, to my astonishment, appeared to find a positive pleasure in it. I noticed that his eyes watched her as she moved about the room, and once I could have sworn I heard him heave a deep sigh. Perhaps she reminded him of someone he had known in that mysterious past of his, to which nothing would ever induce him to refer. Taken altogether, he was a queer mixture was John Flaxman.

As for Miss Moira herself, every day saw a difference in her. Her once hollow cheeks had filled out and had taken to themselves the bloom of health—her eyes had lost their frightened look entirely. She had improved her wardrobe with all a woman's cleverness and daintiness, while she treated Flaxman and myself as though we were two elder brothers who stood in constant need of all her care and attention. By degrees she had entirely taken over the management of the house, thus relieving Flaxman and myself of one of our most irksome responsibilities. Under our régime the matutinal interview with our Chinese cook ran on something like the following lines.

Scene: The kitchen.

"Morning, John!"

Grunt from John, as he dusts an invisible crumb from his spotless table.

"What have got?"

"Col-lee mullon yeslay (cold mutton) makee one same cullee (make curry), potato pie think? All same leesehole (rissole)."

By this he desired to inform me that there was sufficient mutton remaining over from the previous day, which, by his dexterous manipulation could be turned into a curry, a potato pie, or that culinary standby, the accommodating rissole. Cattle and sheep stations are not proverbial for their variety of diet; on the one it is all beef, beef, beef, fresh occasionally, salted usually; on the other it consists of the eternal mutton, roast, boiled, hashed, or stewed, according to the taste and fancy of the eater.

Now all this was changed; Miss Moira assumed direction of affairs, and we were absolved from our visits to the kitchen. At first the cook was disposed to resent the intrusion of a female, but he gradually became accustomed to it, until at last, in his own pig-tailed way, he enrolled himself as one of her most ardent and devoted admirers. "Allee same one piece woman, velly good," he was once heard to remark, and after that there could be no doubt as to his approval. We congratulated her on her victory, but she took the matter very calmly, as she did most things.

"John and I thoroughly understand one another," she declared. "I praised his pastry, and so won his regard for ever. He is pliable enough, if he is properly managed."

"Most of us are," I put in. "To borrow a simile from our Chinese friend, we are all pastry in a woman's hands."

"I am afraid you forget that in order to become pastry you must originally have been dough," was her laughing reply, "and that sounds scarcely complimentary, does it?"

"Fairly hit, my boy," cried Flaxman, who was making a cracker for his stockwhip on the verandah outside, "if you will play bowls or compliments, you must expect the rub."

"Compliment or no compliment," I answered, "it's the truth, is it not, Miss Moira? There is scarcely a man in the world whose life is not influenced, one might almost say moulded, by some woman, for good or ill. I wonder how many men there are in Australia at this minute eating their hearts out in exile, who but for some woman would be living their lives out in peace in England?"

At that moment I heard the crack of Flaxman's chair as he rose from it and went down the verandah towards the steps. I immediately wondered whether, metaphorically, I had trodden on his corns by my foolish speech. I sincerely hoped not, for I would not have given the poor old fellow a moment's pain for anything. He, at least, so I firmly believed, might be classed among those to whom I had just alluded. I fancy Miss Moira knew what was passing in my mind, for she looked at me and then at the window; after which, with what was for her an unusually quiet air, she departed on household duties intent. When she had gone I could have kicked myself most heartily for my stupid speech. I had said it without thought, and by doing so had given pain to the two people I liked best in the world. That was always my way. My heart was in the right place, but that unruly member my tongue would persist in getting me into trouble, however much I might try to prevent it.

At the commencement of the week following it became necessary for me to go north in order to purchase some stock for which we were in treaty. It was a long and tiring journey, and, as I brought the cattle back with me, nearly a week elapsed before I reached home again. Needless to say I was by no means sorry when I saw ahead of me the white roofs of the head station rising above the trees. Having seen the cattle disposed of, I gave up my horse and made my way to the house. It was nearly time for our evening meal, and I was as hungry as a hunter. But it was not of that I was thinking, but of Miss Moira. Since I had been away I had thought more than a little of her, more perhaps than was altogether good for my peace of mind. During the cold, dark nights, when I had been on watch with the cattle, and when the only sound to be heard was the croaking of the frogs down at the waterholes, the occasional lowing of some uneasy beast, and the cry of a night bird in the scrub, I used to think of her, and wonder at the strange chance that had brought her into my life. I used to picture her moving about the rooms, seated at the piano or presiding at the tray at table, until I almost felt as if I were actually present with her.

That I was over head and ears in love with her I knew only too well, but whether she, on her side, entertained any feeling other than kindness for me I could not, of course, tell then. Why she should do so I could not think—it was true I had found her in the storm and had brought her to the station, but I had done no more. On the other hand, Flaxman was cleverer than I in a hundred ways; he was handsomer by a great deal, was the possessor of a more polished manner; and for these reasons, and many others, was more likely to catch a maiden's eye. For the first time since I had known him I felt jealous of him; but, in justice to myself, I must say that I tried to put the feeling away from me. What right, I asked myself, had I to be jealous of Flaxman, or indeed of anyone else? Yet the wretched fact remained; it was so, and it would not be denied.

I ascended the verandah steps and passed into the hall. The sound of music came from the sitting-room, and from the touch I knew that it was Flaxman playing. Vaguely irritated, I strode to my own room, tossed my hat and valise on to the bed, and then made my way to the room where I had no doubt I should find them both. As I reached the door a burst of laughter from within caused me to stop before entering. I felt as if I were playing the part of the unwelcome guest at the marriage feast. I cursed myself for a fool, and opened the door. It was a homely scene that presented itself to me. Flaxman was seated at the piano, with his back towards me. Miss Moira was reclining in a low chair beside the fire, knitting. Opposite her, to my intense surprise, was an elderly lady of most imposing appearance, with snowy hair, worn in ringlets, gold-rimmed spectacles, and a general air of respectability that was almost awe-inspiring. It was a matter of some moments before I recognised in her the widow of the parson of a township thirty miles or so away. But what on earth was she doing here? That was what puzzled me. She seemed to be quite as much at home as the old cat dozing before the blazing logs.

The sound of my entrance made the two ladies look up, and the exclamation of surprise to which Miss Moira gave utterance brought Flaxman wheeling round on his stool to face me.

"Welcome, old fellow," he cried, hastening forward to greet me. "We were only talking of you half an hour ago and wondering when we should see you, were we not, Moira?"

I started as if I had been stung. So they had even got as far as this during my absence. He called her by her Christian name and she did not object to it. I felt more like the unwelcome guest than ever, particularly when I noticed that Moira seemed to hang back behind Flaxman, with a shyness I had never noticed in her before. It was almost timidly that she offered me her hand and bade me welcome home. My heart sank down and down, for I feared the worst. I tried hard to pull myself together, but in vain; the jealous dog was on my shoulder, ready to show his teeth on the smallest opportunity.

"I think you already know Mrs. Dawson, do you not?" enquired Flaxman, with a little motion of his hand towards the widow, who, like the others, had risen and was standing before the fire.

"I believe I have that pleasure," I remarked, but with no great show of cordiality. "I think I met you the last time I was in Marabah."

"I remember the occasion perfectly," she replied in a voice like that of a tragedy queen. "My poor dear husband was alive then, ah me!" She heaved a heavy sigh as she thought of the dear departed. This was, of course, only for effect, since it was notorious that they had led a cat-and-dog life together for years. On which side the fault lay I am not prepared to say.

"Mrs. Dawson has been kind enough to come up and pay us a short visit," my partner continued. "I am afraid she must find it very dull, but she is good enough to pretend that she does not. Now that you have returned we must see what we can do to amuse the ladies."

I am afraid I sniffed scornfully. If Flaxman imagined I was going to trot Mrs. Dawson about the station like a bear-leader while he paid court to Miss Moira, he was very much mistaken. I would not do that for him or anyone else, and the sooner he realised that fact the better it would be, so I told myself, not only for him, but for all concerned. I am afraid I was in a very bad temper indeed, and it threatened to grow worse as the evening progressed. What a poor, weak-minded fool I was! However, I was destined to pay dearly for it later on.

All this time Miss Moira had stood quietly in the background. Once or twice she looked at me as if she divined that there was something wrong and was not able to tell what she could do to set matters right. I turned to address her, and as ill-luck would have it, I had scarcely uttered a word before Flaxman, who was kneeling at the fire, putting some logs on, said without looking round:—

"Isn't it time for us to get ready for dinner? Surely it must be nearly seven, Moira?"

Of course, being in the humour I was, I must needs take this as meaning that he was anxious to prevent me from speaking to her.

"Surely the dinner can wait for a few minutes," I said pettishly. "I've no doubt it won't spoil while I ask Miss Moira what she has been doing with herself during my absence."

I had no sooner said it than I realised what a tactless speech it was. In the first place, I had snubbed Flaxman; in the second, I had implied that the dinner would in all probability be a poor one, which was a deliberate slight upon Miss Moira's house-keeping; and in the third and last place, I had as good as said that the young lady in question must of necessity find the time hang heavily upon her hands when I was away from home. Whether she saw what was passing in my mind or not, I cannot say, but she replied without hesitation.

"Everything has gone on very much as usual," she answered. "I have had the house to look after. I have had several nice rides on the mare you gave me. She is as quiet as a lamb now, by the way, and looks so beautiful. You will see a difference in Fly's puppies, I expect, they have grown a great deal. Poor old thing, she has missed you."

"That's more than other people have," I thought to myself bitterly. "It's a trifle hard to a man when only his dog, poor dumb creature, seems to have felt his absence from home." However, thank goodness, I had, for once, sufficient sense to keep these thoughts to myself. Had I given utterance to them, I dare not think what the consequences would have been. We talked together for a few moments longer, and then, without further opposition on my part, went off to our respective rooms to prepare ourselves for the evening meal.

I had just changed from my travelling clothes into those I usually wore at home, when Flaxman entered the room. I thought at first that he had come to remonstrate with me for my sulky behaviour in the sitting-room and to find out in what way he had offended. I soon discovered, however, that this was not the case.

He had merely come in for a chat while I dressed, as he very often did. Despite my wretched temper, I could not help feeling my heart warm to him as I saw him in my looking—glass seated on the bed, watching me with a smile on his kindly face. He was a man with whom anyone would find it difficult to pick a quarrel, and yet that evening I had been quite prepared to do so, indeed I had been almost anxious to do so.

"Well, how did you get on?" he enquired. "Did the cattle come up to your expectations?"

"In every way," I answered, manipulating a tie as I spoke. "They're a first-class lot and should do well in our country. I got them cheaper than I expected. I fancy old MacPherson wants money—at least, I gathered as much from what one of his overseers let slip. If all goes well, we shall turn over a snug profit by next season."

"Bravo, old fellow, you're a wonderful hand at scenting out a bargain. At any rate, I'm glad to have you home again. I did not think you could possibly be here before Saturday."

"I should not have been, but for the river falling. We were able to cross just above Arbuthnot's boundary, so saved a couple of days—a saving for which both I and the cattle were more than grateful. If we had had any more rain it would have meant going round by the Rocky Waterhole, and that's far from being a part of the country that I care about. Any news here?"

"Nothing of any importance," he replied. "There was a slight freshet on Monday, so we moved the stock from number three paddock up to number five. On Wednesday, that is to say yesterday, the stores came up, and I sent out the ration cart to the huts. That's all there is to tell, I fancy."

There was a little pause, after which I said, "By the way, how did Mrs. Dawson happen to get up here? She was about the last person I expected to see."

We were facing each other now, and it seemed to me that he looked a little uneasy. Once more I began to grow suspicious. I wondered what excuse he would make to account for her presence. He did not attempt to make one, however. His answer was perfectly straightforward, as I should have known it would be.

"I asked her to come up and spend a short time with us," he said. "For some while I have thought it was scarcely fair of us to debar Miss Moira from the society of her own sex. Feeling sure that you would agree with me, I wrote to her, she accepted, and I sent the buggy to the mail change to meet her. Perhaps I should have waited until you came home, but the opportunity seemed too good to be missed. You are not annoyed about it, are you?"

"Why on earth should I be?" I asked, but none too cordially. "You have a perfect right to do as you please, and, of course, we must make Miss Moira as happy as we can. That goes without saying."

"I'm glad you take it like that," he continued; "I was half afraid you might not like it. Now, let us come and have dinner. I expect you are ready for it."

When we reached the dining-room we found the cloth laid and everything ready for our meal. Though, of course, I did not say anything on the subject, I could not help comparing the table as it was now, with what it had been, say, a year before. Now it was daintily decorated, the glass and silver sparkled upon the snowy napery; aforetime we were content with pewter plates, forks and spoons, while our glass ware might have been dropped or thrown about without the least fear of any damage happening to it. And this change we owed to Miss Moira, the girl whom I had rescued under such extraordinary circumstances a few months before. For that, at least, we should have been grateful.

For upwards of a fortnight Mrs. Dawson remained with us, and by the end of that time I had quite come to see the wisdom of Flaxman's action. There could be no sort of doubt that it gave Miss Moira pleasure to have a female companion, one with whom she could talk the talk that women love and of which Flaxman and I were necessarily incapable. When one got to know her, the widow proved a kindly old soul, and while perhaps her best friend could not have called her intellectual, she was quite clever enough to comprehend the position of affairs and to act accordingly.

As may be supposed, I was quite ready to enjoy a holiday after my long and tire—some journey. I had worked hard, had made money for the firm, and felt entitled to a spell. Winter was well advanced, and, so far as I was concerned, work on the station was practically at a standstill. I was thus able to devote more time to the amusement of Miss Moira and her companion than I should otherwise have been able to do. I took them for drives here, there, and everywhere, pointed out the beauties of the run, such as they were, and generally did my best to interest them. And with each day my love was growing stronger and stronger. Sometimes it was as much as I could do to keep it back, so strong was the craving to let her know how much she was to me. But I dared not do it. What, I had to ask myself, would my position be should she tell me that she did not love me? In that case it would be necessary for one of us to leave the station, for we could not live under the same roof together. And who would have to leave?

At last Mrs. Dawson's stay came to an end, and I drove her to the mail change eight miles away, where she was to catch the coach for home. That she was sorry to go there could be no doubt; she had taken a sincere liking to Miss Moira, which was heartily reciprocated. As we drove along she spoke of her.

"She is a wonderful girl," she said. "I don't think I have ever met another like her. He will be a lucky man who wins her for his wife."

To this I offered no reply, for the simple reason that I felt I could not speak without betraying my secret. She did not appear to find anything extraordinary in my silence, or if she did she did not comment upon it. But she had not done with the subject yet.

"Yes," she continued, "he will be a lucky man who obtains the hand of Moira Pendragon in marriage. Pray, have you noticed anything lately?"

"In what way?" I asked. "Do you mean in reference to Miss Moira? If so, I am afraid I have not."

"Well, yes, it refers to her of course," she went on, "but I am thinking of Mr. Flaxman. Has it ever struck you that he admires her?"

So she had noticed it too, had she? I felt the old demon of jealousy spring to life within me immediately. If she had noticed it, then it must be so, and my friend was my rival after all.

"I do not see how anyone could fail to admire her," was my reply. Then, after a short pause, I added, "Does it strike you that he means anything by the admiration he entertains for her?"

"I cannot, of course, say for certain," she answered, "but in my own heart I feel confident that he does. One has only to watch him when he is in her company to realise that in Moira he has met his fate."

Every word she uttered stabbed deeper and deeper into my heart, and yet, though I winced under the pain, I did not attempt to escape from it.

"What you say naturally surprises me," I began. "It is also a little disquieting, for Flaxman is not only my partner, but my best friend. If he were to marry, it would make a vast deal of difference to me, and I am afraid I am selfish enough to think of that."

"Perhaps I should not have spoken my mind so freely," was her reply. "But I felt sure you must have noticed it as I did, and have drawn your own conclusions. The matter seemed so obvious."

The horses had covered nearly a hundred yards before I put my next question to her.

"And what do you think Miss Moira's decision would be in the event of his asking her to become his wife?" I queried, though I could scarcely force myself to utter the words.

"I feel sure she would accept him," replied the old busybody. "And I think she would be very wise. He is a charming man, well read, good-looking, and they have so many accomplishments and tastes in common."

I cursed his good looks and his accomplishments, and to prove it gave the near—side horse such a cut with the whip that it sent him capering down the track for a hundred yards or more. Fortunately for her peace of mind the old lady beside me was quite unconscious of the pain she had caused me, and I intended that she should remain so if necessary to the end of the chapter. Five minutes later, when I had steered the conversation into a safer channel, the mail change hut came into view, and almost at the same moment the coach itself turned the corner of the cross tracks and pulled up before the shanty. When we had drawn up alongside, I assisted Mrs. Dawson to alight, and then saw to the stowing away of her luggage on the coach. The driver was ready to start again by the time this was finished, so that there was no opportunity permitted us for discussing the topic in which we were both so much, yet so differently, interested. This was a boon for which, you may be sure, I was grateful.

When the clumsy vehicle had rolled away and had disappeared round the corner of the track, I stayed talking to the change man for a time, then having obtained our mail bag, turned my horses' heads and set off on my drive back to the station. As you may suppose, I had plenty to think about as I drove along, and my thoughts were far from being pleasant ones. What would become of me if Moira became Flaxman's wife, as I felt sure she would do? I should have to clear out of Montalta, for I could not bear that—flesh and blood could not stand it—particularly a man who loved her as madly as I did. The very thought of it well nigh drove me beside myself. God help me for a miserable man, if ever there was one.

The sun was low as I drove up to the head station. There was a thundery look about the sky that seemed to prophesy rough weather in the very near future, and I thanked my stars it was not my fate to have to camp out that night. From what I could judge of it, it looked very much like being a repetition of that eventful one on which I had seen Moira for the first time, dripping, dishevelled, and well-nigh driven mad with terror. I had rescued her then and had brought her to my home, for what? Well, so far as I could judge, for no other reason than to break my heart. And that through the instrumentality of my best friend. It was the irony of fate with a vengeance. I had never loved before, and now that I had met the one woman of all the world for me, she had preferred another to me. For the first time since I had known it, I could find it in my heart to wish that I had never seen or heard of Montalta and that Flaxman and I had never met.

As I have explained earlier in my story, the homestead of Montalta is approached by a circuitous drive—track would perhaps be a better description—which winds through the horse paddock, then passes through some rather fine timber up to the plateau on which the house itself is situated. Needless to say there are gates on either side of the small horse paddock, and as I had no one with me it was necessary for me to get down and open them for myself. I had crossed the paddock and had alighted to open the second, which led into the belt of timber above mentioned, when the sound of voices reached my ears. I recognised them instantly; in fact, there could be no mistaking them. Loth though I was to do so, I could not help overhearing a sentence or two of what they said. It was Flaxman talking.

"But, my dear Moira," he was saying, "forgive me if I say that I cannot understand why you should feel in this way about the matter. I am quite sure that if you will only have patience all will come right in the end."

"No! No! It can never come right," was Moira's sobbing reply. "I must go, come what may."

"Such a thing is not to be thought of for a minute," Flaxman retorted quickly. "I would not hear of it. Do you want to break my heart? If so, you're going the right way to work to do it."

What reply she made to this I cannot say, for they were now too far off for me to hear, even if I wished to play the part of eavesdropper any longer, which I am quite sure that I did not. I accordingly propped the gate open and led my horses through, closing it after me. In order to give the pair time to get well away, I did not hurry myself, and when I remounted to my seat in the buggy I allowed them to walk the remainder of the distance for the same reason. What did it all mean? Why was Moira crying, and, still more important, why did she insist on the necessity of her going away from Montalta? Here was a nice riddle they had given me to solve. That she was unhappy, there could not be the least doubt, but what was it that had made her so? I vowed that, come what might, I would find out, and before very long, too.

CHAPTER IX

GATHERING CLOUDS.

It was with a heavy heart that I drove up to the homestead which I loved so well. What I had heard in those few minutes had been sufficient to shatter even the smallest hopes I might have entertained of winning Moira's love. And at the back of it all was a haunting terror that I could not dispel, do what I would. What could this fear be? This trouble that would never come right, that was driving her away?

It was so unlike her to show fear; as a rule she was so self-reliant, so independent, that this complete breakdown was all the harder to understand. I passed the front of the house and proceeded to the stables, or to be more correct to the shed in which we kept the buggy, for stables we had none, nor did we require them. A few posts with hooks and a bough shade for hot days were all we required. Having seen the horses unharnessed, I strolled slowly back to the house, feeling more like a criminal on his way to execution than anything else. How I was to look them in the face, knowing what I did, I could not for the life of me imagine. I crossed the open space between the kitchen and the house and entered the back verandah. One of the black boys from the camp was seated on the steps waiting for the "young missis," so he informed me.

"What do you want her for, Snowball?" I asked, hoping that she would make her appearance while I was talking to him and thus enable me to get our first interview over in the presence of a third party, even if that third party did happen to be a black fellow. I repeated my question as to what he wanted with Miss Moira.

"Want melcin (medicine) longa me, mine think it," was the whining reply. After which he continued, "Plenty bad this fella. Mine think it got 'um debbil-debbil (devil-devil)."

At this moment the lady for whom he was waiting, and whom the tame blacks of the district had come to regard as a physician of extraordinary cleverness, made her appearance from the house. Seeing me, she looked at me in a timid way, for all the world as if she were frightened as to what I might be going to say to her. Her eyes showed traces of recent tears, and when she spoke I noticed that her voice was not as steady as usual. It could have been no small matter that had brought about this state of things.

"Well, Snowball," she began, "what is it now? Have you been drinking rum again? You promised me you would never do so again. Do you remember that?"

"Not rum, Missis," the native replied. "Very bad this fella. Like 'um die mine think it."

He began to groan and rub himself as if in proof of his assertion.

"Why do you bother yourself with him?" I asked. "The fellow is only imposing on you. That rascal at the River Bend grog shanty has been letting him have rum again, and this is the result. Leave me to deal with him. I have some medicine by me that I fancy will about meet his case."

"No! no!" she answered, with a forced smile. "I cannot let you play with him, but if some day when you are passing that way you would call in and give that rascal Giles a good talking to it would be more to the point. It does seem a shame that, in spite of all the warnings he has received on the subject, he should persist in giving this poison to these poor creatures. It maddens them, and then they come to me to be put right again. If I were a man I should feel inclined to horsewhip him. He richly deserves it, if ever a man did."

"Even that might be managed without very much difficulty," I replied, feeling that in my present humour it would do me a vast amount of good to treat the man in question in the manner she suggested. "I'll bear it in mind the next time I'm passing that way, and it won't be my fault if the scoundrel does not remember it for at least a week or two. I've had a rod in pickle for him for some time past. You let me catch you down at the grog shanty, Snowball, and I'll give you waddy till your own lubra won't know you. Don't you forget that."

The black whined something to the effect that he had not been near the place in question, but Miss Moira cut him short by telling him to remain quietly where he was until she brought him some medicine. She there-upon returned into the house, and I followed her. We had scraped through our first interview safely; I had now to meet Flaxman and see how he would comport himself towards me. If he could look me in the face as calmly as he was wont to do, then I should know him for one of the most consummate actors I had ever come in contact with.

We did not meet, however, quite as soon as I expected, for he had gone down to give an order at the men's hut and did not return for upwards of an hour. When he did he went straight to his room, so that I did not get an opportunity of speaking to him before the evening meal. When we did meet, Miss Moira was in the room, so that conversation, save on everyday topics, was impossible. That, for some reason or another, he was ill at ease I could plainly see, not only from his disjointed conversation, but from the way in which he glanced almost apprehensively from time to time at Miss Moira, who sat pale and, so it seemed to me, care-worn at the further end of the table. All things considered, it could not have been looked upon as a cheerful meal, and I think we were all united in attributing this to the departure of Mrs. Dawson, who thus, for once in her life at least, became of real use to her fellow humans.

Our meal finished, we adjourned as usual to the sitting-room next door, but on this occasion, and not a little to my surprise, there was no suggestion of any music. Flaxman ensconced himself in an easy chair with a scientific work he had received by that day's mail, Miss Moira occupied herself with her sewing, while I endeavoured to interest myself in the pages of the Australasian, and failed signally in the attempt. Taken altogether, we were as miserable a trio as could have been found between Cape York and Sydney Heads. Once I did my best to promote conversation on the subject of a notorious forgery case then sub judice. The effort, however, was in vain. Miss Moira frankly confessed that she knew nothing about it, while Flaxman propounded a theory which was absurd to the borders of lunacy, and which proved to me beyond a doubt that he had not paid the least attention to what I had been talking about. Thus discouraged, I succumbed to the general inertia. About ten o'clock Miss Moira rose, and saying that she was tired, went off to bed. As she gave me her hand, I looked into her face, but her eyes would not meet mine. She glanced swiftly up at me and then down at the floor—I could feel that she was trembling, though why she should have done so I could not for the life of me imagine. She knew well enough that I was her friend, that there was nothing I would not do to help her at any cost to myself. And from what I could see of it, she stood badly in need of help just then, if ever a girl did. Then the door closed upon her, and she was gone. Flaxman and I were alone together.

It is all very well to make up your mind that you will do a thing which is unpleasant but necessary; it is quite another to do it. I found it so in this case. I was fully determined that as soon as a fitting opportunity presented itself I would take the bull by the horns and ask my partner straight out what he believed to be the matter with the girl. But now that the actual moment arrived for carrying that scheme into practice I found myself shirking it like the despicable coward that I was. And yet I knew in my heart of hearts that the question must not only be put, but also that it must be answered, and that without delay. The mere thought that Miss Moira had declared her intention of leaving the station made this imperative.

But how was I to begin? Flaxman was still engaged with his book, pausing now and again to verify a calculation or to mark a passage for future reference. The clock ticked steadily on the mantelpiece and the logs crackled in the fireplace. That was the only sound to be heard in the room. At last I could bear the suspense no longer.

"You seem to be very interested in that book," I said, by way of making a beginning.

"I am," he answered, without looking up. "I've always been fond of mathematics. The subject has a great fascination for me. Under other circumstances I fancy I might have made a name for myself in that line of study. As it is—well, you know the rest."

He gave a queer sort of a smile and a shrug of the shoulders, as much as to say, "See what I have come down to."

I knocked the ashes out of my pipe against the side of the fireplace and then slowly refilled it. Now that the crucial moment had come I wanted to gain time.

"I say, Flaxman," I began, "there's something I want to ask you. I should have done so earlier in the evening, but I did not have an opportunity."

"What is it you want to ask me?" said Flaxman, closing his book, but keeping the place with his finger. He must have realised from my manner that something out of the common was about to happen. Possibly he may have guessed what it was.

"Have you noticed any change lately in Miss Moira?" I inquired, feeling that I was now fairly committed.

"What sort of change do you mean?" he replied. "Don't you think she looks well?"

"I am not referring to her bodily health," I answered. "But it seems to me that she is not as happy as she used to be. Tonight, for instance, she scarcely spoke, unless she was spoken to."

"Very possibly she may have a headache," he continued. "The day has been thundery, and, as you know, that usually upsets her."

"But I am convinced that she is fretting, that she is unhappy about something," I went on. "One had only to look at her face at dinner to see that she had been crying. Now, what made her cry? Have you any sort of idea? You have been more in her company to-day than I have, so surely you must have noticed something."

Flaxman hesitated before he replied, and I could not but notice the fact. My suspicions were momentarily increasing. He was in the secret, and he was acting a part in order if possible to put me off the scent. But I was determined to penetrate the mystery if I could manage it.

"My dear old fellow," he went on, "you give me credit for more penetration than I possess. I certainly have been in her company a good deal to-day, and have noticed, I confess, that she did not seem quite as cheerful as usual, but I am quite unable to tell you what occasioned it. You refuse, you see, to accept my suggestion with regard to the thunder."

"Because I am quite sure it has nothing whatsoever to do with it," I replied. "Thundery weather may have a depressing effect, and I know that she is susceptible to its influences, but it does not make her eyes swollen with crying or depress her to such an extent that she will not speak and scarcely dares to look her friends in the face. No! old man, there's more behind this than meets the eye, and you know it. If she is in any sort of trouble, I think I have a right to share the secret with you. It is not fair to let me be kept in the dark like this."

"But, my dear fellow, what should put it into your head that you are being kept in the dark, or that there is any secret which you ought to share in? You are taking matters far too seriously, believe me, you are. Remember, after all, she is little more than a girl, and girls are the slaves of all sorts of whims and fancies. Doubtless, you will find that she will be quite herself tomorrow, and you, on your side, will be laughing at yourself for having been so concerned about her."

Plausible as all this was, it did not in the least shake my conviction, not only that there was something wrong, but also that Flaxman was aware of it. The fact that he would not confess it, or share his knowledge with me, fairly roused my temper. It was not fair to me. If he loved her and she loved him, why on earth did he not say so straight out and let me know the truth? Then, at least, I should be aware how I stood. As it was, I was neither one thing nor the other. I loved Moira with all the strength of which my nature was capable, but how could I tell her this, feeling as I did that her love was given to another? For the same reason, although I knew that she was unhappy, I could not interfere or attempt to set matters right. All that was needed was that Flaxman should speak out, which was the one thing of all others that I could not induce him to do. I determined, however, to make one more endeavour. If that failed, there would be nothing for it, but to let matters take their own course and abide by the result. The prospect was by no means cheering.

"It's all very well for you to be so certain that there is nothing wrong," I said at last, "but, for my part, I am sure there is. The girl is not herself at all. The first opportunity I get I shall try to induce her to confide in me and to tell me what her trouble is. It is evident you don't care."

He once more closed his book and looked up at me, steadily and unflinchingly. Had I not been angry and therefore a fool I should have seen in his face that all my suppositions, such as they were, were wrong. However, the most obvious is as often as not the least discernible; the small deer sees what the elephant overlooks. And it was so in my case.

"What makes you think I do not care?" he asked very slowly. "Does it not strike you that that is rather a strange thing to say, seeing that Miss Moira and I are friends?"

Then I lost my temper altogether: his manner was more than I could possibly put up with.

"Are you quite sure that you're not something more than friends?" I sneered. "Oh, you need not think you can put me off the scent. I am a little wiser than you suppose me to be. I haven't knocked about the world without learning to keep my eyes open."

"By heavens, this is too bad," he cried, springing to his feet and almost over-turning his chair as he did so. "Are you mad that you talk to me like this? I'll not put up with it. It is more than flesh and blood can stand. I never thought you, of all men, would have said such things to me."

"I notice that you do not deny the truth of my words, although you object to them," I went on, my temper rising momentarily higher. "That, I should say, would be more to the point."

He threw at me a look which I shall not forget to my dying day. I can read its meaning now, in the light of after events, but I was too much beside myself with rage to do so then.

"You are insulting me," was all he said, and made as if he would leave the room. "If you do not respect me, you might at least respect her. Some day, I pledge you my word, you will be sorry for this. But it will be too late then."

Surely the spirit of prophecy must have been upon him at that moment, for what he predicted then has certainly come to pass, to my bitter shame be it said. Yet, God help me, could that scene be re-acted, I fear I should again behave as I did then. It is a pitiful confession to have to make, but, alas! it is the truth. But to continue my narrative.

I have said that Flaxman made as if he would leave the room. He did not do so at once, however, but stood at the door for a few moments, looking back at me with an expression of deepest reproach upon his face. Then he passed out, leaving me in the room alone.

"Let him go, the sneaking hound," I muttered, for I am determined to set everything down. "He little thinks what I heard down at the gate this afternoon. However, he has not done with me yet. If I can be nothing else to her I can at least stand by her like a brother, and, by heaven, I will too—so let my fine gentleman beware of me. I'm a man, not a school-miss, as he'll find to his cost."

Patting myself on the back thus, I mixed myself a stiff glass of grog and tossed it off. Under its magic influence I began to see matters in an even clearer light than before. I recalled little circumstances which had hitherto escaped my memory, and which now only served to increase the load of guilt my unhappy partner was carrying. A second glass of grog convinced me beyond all possibility of doubt that it behoved me to call him to account for his treatment of the girl—always, of course, in my self-appointed capacity of brother. A third showed me how happy I might have been with her had fate been kinder; after which I went off to bed firmly resolved to set matters right on the morrow.

On the morrow, as it happened, I rose with a splitting headache and a general feeling that nothing was right with the world. On first waking I had only a confused idea of all that had occurred on the previous night. Then, as memory returned to me, I began to realise something of the serious nature of affairs. One thing was quite certain, and that was the fact that Flaxman and I must come to some definite understanding on the subject as to which we had fallen out. Until that was done, life would be well nigh unendurable for both of us. As for myself, I had not abated one jot of my determination to champion Miss Moira's cause; if anything, my intention to do so was even more firmly rooted than before.

It was a strange trio that sat down to breakfast that morning. I was not hungry, Flaxman scarcely touched anything, while Miss Moira presided at the tea tray, but, beyond playing with an infinitesimal piece of toast, made no pretence of eating at all. I could see from the furtive glances she stole at both of us from time to time that she knew that there was something amiss with us and that she feared it was on her account. To try and divert her thoughts I started some topic of conversation, I forget what. Flaxman joined in it, probably with the same intention, and for perhaps a minute and a half all went well, then it dwindled down, no one offered any further remark, and quiet reigned once more. None of us had the pluck to start a fresh subject, so the remainder of the meal was eaten in silence. I was the first to rise, Miss Moira next, and Flaxman last. I informed the company generally that I should not be in to lunch, as I had made up my mind to ride out into the back country to see how much damage the flood had done. I fancied I detected a look of relief on the faces of my two companions, and the thought was far from pleasing to me. It was evident that they deemed me safest out of the way; at any rate, for the present. No man likes it to be thought that his company is not welcome, and it was certainly so in my case. They wanted to get rid of me, did they? Well, they should do so. But his star help Flaxman if he played me false in my absence! The vengeance I would take in that case would be one that he would not be likely to forget for many a long day to come. Poor blind fool that I was, I still persisted in believing that all I did was right, and that all they did was wrong. For pig-headed obstinacy a mountain—battery mule could have given me points and a beating.

Having announced my programme for the day, I lit my pipe, and calling up one of my terriers, of which I had about half a dozen, I left the house and strode off to the store, before which a group of the hands was waiting for their tasks to be allotted them. When I had made my arrangements, and had selected two of their number to accompany me, a move was made to the stockyard, where the black boys had run up the horses. In something under a quarter of an hour all had dispersed in various directions, and I and my companions were riding down the track that led along the valley towards the part of the run I was anxious to inspect. It was a perfect winter's morning, as winters are reckoned in that part of the world. The dew lay heavy on the grass and bushes, and the mist of morning was drawing off the hill tops before the increasing heat of the sun. Pink-breasted galas, disturbed by us, rose like clouds before us and wheeled high above our heads in the brilliant light, turning from white to pink and back again to white, to settle on some new feeding ground a mile or so away to our right. Now and again a great blundering kangaroo would go skipping across our path, pursued at a respectful distance by the terriers, who knew too much to endeavour to come to close quarters with those terrible hind legs. A young wallaby sat on a rock and studied us attentively, then scratched his nose with his absurd little paws, cast an apprehensive glance at the dogs, came to the conclusion that they were not to be trusted, and disappeared from view with one bound, much to the amazement of a flock of white cockatoos, who shrieked discordantly at him from the neighbouring tree-tops. It was just the morning for a ride, and on any other morning I should have thoroughly enjoyed it. On this particular occasion, however, I could see nothing good in it. Everything was distorted and warped by the fire that was raging within me. I could not see any beauty in the landscape, or feel any warmth in the sunshine. Beyond giving some instructions to the men who accompanied me, I don't think I spoke half a dozen words in the first ten miles. The very tobacco I was smoking did not seem to taste the same as usual, nor did the animal I was riding, my favourite hack by the way, appear in any better spirits than myself. And that reminds me, I wonder if you have ever noticed, I have done so times out of number, how quickly a horse who is accustomed to you gets to know the sort of humour you are in and immediately adapts himself to it? Perhaps you mount him on some fine spring morning, full of life and the joy of living. He knows the feeling and reciprocates it, tosses his head, plays with his bit, and passages just to show you that he is as ready for a gallop in the fresh bracing air as you are. On the other hand, we will suppose that you are depressed, out of spirits, and not inclined for boisterous fun; observe then how he adapts himself to these altered circumstances. He proceeds soberly upon his way, as if he were wondering what he could do in his small way to help you, and has at last come to the conclusion that the best line for him to adopt would be to carry you discreetly, neither too fast nor too slow, and to wait with equine patience for the cloud to lift from your shoulders and for the sunshine to burst forth once more. No, I shall never be convinced that horses do not understand a man's feelings almost as well as he does himself. Why, of course they do!

It was close upon eleven o'clock by the time we reached the place I was anxious to inspect. The flood which I had been dreading had not done as much damage as I had expected; nevertheless there were several matters which required attention; several panels of fencing had in one place been washed away, and the gap thus made required to be filled in to prevent the cattle getting through into the adjoining property; further down two beasts were discovered bogged and too much exhausted to extricate themselves from what would, undoubtedly, have meant certain death to them had we not providentially arrived upon the scene when we did. Next, there was the stockman's hut to be visited at the Twelve Mile Crossing and the list of his wants to be obtained against the next despatch of the ration cart. To the tale of his woes I paid no attention, for the man, though a hard worker, was a born grumbler, and had I had the patience to stop and listen to him I should without a doubt have been induced to believe that of all the sons of men he was by a great deal the most miserable.

An eight mile ride along the boundary brought us to the coach track, and a mile further on to the mail change, where, for the good of the house and other politic reasons, I pulled up and treated the men to a glass of grog each, to which you may be sure they offered no sort of objection. After that we resumed our ride until we once more saw the roofs of the head station rising before us. As we came closer I found an unaccountable nervousness coming over me. I tried to explain it away, but in vain.

On reaching the store I dismounted and having unsaddled my horse turned him loose. For upwards of a minute I stood watching him as he trotted off to join his comrades, and then turned to enter the store, expecting to find Flaxman there. I was met, however, on the doorstep by the storekeeper, who informed me that my partner had gone up to the house some few minutes before my arrival. He asked if there was anything he could do for me, but I told him no, I would go in search of Flaxman myself. Heavy clouds had been threatening us all the afternoon, and as I walked towards the house rain commenced to fall. It was growing dark, and the wind moaned drearily through the scrub timber behind the homestead, as if with the desire of making me even more miserable than I was already. If the truth must be told, I was suffering from about as bad an attack of the blues as a man could well experience, and, so far as I could see, there did not appear to be any prospect of matters improving—a pleasant look-out for all parties concerned. Miss Moira's sorrowful face had been haunting me all day long, and now I seemed to be able to see it gazing at me in the gathering gloom. According to my usual custom, I made my way to my bedroom and changed my things before going on to the sitting-room. On this occasion it was a matter of necessity, for I was not only wet, but plastered with mud from head to foot. I could well imagine Miss Moira's housewifely horror should she catch me tramping about her spotless floors with such grimy boots as I was wearing.

Having brought myself within a measurable distance of a civilised being once more, I left my room and proceeded to that in which I felt sure I should find the others. Somewhat to my surprise Flaxman had the apartment to himself. He was standing at the window, his hands behind his back. His head was bowed, and his whole bearing spoke of the deepest dejection. In his right hand he held a letter. Was it something contained in that that was agitating him so? I was soon to learn.

CHAPTER X

"CAN FRIENDS PART SO?"

Flaxman evidently had not heard me enter the room, for he did not turn round. For a few moments, perhaps while a man might have counted ten slowly, I stood and watched him. Then something that was very like a sob escaped him, and I saw his hands clench, as if he were battling with himself in an endeavour to suppress his emotion. Not being anxious to allow him to suppose that I was prying upon him, I stepped from the rug on to the polished floor and the sound brought him round face to face with me. Two large tears were coursing down his cheeks, and he made no attempt to hide them from me. Again I asked myself what had happened to bring about this extraordinary state of affairs. Had it been mail day I might have been tempted to believe that he had received bad news from the Old Country, but there would not be another mail for more than a week, so that that could not be held accountable for it. That he was really upset, as I had never seen him before, was as certain as that I was in the room, looking at him. And yet I knew him for a man who did not, as a rule, show emotion very easily.

On seeing me I noticed that he thrust the letter he held in his hand into his pocket, as if he did not desire that I should become aware of its existence. Whatever anything else might be, that scrap of paper at least had an important bearing on the affair.

"There is a letter for you upon the mantelpiece," he said, doing his level best, I could see, to speak calmly, and succeeding very badly in the attempt. "You had better open it."

I turned to the place in question and found there an envelope addressed with my name. I knew well enough before I opened it from whom it came, though, strange to say, I had never seen Miss Moira's writing before. During the time she had been with us, she had neither written nor received any letters, so that there had been no chance of my becoming familiar with her penmanship. I took it down and opened it with a sinking heart. I could guess what it contained before I started to read a word. I remembered her cry on the previous day—"I must go away! I must go away!" The letter was a short one—only a few brief sentences. It read as follows:—

"DEAR FRIEND,—Before you receive this I shall have left Montalta for ever. I feel now that I was wrong ever to have come. But how thankful I am to you for all you have done for me, I think you know. I shall always pray to God to bless you for it. Good-bye.

"Your grateful friend.

"MOIRA PENDRAGON.

"P.S.—I beg of you not to attempt to find me, for I assure you your search will be in vain."

For more than a minute I stood looking at the paper in my hand and trying to collect my thoughts. Moira gone! Could such a thing be possible? Were we never to see her again? These were the questions that tumbled over each other in wild confusion in my brain. What was the reason of it all? She had seemed so happy with us until the last week or so, that no one would have dreamt she was on the verge of leaving us. The whole thing was incomprehensible to me; it was more than that, it was unbelievable. At last I found my voice. Addressing Flaxman, who was still standing at the window, I said, "What hand had you in this?" He looked at me in amazement, as if he marvelled that I could ask such a question.

"What hand had I in it?" he repeated. "Good God, man, do you want to drive me mad with your questions? If so, you're going the right way to work to do it, I can tell you that. Do you think I drove her away from the place? Do you think it was by my wish that she went away from comfort to misery, perhaps to starvation? Great heavens, I would have given all I possess in this world to have been able to prevent it. She gave me no hint of her intention or I should have done my utmost to stop her, whatever the consequences might have been. Surely you know me well enough for that. If not, you're far from being the friend I took you to be."

I laughed scornfully, and as I did so I saw his face flush crimson. To think that we should ever have come to such a pass as this. It seemed well-nigh inconceivable.

"This is just the right time to talk of friendship, isn't it?" I cried, with scathing irony. "I admire your good plain commonsense. Perhaps you would like to discuss Shakespeare and the musical glasses while you are about it? There is nothing like putting in one's time profitably. You regret that she has left us; you would have prevented it had you known. Yet you were on the spot and knew nothing of it. The consequences would have been nothing to you, you declare. Well, you have the consequences to amuse yourself with now, if they are of any solace to you. Bah! I believe you knew it all the time; I believe that you connived at it. John Flaxman, I have had my suspicions for some time past, and now they have been confirmed. Let me tell you to your face that I distrust you from the bottom of my heart. Now I've said it and the murder's out."

He took a step towards me, his hand raised as if he would strike me. His face was now white as a sheet and I could distinctly hear his breath come in gasps.

"You dare to tell me that you believe I connived at her leaving this place?" he cried, his voice almost guttural with passion. It is the quiet man whose anger is most deadly when once thoroughly roused. "Then I tell you you lie, and that you know it."

"Show me that letter in your pocket then," I retorted. "Let me see that before I believe that you have no hand in it."

His expression and his manner changed as if by magic. The hand he had raised dropped to his side and his face began to flush once more.

There was a short pause, after which he said hesitatingly, as if he were not sure of the reception his words would receive:—

"I cannot show it to you."

"You cannot show it to me," I echoed mockingly. "That is good news, indeed, and may I be permitted to ask the reason that prompts that decision? There is my letter," (here I threw it down upon the table for him to see). "You are quite at liberty to read it, if you please. Why may I not see yours in return?"

"Because I cannot show it to you," he replied doggedly. "It would be abusing a confidence were I to do so. I must ask you to accept the explanation for what it is worth. I can give you no other."

"I can quite believe that," I sneered, "and I will take it for what it is worth— which is nothing, literally nothing. You know that as well as I do. You have already told me that you were not aware that she contemplated leaving us, yet a thought has just struck me which may throw some light on the case. Possibly you may remember that last week you talked of paying the South a visit in a few weeks. Doubtless you will do so now. It is a pretty little plot, but it seems to me as if it has miscarried somewhere."

"What do you mean?" he asked, staring at me with dilated eyes. "What is this vile thing you are endeavouring to insinuate? Speak out like a man and say what you have in your mind. You can't insult me more than you have done already. What do you charge me with?"

"I charge you with nothing. I make no insinuations. I simply leave you to your own conscience. You can settle with that."

"I demand that you shall tell me what you meant when you said that," he repeated angrily. "I do not want any further subterfuges. You have brought forward the fact that I talked of going South in connection with this affair, and I wish to know what you mean by it. You shall tell me, even if I have to force you into doing so. As a gentleman, I put you on your honour to do so."

I had not bargained for this, but my blood was up and I was reckless as to the consequences.

"Very well, since you will have it, I'll speak out as you bid me," I answered defiantly. "What I charge you with is inducing Miss Moira to leave this house in order that you may meet her elsewhere. The reason that prompts such hole-and— corner work is best known to yourself."

The words had scarcely left my lips before he had sprung at me, and had struck me such a severe blow upon the mouth that I could feel the blood trickling down my chin a moment later. The force with which it was dealt was sufficient to drive me back a couple of paces. Then, may God forgive me, I knocked him down. It was done in a fit of passion it is true, and in return for a blow dealt to me, but I give you my word, sworn by all I hold sacred, that if I could recall it now, I would willingly lose the hand that gave it. For a moment he lay upon the floor as if stunned, then he staggered to his feet. Having done so, he gave utterance to this extraordinary confession:—

"You did right," he said, speaking calmly and deliberately, as if he had carefully worked the matter out. "I forgot myself and struck you; you only punished me according to my deserts."

To my eternal shame be it set down that my only reply was a laugh. Idiot that I was, I imagined he had been frightened by my blow and had turned craven. Now, of course, I can see it all in the proper light. But then I was so blinded by my jealousy and the hatred it engendered in me, that I was incapable of believing in anything or anybody.

"Now that you know what I think," I answered, "I'll leave you to chew your cud in peace. I hope your reflections may bring you happiness. You may expect me back when you see me."

So saying I flung out of the room, and in less than a quarter of an hour was galloping down the track in the direction of the township. At the best of times it was none too safe a road, but in the pitch-blackness of a stormy night it was positively dangerous. I gave no thought to that, however, but rode as if for my life, regardless of everything save my whirling, maddening thoughts, my love for Moira, and my hatred of the man who, I implicitly believed, had robbed me of her. My only regret now was that I had not thrashed him more severely, as soundly indeed as I believed that he deserved.

Overhead the storm roared, the wind lashing the trees with remorseless fury. The lightning flashed, the thunder crashed, while now and again in the lulls I could hear the tumult of the torrent in the valley below me. It was such another night as Tam—o'-Shanter must have been abroad in, and again such another as that on which I had first met the girl who was the primary cause of my present happiness. How much had happened since that momentous night! I had learnt to love, and I had also learnt to hate. I had believed myself one of the happiest of living men, and I now knew myself for one of the most miserable. To find relief I urged my gallant little horse to greater efforts. He was a game beast, and needed no spur to induce him to do his best. Regardless of the state of the track, which as often as not was merely a matter of conjecture, we sped on and on, sometimes tumbling and slipping, but with never a thought of caution. More than once, nay, at least a dozen times, a vivid flash of lightning showed me how near I had been to death's door. Once we were scarcely half a horse's length from the edge of a deep ravine, through which a swollen stream ran like a mill-sluice bounding down the hillside, missed the horse's head by scarcely two yards, crossed the track and disappeared with a crash into the valley below. The animal's sudden stop came within an ace of throwing me headlong out of the saddle. But even that narrow escape did not steady me.

"Come up, old horse," I shouted. "We were not born to be killed in that clumsy fashion."

Once more I set him going. We had put more than ten miles behind us by this time and were within an appreciable distance of the township. At the pace we were travelling, all being well, we should be there in less than half an hour. But would, or could, the animal hold out so long, was the question I should have asked myself. But I never thought of it. All I wanted was to get to my destination and into the society of men who could help me to forget what I was suffering. And what was Moira doing meanwhile? She had left the station on foot, so I had ascertained. Where could she be, then? Wandering in the scrub in all probability, as I had found her on that night when we had first met. I cursed Flaxman again, and rode on even harder than before. The thought of that poor girl wandering alone in the storm maddened me. Why was it Flaxman had not gone to her assistance? Had he told me a lie, I wondered, or was he tired of her and resolved to abandon her to her fate? Suspicion induced me to believe the first; common humanity forbade me to credit the second. No man could surely be such an out-and-out scoundrel as that. However, it was no business of mine now. All I had to do was to endeavour to forget that we had ever met.

At last and none too soon, for my horse was completely done for, I saw ahead of me the lights of the little township twinkling like so many stars on the plain. Thank goodness, we were there at last. From the point where one obtains the first view of the little settlement the track slopes somewhat steeply for between half and three—quarters of a mile. The main street of the township, if street indeed it can be called, consisting as it does of three hotels (save the mark!), a blacksmith's shop, two stores, a policestation, and half a dozen wooden cottages, is as broad as any in the Empire, and probably muddier than most. After a storm, such as was then raging, it is well nigh impassable, either for man or beast.

"At last, at last," I muttered to myself as I galloped down the hill. "If I don't make this rat-hole of a place sit up to-night, it won't be my fault. I can assure them of that. Hold up, old horse, I know you're done for, but in a few minutes you shall rest for as long as you like."

I little guessed how true my words were destined to prove. As I entered the street the poor beast reeled and almost fell. A few yards further on he did so again; then, within a dozen paces of the verandah of the "Jolly Bushman," he gave a lurch, pitched forward on his head, and rolled over, almost crushing me beneath him. Covered with mud, I scrambled to my feet; but the horse lay just as he had fallen, his neck stretched out and his breath coming in long gasps.

"God help me, I've done for a better brute than myself," I muttered as I looked down at him. "I've ridden him to death."

At that moment the landlord of the inn made his appearance in the verandah with a lantern. I hailed him, and he immediately came out to me.

"Why, surely it's never you," he cried, when he became aware of my identity. "You're just about the last person I expected to see on a rough night like this. What does it all mean? Nothing wrong at Montalta, I hope? Bless my heart, just look at your horse now! Why, he's clean knocked out of time. You've fair ridden him to a standstill, if you haven't done worse. Here, hold the lantern while I have a look at him. You've some rare good cattle over at your place, and you don't want to lose any of them."

While I held the lantern he knelt down in the mud beside the horse and carefully examined him. As he did so the animal half raised his head, gave a long groan, and then lay still. The fat little publican rose to his feet.

"It's no use bothering any more about him," he said. "He's done his last journey. I'll get a couple of my lads to pull him into the yard for to-night. The saddle and bridle we'll take inside."

Poor old horse, he had paid the penalty of a man's anger, and here was the result. How often is it not the way! A hasty deed, a fit of anger, a wrong impulse momentarily gratified, and as often as not some innocent man or beast is drawn into the net and directly or indirectly may be called upon by fate to suffer for it. I had an excellent example before me now.

I followed the landlord into the hotel and made for the bar, which I found crowded to its utmost holding capacity. A shout of welcome greeted me, for I had not been in there for upwards of a year. By way of setting the ball rolling, I called for drinks all round. From that moment I put all thought of Montalta, of Moira, and of Flaxman behind me. Nothing mattered now, I told myself. Let care go to the deuce, I cried. Whatever the upshot might be, I was determined to enjoy myself, and in so doing to forget the past. But I was destined to make a discovery that many men had made before me, namely, that care is not so easily relegated to the background as some folk would imagine. However successful one may think oneself at night, there is always a to-morrow to be considered, and experience proves that that selfsame to—morrow possesses the unhappy faculty of adding to rather than lessening the load of care that is already being carried.

It was almost daylight when we broke up, and yet I was loth to permit anyone to leave, for I feared lest with his going I should find myself in the Slough of Despond again. But one by one they dropped away, until the landlord and I found ourselves alone together. Even he, accustomed as he was to late hours, began to think it was time to think of going to bed, and, seeing that there was nothing else for it, I was at length constrained to agree with him. I accordingly followed him along the wooden passage to the room in which he had already placed my valise. It was at the corner of the house, and looked out across the little plain towards the ranges through which I had ridden so recklessly that evening. The wind howled mournfully round the corner and the rain lashed the roof, as if it were desirous of beating it in. Before commencing to undress I took up the candle and looked at myself in the glass. It was a flushed face I saw there; but I was not thinking of that, I was looking at my still swollen underlip and recalling the circumstances under which I had received it. Then I went to bed and slept soundly until well after ten o'clock. How I hated and despised myself when I woke, I cannot tell you. But that I was weak enough to feel that Flaxman would believe that I was repentant, I would have borrowed or purchased a fresh horse and have returned to the station as soon as I had breakfasted. The thought that he might do so, when my experience of him should have made me know better, fired me anew, and I vowed that, come what might, I would not give him the opportunity of saying that. Rather than do so, I would remain a month in the township if necessary.

Half an hour or so after breakfast some of my companions of the previous night began to drop in; some remained to lunch with me, and began to play billiards afterwards; others merely drank their morning draughts, and then returned to what they somewhat facetiously described as their "business," though I must confess I was completely at a loss to understand what it consisted of, seeing that no one seemed to be stirring in the main street save two drunken station hands, who were quarrelling and preparing for combat at the further end, and the police sergeant's black cat, which was craftily stalking a bird on that functionary's paling fence. In the evening the usual sort of carouse again took place. It was not by any manner of means an edifying spectacle. Some of the company were soon hopelessly intoxicated; some became quarrelsome, some merely maudlin, others burst into melody without regard to their audience or to the requirements of time or tune. Among the number present was one man, an overseer on a neighbouring station, who had come in that day with the avowed intention of, to use a Bush expression, "knocking his cheque down." He was doing this to such good purpose that there promised to be but little of it left within the very near future. He was a big, clumsily-built fellow, like myself of Colonial birth, with a crop of brilliant red hair and the largest hands and feet I had ever seen on a human being. He had the reputation of being a bully on his own station, and now being well advanced in liquor, it appeared as if he were quite prepared to give us a sample of his powers at a moment's notice. Milligan was the gentleman's name, and for some reason or another he had been nicknamed "The Tipperary Boy." If wildness and a love of fighting went for anything, then the sobriquet was certainly an appropriate one.

The evening was well advanced before he favoured me with his attentions. Then when I was engaged in conversation with a quiet little man, who was book-keeper for a squatter a few miles out of the town, he came up and sat himself down beside me, smacking me familiarly on the back with his enormous right hand as he did so.

"Well, my buck," he began, "and how's the world treating you? I haven't set eyes on you for a month of Sundays. Painting the town red, I suppose, eh? Lord bless you, why didn't you go down to Sydney? You could have enjoyed yourself there. Now I remember the last time I was down I—" Here he proceeded to favour us with some highly-spiced particulars of his adventures in the New South Wales metropolis that would not have discredited a Bowery Boy at his best. They not only did not interest me, they bored me nearly to distraction. He reeled them off one after another until I ceased to pay any attention to him at all, and resumed my talk with my previous companion which he had so rudely interrupted. My temper was none too sweet that evening, and it would have required but small encourage-ment to have induced me to tell him to go away and leave me in peace. However, I had no desire to create a scene, if not for my own sake, at least for my friend the landlord's. When once a fight becomes general in a Bush public-house he is a wise man who can tell when it will finish. I have known a whole house wrecked on such an occasion, and the owner come within an inch of losing his life for endeavour-ing to protect his own property. Bush spirits, manufactured as often as not on the premises, can be trusted to raise the devil that lies dormant in most men quicker than anything else I know in this world. And when he is once released, he is seldom to be laid by the heels again until he has been pacified with blood. Unless such a thing should be absolutely necessary, I was not going to be the one to give it to him.

For some moments after I turned my back upon him, Milligan continued to talk, apparently oblivious to the fact that I was no longer listening to him. Then he became aware of what had happened, and an ominous silence ensued. In all probability he was endeavouring to make up his mind as to what course of action he should adopt. He knew something of my reputation, and I fancy was aware that I was not the sort of man to stand much nonsense, particularly any attempt at bullying, such as he was known to be so fond of. Almost in a moment his mood changed to one of the utmost friendliness. He informed me with an oath that we were the best of pals, and in figurative language gave me to understand that on the whole he even preferred me to his own brother.

"Why shouldn't we be friends?" he inquired. "We've known each other a long time now. You've stayed over at my place and I've stayed over at yours." Then, raising his voice and preceding it with a loud guffaw, he continued, "I say, old boy, what's become of that deuced pretty girl I saw over at your place last time I was there? She was a stunner and no mistake, with the rummiest sort of a name that ever I ran up against. What was it now—something like Penny-pop-gun, wasn't it? I'm sure I disremember," he added with a grin.

I stared at him in amazement. That he should even have dared to refer to Miss Moira in such company was in itself sufficient to put me into a frenzy of rage. To speak of her as Miss Penny-pop-gun was worse than anything.

"I'll trouble you to leave the lady in question out of the conversation," I said. "I object to her name being introduced."

This was the opportunity he wanted, and the fighting element in his blood having now gained the ascendancy he was both ready and eager for battle. I consoled myself with the reflection that it would have been bound to come sooner or later.

"So you object to her name being introduced, do you?" he said, mimicking me. "Maybe you don't think we're good enough to say it. Poor, rough men like us mustn't presume to speak it. Listen to that, boys." This last was addressed to the room in general. Some, seeing trouble looming ahead had the good sense to hold their tongues; others laughed, as if in appreciation of a good joke; while others, who for some reason or another bore me no good will applauded with cries of "Good for you, Tipperary Boy." Thus encouraged, he turned once more to me with the same diabolical grin upon his face.

"Perhaps your lordship wouldn't mind condescending to tell us why we're not to mention the lady's name? We all know each other here, and I've been intro uiced to the lady myself."

"You're not to do it, because I forbid," I answered. "That should be enough answer for you. If you do you'll regret it. I can promise you that."

"To hell with you and your forbids," he shouted, flourishing his fist. "Who are you to tell me what I shall say or shall not say? I guess I'm as good a judge of what's what as you are, or anyone else, though I don't boss it at Montalta like some people."

It was quite evident that he was fairly spoiling for a fight. If he persisted in his present line of conduct, he would find that I was quite ready to oblige him. However Miss Moira might have treated me, I was not going to have her name bandied about by a lot of drunken rowdies in a township bar-room—it was not likely!

Milligan had done his best to rouse me, and had failed. Now he tried another plan.

"Boss," he cried to the landlord, "drinks all round. It's my shout. Hurry along now, for I'm going to propose a toast."

Realising what he was about to do, a complete silence descended on the room, which lasted while the drinks were being served. I rose and faced him; but for reasons of my own declined to partake of his hospitality. Looking round him to see that all the glasses were charged, he shouted, "Boys, here's a health to Miss Penny—pop-gun, and no heel taps."

He tossed off the contents of his tumbler, but before he had finished I had tossed the contents of my own full and fair into his face.

"Now," I said, "since you're so anxious to receive a lesson, I'll do my best to oblige you. Landlord, I call you to witness that this fight was forced on me."

The landlord nodded, and continued to polish his glasses behind the counter as if nothing out of the common was about to happen. Meanwhile, some officious partisans had removed the table from the centre of the room in readiness for the conflict.

There are always people to be found who would rather see others fight than do so themselves.

CHAPTER XI

MOIRA IN PERIL.

The news that there was to be a fight between myself and Milligan, or the Tipperary Boy, as he was more often called, soon spread through the township, and, in consequence, by the time we faced each other in the centre of the floor, from which the furniture had been removed, as I have already described, the large room was packed to the point of suffocation, and the air was rank with the odour of stale smoke, drink, and wet clothes. I glanced at the landlord, who was still industriously polishing his tumblers, and noticed the look of encouragement on his face. He had his own reasons, and they were not a few, for desiring that someone should "cut the comb" of this notorious bully, who whenever he came to the township had an unpleasant habit of making himself objectionable to almost everyone with whom he was brought in contact. In fact, to such an extent did he carry this practice that during the period he remained in the place the majority of the usual frequenters of the house betook themselves and their custom elsewhere, naturally not a little to my friend's chagrin. To expostulate with him was only so much waste of time; to threaten him with expulsion would have been as idle as to attempt to stop the wind from whistling round the corners of the house or the stars from shining. Hitherto, with one lamentable exception, in which, by the way, a man was well-nigh killed, no one had attempted to use force with him. Now, so it appeared, I was about to try the experiment. He had deliberately and maliciously insulted Miss Moira, and I was determined to make him pay for it, if it cost me my life. At last I had found someone upon whom to work off my rage. The task was likely to be a big one, but I was only the more content. As I took off my coat and rolled up my sleeves, I took careful stock of my adversary; he was at least a man worth fighting: his muscles stood out on his arms as thick as bananas, to use a Queensland parallel, while the expression on his face showed that it was his firm intention to give me a sound thrashing in return for my insulting treatment of him.

The partisans of either side were noisily arranging as to who should act as timekeeper and who as referee, when the swing-doors leading into the verandah opened, and a newcomer, such as is not often seen in the Bush, entered the bar. That he was a swell and a new chum admitted of no doubt. He was tall, handsome, with a long wavy moustache, slimly built, wore English riding breeches, that is to say, tight at the knees and baggy above, and sported an eyeglass in his left eye. What was more extraordinary still, he actually wore gloves, just for all the world as if he were doing the block in Collins Street on a summer afternoon. He strolled across the floor without apparently noticing what was going on, and approached the counter. The landlord rose to greet him, whereupon the stranger inquired whether he could be accommodated with a room for the night. On being answered in the affirmative, he called for a glass of whisky, lit a cigarette, and turned to watch what was going forward between Milligan and myself. Though it has taken some time to tell all this, in reality it occupied only a few minutes. It was sufficient, however, to distract the attention of the company for the time being from my enemy and myself, and you may be sure this was not at all to Milligan's liking.

To adopt a theatrical expression, he was playing to the gallery, and liked to "have the limelight full upon himself."

However interesting it might prove to some people, it is not my intention to give a detailed description of what occurred during the ensuing quarter of an hour. Let it suffice that if our respective supporters wanted a fight for their money, they got it and to spare. We were both fully aware that our future peace and comfort depended entirely on the issue of the struggle, and that the vanquished would have to sing small for the remainder of his residence in the neighbourhood. That at least was enough to make each of us do his utmost to come out on top, as they say in the Bush.

That the Tipperary Boy was wanting in pluck no one, not even his bitterest enemy, could have said. He fought, if not with skill, at least with dogged determination. He had a fist like a sledge hammer, but he lacked science. At the end of ten minutes he was out of breath, and at the end of a quarter of an hour he lay like a log on the floor, and several of his most enthusiastic supporters, who had championed his cause through fear, were hastening to assure me that they had only done so in order to insure his getting the licking he had so long deserved. That is the way of the world. Had I come out underneath, doubtless my so-called friends would have behaved in exactly the same way to my antagonist.

Having put on my coat, I walked across to where my late opponent was seated and held out my hand to him. "Shake hands, Milligan," I said; "let bygones be bygones. If you are willing, I am quite sure I am."

"Good for you," he answered promptly, and took my hand as he spoke. "What's more, since you take it this way, I don't mind owning up that I was wrong to speak of the lady the way I did. If there's any man hereabouts who thinks otherwise, just let him step out and say so, and I'll show him that the Tipperary Boy can give a beating as well as take one. Where is he now?"

There was no answer to his question, which seemed to prove that the justice of his assertion was admitted by all. He thereupon invited me to drink with him, and needless to say I did not refuse. Since he took the matter so well, it would have been the most foolish policy possible on my part to have done so. We accordingly drank with the customary "here's luck," and here the matter ended to our own and everybody else's complete satisfaction—always excepting those who had their own private grudges against myself, and who, doubtless for that reason, would very willingly have seen me vanquished.

At last that extraordinary evening came to an end, and one by one the company dispersed to their various homes. The storm still continued with increased rather than abated violence, and as I had done more than once before that night, I thanked my good fortune that I was not camped out in it.

When old Dick Grebur, the principal storekeeper, who was invariably the last to take his departure, had bade us good-night and gone out, we, the landlord, the stranger, and I, drew our chairs up to the fire and relit our pipes. It was then that I had the first real opportunity of observing the newcomer. In view of the story I have to tell, a short description of him may not be amiss. I have already said that there could be no sort of doubt as to the fact of his being a new chum. It was written on his face, his clothes, and more than all on his manners. Among other characteristics, he was the possessor of a curious drawl, combined with a strange clipping of his terminal "g's," which I have since been told is considered correct in a certain section of English society.

His face was in a measure handsome; the forehead, however, was perhaps scarcely as broad as it might have been, while the eyes were set a trifle too close together to be really pleasing. A heavy moustache hid his mouth. His hands, I remember noticing, were long from wrist to knuckle, but were spoilt by the fingers, which were short almost to the verge of deformity. They were also coarse and thick, and I noticed that the left hand had been broken at some time or other.

"Do you often have these little affairs of honour, may I ask?" he inquired when the door had closed on Grebur and we had settled down to our pipes. "I had an idea that this eminently satisfactory way of settling one's differences of opinion had quite ceased to exist. Gone out, in fact, with the citizens of Roarin' Camp, Sandy Bar, Jack, and all that Old Tenessee sort of thing, don't you know? I never thought I should have the good fortune to come across it in Australia. I had an idea that you contented yourselves with kangaroo huntin', ridin' buck jumpers, and all that sort of thing."

For the life of me I did not quite know how to take this speech. It seemed as if he were slyly poking fun at me, and yet his face was all seriousness, his manner as courteous as I had any right to expect it to be. From some remark he let fall, I discovered that his name was Vandergrave, and that he had come to Australia from England, via America and Japan. He had always had a longing to see something of the Australian Bush, he said, and he had been advised that Northern Queensland would show it to him as no other part of the Island Continent could do. After a time he began to ask questions concerning our own particular neighbourhood, the size and number of the various stations, and their owners' names. Before I could do or say anything to prevent him, the landlord had informed him that I was part owner of two of the largest properties in the district, which he described after his own fashion as being "out and away tip-top, and don't you forget it." Queensland hospitality, and indeed for that matter of the Bush generally, is proverbial, so that under the circumstances I had no option but to inform him that if he should chance to be in our neighbourhood it would give both my partner and myself great pleasure to put him up, and to show all there was to be seen.

"Your partner's name I think you said was—?"

"Flaxman," I replied, though I could not for the life of me remember having mentioned it before.

"Ah! yes! Flaxman, of course—a rather unusual name," he replied. "Well, it's really very kind of you to offer me your hospitality, and if fortune should bring me in your direction I shall avail myself of the chance of seeing your runs. Like most Globe trotters, I am writing an account of my travels, and information obtained first hand is, of course, very valuable and occasionally hard to obtain. And now, if you will excuse me, I think I will bid you 'goodnight.' I have had a long day in the saddle, and I am not so accustomed to it as you Australians are."

Having knocked the ashes out of his pipe, he left the bar, and the landlord and I very soon followed his example. My head was still ringing from one of Milligan's blows, and as I contemplated myself in the little glass on my dressing table (an old packing-case draped with gaudy chintz), I reflected that I should probably have a very fair sample of a bruise to exhibit to my friends on the morrow.

The storm had continued raging all the day, and as night set in it became worse than ever, and the wind howled and shrieked around as if it were anxious to tear the ramshackle wooden building to pieces. Again I thanked my luck that I had a roof over my head, to say nothing of a nice warm bed to curl myself up in. I blew out my candle and composed myself for slumber, but sleep would not come. I began to think of Moira and of my love for her—where she was, what she was doing? Had she, as I supposed, gone out of my life for ever, and was the man whom I had looked upon as my best friend the traitor? Whether my fight with Milligan had knocked sense into me or not, I could not say; I only know that to my great surprise I found myself thinking of Flaxman in a more kindly spirit than I had done for a long time past. I remembered his gentle ways and his undoubted affection for my unworthy self. It had seemed scarcely anything at the time; now, however, it produced a very different effect upon me. Could it be that I had been mistaken after all, and that Moira had left Montalta for some other reason? The more I thought of this, the more it seemed borne in upon me that it behoved me to make some attempt to repair the breach that my own stupidity had made between us. Then, working together, we could surely arrange some scheme for Moira's future welfare and happiness.

The rubicon once passed, I was able to look at the matter from a point of view that only a few hours before I should have considered impossible. Any way I regarded it, one thing was as clear as noonday, and that was the fact that Flaxman was a thousand times better fitted to make her happy than I was. On that score there could be no sort of doubt.

How long I lay thinking of this I cannot say, it may have been an hour, it may possibly have been more. At any rate I fell asleep over it. I could not have slumbered very long before I was awakened by someone shaking me violently by the shoulder. With the instinct of self-preservation, I hit out with all my strength, and was rewarded by hearing a loud crash and the sudden extinction of a light which had just begun to break upon my half-opened eyes.

"Well, I'll be jiggered," remarked a voice in the darkness, that I instantly recognised as my landlord's. "Here I come to call him an' to tell him there's a friend to see him, and he knocks me head over heels on to my own crockery. Seven an' six won't pay for what you've broke, my beauty."

I struck a match and set my own candle going. If I had not been angry at his disturbing me, the picture would have been an amusing one, for my companion and host was seated, clad only in his night apparel, in a pool of water on the floor, caressing what remained of the broken pitcher and surrounded by fragments of assorted china ware. There was an expression of indignation on his usually placid countenance.

"What on earth is the matter?" I inquired, sitting up in bed to look at him. "Have you taken leave of your senses that you come and wake me up at this time of night?"

"Leave of my senses be hanged," he retorted. "I was only doing you a kindness. Here's your partner, Mr. Flaxman, turned up looking for you. By the state he's in I should say he's been bushed. I thought, maybe, you'd like to know it, but it seems I was mistaken."

"Flaxman here?" I cried, scarcely able to believe my own ears. "What the deuce does this mean?"

"You'd best get up and find out," was the landlord's laconic reply. "Meantime, look out where you tread, for the floor's just covered with pieces. If folks would think before they hit out there wouldn't be so much mischief done in the world. That's the way I look at it myself."

Before he had finished speaking I was out of bed, pulling on my clothes with feverish haste. What on earth had brought Flaxman to the township, and at such an hour of the night? Had he been bushed, as the landlord suggested, or had he really come in search of me? However, I should very soon know.

As may be supposed, my dressing did not take long, and I was presently following my host down the wooden passage to the bar. There I found Flaxman, standing in a pool of water which was draining from his soaked clothes. A more miserable picture than he presented at that moment I don't know that I have ever seen. His hair, which he always wore somewhat long, was wet and dishevelled, his face was white and drawn, while his great dark eyes seemed to have sunk further into his head than was natural. He was standing before what remained of the fire, evidently awaiting my coming with no small amount of impatience. Directly he saw me he hastened forward with outstretched hands.

"My dear old fellow," he cried, "forgive me for coming to you at such an hour of the night. But I felt that I must do so. My life was growing unendurable. Another day would have made me a fit patient for a lunatic asylum."

At this point the landlord left us alone together, but not before he had mixed a couple of hot grogs. If ever a man stood in need of one, Flaxman was certainly that one. With his hand in mine all my old liking for him returned. Instinctively I felt there was no longer any reason why I should doubt him.

"But what has brought you?" I asked. "You do not mean to tell me that you have ridden all this way and on such a night simply to see me? You might have met your death in the scrub."

This was perfectly true, for I knew that had he lived to be a hundred nothing would ever have made a Bushman of him.

"I could not wait," he replied. "I have had some news of Moira, and it has frightened me more than I can say."

"What is it?" I asked, with a catch in my throat and a sudden feeling of nausea, that told of the intense anxiety which I laboured under when I heard his disquieting words. Standing before him, with my fists clenched tightly and every nerve in my system strained to the utmost, I was prepared for news of the direst intent, knowing only too well that Flaxman would never have undertaken the risk of such a wild night-ride in this fearful weather unless the situation was one of the utmost importance, and moreover remembering, as I did, the nature of our parting only the night before, As I looked at the haggard, deathly-white faced man who stood before me, I cursed myself inwardly that I had treated him so badly by allowing my jealousy to get the upper hand of me, and in one bitter moment to undo the best and sincerest friendship that two men could form. Now I felt that I would have given my right hand to have been able to recall the words that I had so rashly given vent to, for I had stabbed both his heart and my own, the hurt of which could never be entirely cured.

Gazing into the weary eyes, with their deep black rims showing only too well the mental and physical strain that he had suffered, and was suffering, all my old affection for the man returned, and the longing to be forgiven for the wrong that I now knew I had done him filled my heart.

"Flaxman," I cried, the tears welling up in my eyes as I did so, "I have been a brute, a jealous, cruel brute, I know, and I cannot expect you to look at my conduct in any other light, but can you ever forgive me? I know I don't deserve to be spoken to again, but I realise now what it would be to lose your friendship for ever. It is my jealousy that goads me on and makes me do and say things that are unworthy and unjust. I hate myself for it more than I can say, but I could not bear that Moira should love you more than she did me. Now I see clearer that you are the better man to make her happy."

"Hush, hush, George," he replied, "you must not talk like this, you don't know what you are saying; to-morrow, yes, tomorrow, when I am better and calmer, I will tell you all, so that you may judge for yourself. Now, what I want is your forgiveness and help; you know that you have mine. We must not quarrel, old boy; life is too serious and too short. We must never allow anything to come between us in our friendship. No, not even a woman, not the most beautiful woman in the world, must we?"

He held out his hand, I took it in both of mine, and neither of us spoke. I knew that his kindly, sweet nature had forgiven me. To my dying day I shall remember the episode; it is burnt into my brain as with a branding iron.

After a few moments of silence had passed, I pulled myself together, and bringing a big wicker chair forward pushed him into it.

"Now tell me your bad news. I can bear it, only let me hear everything. Is—is Moira dead?"

As I uttered the last words there came over me a feeling of dread that was indescribable, a feeling that sent a chill through me and made me shudder. In my mind I seemed to picture the body of Moira lying dead at my feet—Moira, the girl who had entered so eventfully into my existence, and whom I had learned to love so dearly. The mere thought of her death was enough to terrify me.

Flaxman was quick to notice the effect of my words, for he replied:—

"I am afraid that I distressed you more than was necessary, but the strain I have gone through lately has greatly affected me. Perhaps it is not as bad as I imagine."

"But you don't tell me, old man," I cried impatiently. "How on earth can I be expected to judge; come, tell me—is she dead?"

"Not yet, I think, but very, very seriously ill."

"Where?"

"Well, I will explain all. Yesterday afternoon I was worn out with worry and anxiety, and had a bad headache, so I went to my room and lay down; after a while I fell into a doze. Suddenly I was awakened by hearing someone walking along the verandah outside my window. Thinking nothing of this, putting it down to one of the hands, I turned over and tried to go to sleep again. Then there came a tremendous growling and barking from Judy at the other end of the verandah. I was off the bed in a second, and out of the window like a shot, just in time to see a big man come stealthily out of Moira's room. Directly he caught sight of me he made off, followed by the dog.

"It did not take me long to be on his track, you may be sure, for I at once realised that he was not a desirable character from the appearance he possessed. I can describe him exactly; in fact, I could pick him out of a hundred men with the greatest ease. He is very tall, I should say about six foot six, very broad, with rough red beard, and bushy eyebrows and big ears standing out; he wore a dirty red shirt, very much patched, and a battered hat with a hole in the crown as if a shot had gone through it. I noted all this as I ran after him, with Judy at his heels growling away and showing her teeth pretty seriously, I can tell you."

"Well, go on," I said eagerly, as he paused to take a drink.

"Judy was too troublesome for him," he continued, "so turning round suddenly he swung his whip and caught her clean on the skull, which knocked her out at once. If I had only got a six-shooter I should have shot him dead then and there, the brute."

"Did it kill her?" I asked anxiously, for she was a favourite terrier, and there's nothing that a man dislikes so much as another man killing his favourite dog.

"No, she's all right again, but it was a bad blow given by a dexterous hand that makes no mistakes. However, to continue, I called loudly for assistance as I ran on, and Blake, hearing me call, came running forward to stop the ruffian, but, as they met, he received a blow which knocked him out. I could not wait to attend to Blake, as I saw the chance now of getting the man into my power, for he stopped and looked about as if searching for something; as he did so, I noticed his horse tied to a tree, slightly to my right. Evidently in the excitement he had gone too far, and my opportunity had occurred, so I at once started off to get to the beast first. I was a bit of a sprinter when I was at the 'Varsity, and you may be certain I did my little best at this moment. I fairly flew over the ground; the man saw his mistake and came after me like a flash, and I can assure you no race run at any athletic sports in the world could have been more exciting or more straining. That he was gaining upon me at every step was certain, and as I tore on I seemed to feel his hot breath upon the back of my neck, while I imagined him raising the heavy whip, that had already done so much damage, to bring the butt end down with a thud on my head—that made me move on without a doubt. I was about ten yards from the horse, who was standing with ears forward, as if taking the keenest interest in the exciting race going on before him, and it needed only a great effort on my part to get to him first, for the man was still some distance away, although in my anxiety I had imagined him nearer. Just as I reached the animal, and was about to untie the reins I heard a thud, and looking round saw that the fellow had tripped and fallen. In the twinkling of an eye I was upon him, and then began such a struggle as I am never likely to go through again.

"It did not take me long to realise that I had met with an antagonist of no mean order. He had fallen on his face, and this had slightly knocked the breath out of him, together with the hard run he had been through.

"By the time I got to him he was on his hands and knees, and I immediately set to work to use all the old wrestling arts that I knew as a younger man in my Cornish home.

"But it was perfectly obvious to me that I was no match for this ugly customer. He held himself in reserve, to regain his wind and strength, and I felt that I stood as little chance of securing him as a child would against a grown man. In a shorter time than it takes to tell I was fairly beaten, and at his mercy.

"He now was kneeling upon my chest, and it seemed that every bone would break with his weight. I saw him looking round for his whip, which he dropped when he fell; his left hand clutched my throat; and then I saw him raise the weapon by the thong end, and I heard him hiss through his clenched teeth, 'Curse you, I'll teach you to interfere with me,' when the whip butt descended on my luckless head, and I knew no more.

"When I came to myself I found Snowball kneeling by my side. I felt deucedly bad in the head, I can tell you, for on putting my hand to my brow I discovered that I had a lump as big as an egg there, and, judging from the skill with which he wielded the weapon, my friend of the red beard must have used all his power upon my poor cranium.

"Looking about in a dazed fashion, I could see no sign whatever of my adversary or his horse; both had long since departed, leaving me to look after myself. Poor Snowball was extremely concerned as to the state of my health, and did all in his power to make my position as comfortable as he could. I gleaned the information that he was on his way to the station to bring me news of Moira, when, to his great alarm, he saw the big man galloping like fury towards him. It did not take him a second to lie prone as a snake and let horse and rider go past him. At this juncture I fainted, and did not regain consciousness until I found myself upon my bed. After an hour or two I was better and able to get up and send for Snowball.

"It appears that when Moira left the station he followed her, for, as you know, he is devoted to her. She was making an effort to get to the coach route, when this ruffian rode up, and after an angry conversation, knocked her down with his whip, and, after robbing her, mounted and made off. As they were only a short distance from the grog shanty that Snowball knows so well, he made all speed, obtained help, and fetched her to the place in an unconscious condition. He then started off to give us information, only to find me in the same state, and through the work of the same dastardly hand.

"The whole occurrence was so extraordinary that the more I thought it over the more mysterious it became. What the man wanted at the station I could not for the life of me understand. Then I remembered having first seen him coming out of Moira's room, so I immediately made my way there and discovered everything upside down, just as if a person had been looking for something in the greatest hurry, but nothing had been taken away.

"From this fact it was obvious that my assailant had not come to the station for the mere purpose of robbery, but with the intention of endeavouring to find something that Moira had in her possession; but whether he was successful or not I cannot say.

"It therefore behoved me to act at once. I weighed the matter carefully over in my mind, and determined to find you without any further delay, for together we could act for the best. I therefore instructed Snowball to remain at the station until our return, and set out for the township, but, unfortunately, I am a very poor Bushman, and the awful storm going on caused me to become bushed, and had it not been for a sundowner I happened to strike, I should have been there now. However, here I am, pretty well done, mentally and physically."

"Yes, old chap," I replied; "now there's nothing for you but rest. You had better come to my room and get some sleep; in the morning we'll get off to the station and put things right."

He agreed, and I led him to my room, and before many minutes had passed he was in a deep sleep, worn out completely with fatigue.

I softly closed the door and went back to the bar parlour, where I replenished the fire, pulled a big chair up to it, lit my pipe, and prepared to think out the very mysterious occurrences of which Flaxman had told me, but very soon I fell asleep, and dreamed that I saw poor Moira being murdered by Snowball, while I myself was bound hand and foot and could do nothing to help her. At last, by almost superhuman strength, I burst the rope that bound me and—woke up to find myself being well shaken by my good friend the landlord, and the daylight streaming into the room.

CHAPTER XII

UNRAVELLING A CONSPIRACY.

It was eight o'clock before I made up my mind to rouse Flaxman out of the heavy sleep of exhaustion that he had fallen into; for, eager as I was to set out upon the task of bringing Moira back once more to the station, yet I felt that it was most essential he should obtain all the rest that was possible under the circumstances, to enable him after the hard doings of the last few hours to cope with the equally hard ones that lay before him. I well knew that the man was not physically strong; in fact, he was almost fragile, and unless I took the greatest possible care, it was most probable that I should have two invalids upon my hands instead of one.

In the meantime I ordered the best breakfast that could be obtained in the place, settled the bill, and arranged with the landlord for the use of a horse in place of the one that I had so wilfully ridden to death two nights before; then I felt that all was ready, on my side, for the earliest possible start.

The storm had ceased in the small hours of the morning, and now the sun was blazing away once more in all its intensity; and as I looked across the wide street and noticed the heat shimmering over the roadway, I knew that the sooner we started the easier and pleasanter our journey would be.

I then made my way to the bedroom, and, after considerable difficulty, managed to get Flaxman into a wakeful condition and told him that we should start to ride back to the station directly after breakfast; then left him to his toilet and went to my meal.

I had only just commenced to help myself to the good and substantial fare that had been placed before me, when the landlord entered the room and came over to my table. After enquiring how I had found Flaxman after his night's rest, he brought a chair close to mine, and I could plainly see that he was preparing to be communicative.

"Mr. Tregaskis," he said, lowering his voice so that the other occupants of the room could not overhear him, "I want to have a talk with you before Mr. Flaxman comes down. I don't usually take much interest in other people's affairs, but seeing that both of you gentlemen have always treated me so well, and, if I may say so, we have always been good friends, I think that it is my duty to give you some information that may be of service to you."

"Indeed, that's very good of you, Johnson," I replied, nervously I confess, for, somehow, I could not but feel disquieted owing to recent events, which had not a little upset my nervous equilibrium.

"I don't know about that," he said; "but this I do know, that when a man treats me decently, I do the same for him; but when one has to deal with the sharp gentry, one must act accordingly."

This latter remark was made with a mysterious air, and with such sincere feeling that I knew the man had a desire to do me a good turn, but was not quite certain how I should take his interference in my affairs; therefore, to put him quite at his ease and more than that, to hear what he had to say—for to tell the truth I was extremely desirous of doing so—I gave him to understand that I was deeply interested, which indeed I was; whereupon, in response to my advances, he opened up his subject to me.

"No doubt you wonder what on earth it is I am about to tell you, but as a matter of fact both you and Mr. Flaxman have an interest in the affair, and therefore I'm going to give you all the information I can, and when you have heard what I have to say, you can discuss the matter with me, or not, as you feel disposed; but, whatever results, I shall always feel that I have done my best for you, sir."

"Upon my word, Johnson," I said, "I hardly know what to say. That you have some valuable information to impart to me, I feel convinced; but you whet my curiosity to such a degree that I really must ask you to gratify it. What on earth is it?"

"Well, without beating about the bush any further," he said, and he leant quite near to me and almost whispered; "there's some conspiracy going on in which you and Mr. Flaxman are concerned. Of that much I am certain. From information, slight 'tis true, but still information I have gathered, I feel I am right and it is my bounden duty to tell you."

"Well, for Heaven's sake, man, do start; I am all attention; but what it can be I'm at a loss to understand."

"Do you remember the cove that came in and sat smoking last night in the parlour with us? A new chum we voted him. The chap who wore gloves."

"Of course I do. He told us he was a new chum, and one could easily see that he was."

"Humph! Well, he isn't, that's a certainty. At first I thought he was, but when I got to bed and began to think deeper about it, I felt I had met the man somewhere before, but for the life of me I couldn't think where. I puzzled my brain over it again and again, and at last fell asleep with him on my mind, and the most curious part of the whole affair is the way that I did recall who he was and where I last saw him.

"I wonder if you remember about eight years ago the notorious bushranger, Black; Captain Black he used to call himself. He received six years' imprisonment for some blackguard job. At that time I was living in the district he frequented, and I can well recollect the exciting moments we spent when the whole neighbourhood was trying to secure him; but, somehow or other, he always managed to avoid capture, until at last he was given away at his hiding-place by one of his pals, who afterwards turned King's evidence. Then the police took him. I was present at his trial, and can remember, as if it was only yesterday, the calm and collected way that he stood in the dock and took his sentence. Whatever other faults he has, there is no doubt whatever the man had great pluck.

"But, by Jove, he used to give us some shocking frights. It seems only a day since the time when I used to lie awake at night straining my ears for every sound, which I felt would be 'Black's gang,' as they were called. However, we were never favoured with a personal visit from the lot, although the next station was. But then, all this is now ancient history. The gang got lagged, and serve 'em right. We've no use for a dirty lot of blackguards like his. They used to say he was well-born, a gentleman, and I firmly believe they were right, at least, judging from appearances, for I never saw a criminal turned out so well in my life, and I've seen a few."

I replied that I had known all about him, and well I did, for he was a veritable Ned Kelly, and the wonderful adventures of the man made a very great impression upon me at the time; I remember I used to picture myself as one of the police who took him, and I envied them their task in securing one of the shrewdest and most dare—devil of criminals.

"It's very curious that just after he had left this morning, I should go to my desk to find a letter I had placed there, and the first thing my eye lighted on was this old paper, giving, as you will see, the whole account of his trial and a portrait of Captain Black."

With that he produced an old and soiled newspaper, and, after carefully smoothing out the creases with his fat red hands, placed it before me. In the text I saw a crude portrait of the criminal. It might have been the man Vandergrave, or anyone else, as far as I was able to judge, but the landlord was so certain that he was correct in his assertion, that I did not argue the matter with him.

"All this is very interesting, Johnson," I said, "but for the life of me I cannot see what this man's history can have to do with me, or Flaxman, unless you think we were members of his beautiful gang. I conclude from what you have told me that you are certain this chap Vandergrave is really Black, and that he has some scheme on hand in which we are mixed up in a mysterious way."

"That's it, Mr. Tregaskis, that's it. It certainly sounds a fairy tale, but it's true, nevertheless, and I will tell you my reasons for thinking so. He ordered his breakfast early this morning, for he was anxious to get along quickly, he said. When sitting down to it, he began in a casual way to pump me with regard to you and your station. How far off was it? Was it a large station? How many hands do you employ? What sort of a house was it? What was the best route to take to get to it? I, of course, innocently enough, told him, as we are justly proud of your station.

"Those few enquiries led to a great many more, and at last he asked me whether there were any ladies up at the station. 'Why?' I asked. 'Oh, I only ask out of idle curiosity,' he replied. 'I remember that when Mr. Tregaskis was settling his difference with the Irish gentleman last evening the latter apologised for speaking of the lady as he did. I assumed, therefore, that a lady does reside at the station.'

"'There may be, or there may not be,' I answered. 'If there is,' I said, 'it's Mr. Tregaskis's business and not mine; I don't worry myself enquiring into other folk's affairs,' for by now I was getting anxious at being asked all these questions, and it made me a bit suspicious, for I felt that the joker wanted to know more than was good for him.

"'I was only curious to know,' he answered. "By the way, what is Mr. Flaxman like? I once knew a Flaxman at Cambridge, a tall fair man. Of course it may not be my man, but it's rather an unusual name, and it would be very interesting if I were to meet an old friend in the wilds of Australia.

"'Is he married?' he went on, and I told him I knew very little about Mr. Flaxman, but that if he wanted to know anything more he could ask the gentleman himself, as he had arrived late last night to see you, and, by Jove, directly he heard this, he went as white as a sheet, and it was some minutes before he recovered; then he made some small excuse, paid his bill, ordered his horse, and went, and in my opinion he was in a devilish hurry to get off. From his talk and enquiries I'm quite sure the chap's not what he sets up to be; in fact, my suspicions were aroused by his hands. If that chap ain't done time, well, I'm not the landlord of this blooming place, that's all."

"Now, that's very strange; I noticed his hands myself last night. It's most curious that he should take such a huge interest in a man he's never met before," I said.

Then I remembered the way he worked the conversation round the night before until the landlord told him we were the largest station owners in the district, and it suddenly flashed across my mind that he knew Flaxman's name without my having told him.

The more I thought of it the more peculiar and mysterious it seemed. Recent events had caused me to be careful; and now I wondered if this man was in any way connected with the red-bearded villain who had assaulted both Moira and Flaxman.

I told the landlord what Flaxman had told me, how he had been attacked by the rascal, but I was careful to leave out any mention of Moira or her disappearance.

When I had finished my story the landlord asked for a description of the assailant.

"As far as I could gather from Flaxman he is very tall, about six feet three, with a red, ragged beard, immensely broad and powerfully built, roughly dressed, and looks like a sundowner or a horse thief."

"My word, that's Mike O'Connor's description to a tee," gasped the landlord in a state of immense excitement. "He's one of the worst blackguards in Australia, been in choky I don't know how many times for bushranging, horse stealing, and devil knows what other crimes. We hoped we'd got rid of the beast for good, as he hasn't been seen in these parts for five or six years."

"Perhaps he's been in prison."

"Most likely, and I wish he was there still. Just fancy, Mike O'Connor! By gad, you'll have to keep your eyes skinned if he's on the job."

"Yes, judging from poor old Flaxman's experience, I shall," I replied, putting down my cup and pushing my chair back ready to rise from the table. "Somehow, Johnson," I said, "I cannot help feeling that this chap Vandergrave, or Black, or whatever he chooses to call himself, and O'Connor, have some design upon us of which we know nothing. But what the reason is, Heaven alone knows. The whole thing is a mystery, and it is incumbent upon us to fathom it; and, by Jove, I intend to do so, whatever the consequences."

With that I rose from the table, filled my pipe, and was about to leave the room when Johnson followed me to the door.

"Mr. Tregaskis, look here. If at any time you want assistance, will you let me know, and I'll be with you post haste? I tell you quite candidly, I don't like the look of things. I know these precious beauties too well to suppose they mean no harm."

"Thanks very much indeed, my friend," I replied. "If the occasion arises, which I pray it may not, you may be sure I shall send you a message."

"And I'll be there for a certainty," he replied warmly. "But, in the meantime, are you going to tell Mr. Flaxman anything of what I have told you?"

"No, I don't think I shall just yet. I may tell him as we ride to the station. Will you please let him know I shall be back before he has finished his breakfast?"

I then strolled out of the house and turned my steps in the direction of the police station, for I was anxious to hear what the superintendent had to say on the subject of the recent occurrences.

As I passed along the footway, smoking my pipe, and trying to analyse the situation in my mind, I suddenly found myself face to face with the most useful man of any that I could meet under the circumstances. His name was Braithwaite, and he occupied the important position of inspecting officer of police, while his duty consisted in visiting the different district police stations and generally seeing that all was carried on as it should be. He had stayed at Montalta on many occasions, we had been drawn into a very close bond of friendship, and I found him a real good fellow in every way.

As we warmly shook hands, he expressed surprise at meeting me parading the street at this early hour in the morning, just as if I were out for a constitutional.

"Well, as a matter of fact, old chap, I was on my way to pay a visit to the police station."

"Eh, what? Going to give yourself up for the crime of still being a bachelor, I suppose."

He always chaffed me unmercifully for the selfish way, as he put it, that I withheld all the good things of the earth stored away at Montalta from the female sex, and that it was a crying shame I should be allowed to remain unmarried, while there were so many charming girls only too ready and willing to make me happy and comfortable for ever.

"No," I replied, "I'm not going to give myself up yet. I want a little more freedom."

"Freedom be hanged, you old dog, you want a wife, and I shall have to see that you get one without further delay. Joking apart, though, what's up?"

"Really, Braithwaite, I'm awfully delighted to see you. You're the very man of all others in the world I want. Can you turn back to the police station and have a chat in private?"

"Certainly, old boy. I'm entirely at your service, but I hope it's nothing serious; you look awfully glum. Is the station burnt down?"

"No, not yet, I hope," I answered as we stepped out side by side.

"Well, you must let me hear all about it," he said.

It did not take many minutes to walk to the police station, which was perhaps the most imposing building in the place. At Braithwaite's invitation I entered and passed along a stone-flagged passage, then followed him into a room at the back, which he used as an office. It was extremely simple in its furniture, containing only a large iron safe in one corner, a roll top desk in the centre, a revolving chair, and a couple of wicker easy chairs. The walls were hung with framed photographs of policemen in the conventional and extremely unnatural attitudes generally adopted by the portrait photographer, while each had stern duty portrayed upon his features. The end wall was ornamented with a neat design carried out in handcuffs, doubtless the work of a hand that could find beauty in the most sinister instruments.

Pushing one of the easy chairs over, Braithwaite produced a cigar-case and handed it to me. I selected a cigar and proceeded to light it.

"Now then, out with it. What crime have you committed?"

"None yet," I answered, "but there's no knowing what I may do, if I'm put to it; and, taking in consideration the circumstances which I am about to inform you of, it looks as if we are in for a bit of trouble, one way and another."

"Oh, indeed! Well, tell me all about it, so that I may judge for myself."

Then I told him everything that had occurred since Moira first came to the station, and withheld nothing, for I knew the man so thoroughly that my secrets were perfectly safe in his keeping. With this feeling in my mind it made the telling easy. I related how I had fought the Tipperary Boy, and of the arrival of the man who called himself Vandergrave; and, finally, the landlord's recent conversation with me, and his assertion that Vandergrave was really Black, and that it was most probably O'Connor who attacked Moira.

When I finished my yarn, Braithwaite sat still in his chair, taking slow pulls at his pipe and blowing the smoke out of the left corner of his mouth. There was a look of earnest consideration in his grey eyes, those eyes that look so straight into one's own that they seem to search into the very brain to diagnose the motives germinating there.

After a minute or two had passed in silence, he rose and went to the door, and called the superintendent. When this officer came, I heard him enter into a whispered conversation, which lasted a minute or two, then the man went away and Braithwaite returned to his chair.

"Do you think, old chap, you could recognise this Vandergrave if I produce a photo?"

"Most certainly I could, for I took careful stock of him last night; he interested me not a little, principally from the fact that I considered him to be a new chum."

"I have no doubt about the correctness of Johnson's assertion that the other fellow was O'Connor, for we have very lately received information that he is in the district, and have had instruction to watch his goings on. In fact, that's one of the matters that brings me here."

"Do you know him to be a bad lot then?"

"Bad lot, by gad! He's about as big a blackguard as there is in this wide world, I should say. There is absolutely nothing too dirty for his hands to touch, and if he wants a thing he'll go to any extremes to obtain it. Yes, Mike O'Connor is a pretty rascal, and a very dangerous one, I can tell you; he and I are old acquaintances. I got him his last two years' imprisonment for horse stealing up in the Turon District. He's got his knife into me, and won't forget to make it even if he gets half a chance."

"By Jove, old boy, I shouldn't like your job. Too many risks for me."

"That's what makes it exciting," he answered with a laugh. "If one had to consider all the risks run consequent upon the threats that are thrown at one, I reckon there wouldn't be many police left. I must confess I like the job, there's a realism about it that keeps the brain and body active."

"So I should imagine; but there's one thing about Flaxman's story that rather puzzles me, and that is the fact that nothing was taken away from Miss Pendragon's room at the station. O'Connor is a thief, and most probably came to obtain valuables of some sort; but perhaps he was disturbed by the dog before he could find anything sufficiently useful to take away."

"Ah, I'm afraid that robbery of valuables was not the object of his visit. For, if it had been so, he would certainly not have chosen Miss Pendragon's bedroom first; besides that, his attack on the young lady proves that he was in search of something belonging to her, for I have no doubt in my mind that he watched her leave the station, and followed her into the scrub, that being the quietest place in which he could carry out his attack; but I don't expect he realised that Snowball was also following. That was a lucky stroke for us. If it had not been for Snowball we should not have known anything. His devotion to Miss Pendragon is most extraordinary; but it was fortunate that O'Connor did not happen to see him, or I fear Snowball would not have been in a position to tell us of any of the occurrences."

"I say, though, what do you think was O'Connor's motive for all this violence?"

"Well, in my humble opinion he desired to obtain some incriminating document in the possession of Miss Pendragon, and he was prepared to go to any extreme to do so. You will see, if we make this assumption our basis, how the whole story weaves itself into a probability. We'll assume, firstly, that Miss Pendragon is in the possession of something, most likely a document, that this O'Connor desires to obtain. Perhaps he has often been to the station and threatened her, he certainly could do so without your knowledge, as both of you are generally away on some distant part of the run during the day, and the thing would be perfectly easy and safe. At last she gets frightened; doubtless the man has become aggressive, and she then thinks that the only course she can pursue is to go away. She writes you a letter and departs; O'Connor has been watching and follows; he attacks her; but not finding what he wants, he leaves her insensible, hurries off to the station, and goes straight to her room; only to be discovered by Flaxman, with the result that we know. It must be an extremely important object that necessitates so much risk. O'Connor would not run his head wilfully into the lion's mouth unless a very great deal can be gained by it."

At this juncture the superintendent returned with a packet of papers, which he handed to Braithwaite.

"I think you will find all you require in this, sir," he said.

"Thanks, leave us for a little."

The superintendent left the room, and Braithwaite opened the packet, taking from it a photograph, which he looked at for a few seconds, and then handed to me.

I took the piece of cardboard with a feeling of the most extraordinary nervousness. It was quite indescribable. I felt as if I was about to look upon something that would cause me intense horror. I gazed at it intently for a minute or two. It was a picture of a man of about forty years of age, and was without doubt a portrait of Vandergrave, for I noted the cynical expression and the features as the same as those of the man that I had met on the previous night, with the exception, of course, that the original of the photograph must have been at least ten years younger when he sat for it.

"Well, what do you make of it?" he asked.

"The man that I met last night, without a doubt," I answered. "I could swear to him in a court of law."

"Well, perhaps you may have to, old chap, so don't be too eager. Now, then, do you want to hear a little of the gentleman's career? It may interest you."

With that he unfolded a paper and read me out some of the details.

"'William Angus Hesketh, alias Forester, alias Black, aged forty-two, formerly resident in England, retired Captain 17th Dragoon Guards, came to Australia with a woman since disappeared; after having resided in the Colony eight years, received two years for forgery; two years later, one year for horse stealing; later, received six years for robbery under arms, together with others, and among the number of his accomplices was Michael O'Connor.' By Jove, I begin to see a light in this darkness. O'Connor is acting under instructions from, we'll call him, Vandergrave. Now I can understand his anxiety to learn whether any woman was at your station, eh?"

"I believe you're right, old chap," I answered; "it's very curious indeed."

"No, I expect when we've unravelled the mystery a little more, we shall find it's simplicity itself. But look here, Tregaskis, I want you to tell me exactly and faithfully all you know about Miss Moira Pendragon."

"I would most gladly, Braithwaite, but I know absolutely nothing. As you are well aware, I found her in the scrub, nearly mad with fright, during a storm in the middle of the night, when her companion, a man, had been struck by lightning and killed."

"Yes, who was that man?" he asked eagerly. He had risen and was pacing up and down the room.

"That's more than I can tell you I tried to get it out of her, but it was impossible; she was silent on the subject, and would answer no questions. She only told me that she hated him, that he had treated her brutally and she was glad he was dead; more than that I could not elicit."

"My dear old boy," he almost shouted, standing before me, "that is the crux of the whole thing. Miss Moira holds some secret connected with this Vandergrave, which he must have at all costs, and he has employed O'Connor to obtain it, by force if necessary. Now, tell me, did you ever hear her mention a paper or anything of the kind?"

"No, she had only the clothes she stood up in, nothing more; everything else she possessed we gave her."

"Still, I'm convinced there's something. If not, why did O'Connor ride back to the station and ransack her room?"

"I cannot say; I'm at a loss to understand it."

We sat silently smoking for a few minutes, until at last Braithwaite collected the papers together, placed the photograph with them, and put all away in the packet.

"Look here, Tregaskis. You will remember I told you that this Vandergrave came to Australia with a woman who disappeared. It is not possible that Miss Pendragon can be this woman?"

"Of course not, man. She told me herself that she was not twenty-two years old, and that she was born in Australia, so she cannot be."

"No, I suppose not. But what happened to the woman then? Maybe Miss Moira is her daughter."

"And who is the man that was killed by lightning? I saw his face, horribly distorted in death, and I don't think I shall ever be able to get it out of my mind."

"Now, Tregaskis, you had better get back, and be off with Flaxman as quickly as possible to the station. I don't think it probable that you will have any more trouble for a bit with O'Connor, it would be too risky for him. If you can put up with me, I will follow you in an hour or two, as I should like to consider this matter on the spot."

"We shall only be too delighted to have you, Braithwaite; for as long as ever you can manage it. You can feel sure of the warmest of welcomes."

"Thanks very much," he answered. "I suppose you will set out to bring Miss Pendragon back to the station as soon as possible. I will bring over the doctor with me in case he is wanted."

"All right." With that I shook hands warmly with him and made my way into the street and back to the hotel, congratulating myself that I had enlisted the services of one of the cleverest of police officials in Australia.

CHAPTER XIII

FLAXMAN HAS A PRESENTIMENT.

On entering the coffee room, if it might be dignified with the name, I discovered Flaxman engaged in eating his breakfast; I therefore sat down at the table with him, and discussed trivialities. I could not help feeling a sense of restraint, though, for so much had occurred within the last few hours, in which he was so deeply interested, and I had gained such an immensity of information consequent upon these occurrences, that it seemed almost cruel not to divulge it to him. But I reasoned it out in my mind that it would be better to wait until we were safely on our way to the station before I told him anything.

I confess that it was with no little impatience that I waited for him to finish his meal. All the time he was eating I was thinking of Moira, and wondering whether she was alive or dead. I knew the rough place that she had been taken to. It was as bad a grog shanty as there was in the district; a bad place for a man, but a thousand times worse for a woman. A wicked hole to be well in, but to be ill there would be more than awful. When I thought of it, something seemed to say in my brain, "hurry, hurry," and a feeling of nervous anxiety took hold of me. I bit the stem of my unlit pipe, until I almost bit it through; and it was only by a tremendous effort that I kept myself from urging Flaxman to make haste. But a good meal was essential to him, so I wrestled with myself and possessed my soul in patience; yet it seemed ages before he rose up and said he was prepared to start; then I was like a colt getting out of a drafting yard when the rails are slipped, and he is allowed to go free.

In a very short while we completed our arrangements, and were in the saddle, waving farewells to our friend the landlord, who called out after us, "Don't forget to let me know." So we began our journey back to Montalta, where I was destined to go through the most momentous event of my life. I could not help contrasting this setting out for the Station that had become so dear to both of us, and where we had spent so many happy and prosperous days, with that of our first start to take possession. Now a feeling was upon me that all this happiness would be changed, and it was a long time before I was able to throw off the sense of apprehension that had come over me.

We rode side by side without addressing a word to one another. Doubtless both of us had our minds too full of the errand that was before us. Once or twice I glanced at Flaxman and noted how haggard and worn he still looked; and I fancied that I could see tears in his eyes. This was acute pain to me, for I knew that I was greatly to blame in the treatment that I had shown him. How I longed to be able to set aside the past, and return once more to the old feeling of comradeship now gone for ever! Things, I felt, could never be the same again. So it is; a few hasty words spoken in heat and anger, and lifelong friendships are undone. Now there was nothing for it but to make the best amends I could.

It was only when we reached the summit of a high hill, from which a magnificent view of the surrounding country is obtained, that Flaxman spoke. This particular spot was a great favourite of his, and he never tired of admiring its beauties. He always drew rein here to gaze with delight upon the superb prospect that lay spread as it were at our feet. Miles upon miles of green grass dotted everywhere with blue gums and oaks, while in the far distance towered the ranges outlined against the azure sky. What an expanse of earth and sky it was, majestic in its sublime grandeur! The road or track that we followed passed at the edge of a steep hill, which dropped away for about six or seven hundred feet. Blue gums and mulga scrub clothed its side, interspersed here and there with great grey boulders. At the foot of this hill was the green valley, made exceptionally charming and fresh by the recent rains. As far as the eye could reach was sunlight and colour, and not a living creature, save an old-man kangaroo, who suddenly caught sight of us and lopped lazily away down the hillside. All around we could hear the cicalas busily chirruping among the trees, and the chatter of the parakeets, and occasionally the call of an old crow engaged somewhere near in the wattle bushes.

Flaxman was an artist and a good judge of views, and this one pleased him more than any other. This time he stopped, and I followed his example, although I was all impatience to bring our journey to an end, and was in no mood, on this occasion, to discuss the beauties of Nature.

He sat perfectly still on his horse for three or four minutes, gazing over the beautiful scene, and taking in all its glories.

"Oh, what a view it is, old boy," he said, and turned to me as if he wished me to endorse what he said, "and to think that it is the last time that I shall ever look upon it."

"What on earth are you talking about," I answered. "Why, my dear chap, you'll see it again hundreds of times."

"No, George, I've a feeling in my inmost soul that I shall never see it again. I don't know what it is that makes me think this, but it is so. You have always laughed at my superstitions, as you are pleased to call them, yet, so certain am I of what I say, that I have taken the precaution of writing a letter to you which I want you to act upon, if anything happens to me. We have been such awfully good friends, old man, that I could die perfectly happy knowing that you will carry out my wishes. Will you promise me to do so?"

"Of course I will. But really you must not talk like this. I am certain that you will live for years yet to enjoy your success. You are seedy and worn out, and things that have happened have got on your nerves. Let's hurry up and get back to the Station. It makes me miserable to see you so glum."

"My dear old friend," he answered, while he looked at me with the old affectionate smile that I knew so well, "our life has been a very happy one together, until—until—forgive me for saying it, until you brought Moira back with you; since then I have not had a moment's peace of mind. You will wonder at my saying this, but when you know all you will not be surprised, but don't think that I was in love with her, for nothing in the world would give me greater pleasure than to see you two married, if such a thing could be possible, and I earnestly hope that I shall live to have my wish gratified."

To say that I was surprised at the turn the conversation had taken was to put it too mildly. I was amazed; I could find nothing to answer, but only sat like an idiot gazing at him in astonishment.

"You look as if you imagine I am mad, George, but I'm not, I never was so sane in my life. I know that you thought I was in love with Moira, but I was not. I had the greatest admiration and affection for her, and when you know all you will appreciate my position. But I can only tell you of one incident in my career—I have a wife. It's impossible for me to tell you more now, for the subject is one that is far too painful to me, but some day you will know everything and can judge my actions for yourself."

I couldn't answer a word, I was dumb-founded. I tried to stammer out a few sentences, but the words stuck in my throat. What a fool I had made of myself all through! What a jealous, unreasonable brute I had been! I could have kicked myself for my idiocy. To think that in my blundering folly I should have attributed motives to him which were entirely foreign to his mind! I felt more contemptible than it was possible to say.

However, I managed to bring the talk into another channel, and as we started once more on our homeward journey, I informed him that I had seen Braithwaite, who was coming up in a few hours to the Station to stay with us, and would bring the doctor with him.

At last we came in sight of the Station, and drew up at the slip-rails of the horse paddock, removed our saddles and bridles, then sent the horses loose, and made for the house.

With mixed feelings I gazed upon our home once again. It seemed to me that I had been away months and months. How delightfully peaceful and quiet it looked, nestling in a wealth of peppermint, orange, and loquat trees, with here and there great gums, and tall feathery bamboos. The shady walks and neat flower-beds filled with great masses of colour, which poured out the sweetest fragrance, all told of the unceasing care and attention paid to the place. The broad verandah, which was built round the house, covered with roses and creepers of all kinds, looked so cool and delightfully homelike, with its striped awnings, that one felt tempted to throw oneself into the deepest and easiest of the big wicker chairs which stood so invitingly about, and sink contentedly into a doze, lulled softly by the humming of the innumerable insects among the trees.

But no, there was a much more important matter to be attended to; so, after giving orders that the tray buggy should be made ready, with a mattress laid on it, so that Moira might travel with all the comfort possible, I went to my bedroom, and after taking a refreshing bath, dressed myself for the journey, and made my way to the verandah, where I found Flaxman also prepared to start.

I had already given instructions that Moira's bedroom should be prepared and everything made ready to receive her, and a note was sent off to the overseer's wife at the distant homestead, asking her to come over and see that Miss Pendragon wanted for nothing. She was a very nice little woman, devoted to Flaxman and myself, and I knew that she would do all that lay in her power to help us, for she was extremely fond of Moira.

At last we were ready to start. Flaxman was to drive the buggy, while I rode old Ready, a big brown horse, a particular favourite of mine, who had carried me for many weary miles on some of our hardest days' mustering at the distant parts of the run.

Snowball, of course, who was already waiting for us at the slip-panels, would trot patiently at our side, never tiring; he was one of the cleverest trackers it was ever my lot to meet, and nothing in the world could put him off. So we started, and I was glad to feel that it would not be many hours before Moira would be safe once again under our roof. Both of us were eager beyond words to reach the "Bushman's Rest," as the grog shanty was so grandiloquently called, though it belied its name most terribly, for the man who entered its portals knew no rest whatever, at least not until the amount of his cheque was liquidated in more senses than one.

When we left the vicinity of the Station, our route lay through the scrub, and then over broad green stretches of pasture land, right at the outlying portion of our run. As we journeyed along we happened to come across herds of our cattle, in such gorgeous condition that I could not resist the temptation to stop and call Flaxman's attention to them, for within a week or so we were to begin mustering a big mob of fat cattle for the market, and in my mind's eye I saw good prices and large cheques. The excellent rains so recently fallen had produced abundant and luscious herbage, and on all sides the stock gave evidence of doing as well as the most exacting of breeders could wish. There was an indescribable charm and delight in gazing upon the splendid beasts lazily feeding on the tender and nutritive grass, the while they swished the flies off their sleek sides with their long tails and moved slowly on a few paces, or raised their heads and lowed to another, while some stood knee deep in the reed-fringed pools, their goodly proportions reflected in the clear water.

There is no picture that can give greater pleasure than that of seeing one's property improving every day, and in my case I had the best of reasons to be satisfied on this score.

After leaving these fresh and fertile pastures we struck our boundary, when the aspect of the country began to change. In place of the delightful green of the watered lands, we began to see the sand, while the scrub became denser; then, as we ascended to the ranges, we came across great grey boulders.

"The Bushman's Rest" still lay some miles to the north, and it meant climbing up for about three miles and then descending. On every side we saw mulga scrub and spinnifex, and here and there a stunted gum. We had to pick our way pretty carefully now, as the ground was strewn with large rocks and the going for the buggy was not of the pleasantest, but it was the quickest route to take us to Moira, and that was enough for us. After what Flaxman told me during the early part of the day I felt almost light-hearted, so I told myself that if all was well I would ask

Moira to become my wife at the earliest possible moment. The very thought of it urged me on.

It took us a long time to reach the highest point that we had to get over; at last, however, we began to descend, and before long we dived once more into the scrub. All the time Snowball was guiding us; soon we came to a clearing, and here he informed us was the spot that O'Connor had chosen to attack Moira. Neither of us spoke, but Flaxman urged the horses on as if the place were accursed. Within another hour we were near enough to see the corrugated iron building that was our destination. It stood upon an eminence quite devoid of trees, or indeed any growth, but the very coarsest of grass. From its position it commanded the most wonderful view for miles and miles over an immense tract of country.

The position chosen was an excellent one; the shanty was to be seen for a very considerable distance by any travellers on the coach track that passed in front of the building, and as the place depended upon the custom of the wayfarer for what little trade it did, this was most important.

It was by no means an imposing hostelry, as apart from its blatant ugliness it stood sadly in need of repair. On the facia board was painted, evidently by an amateur hand, "The Bushman's Rest. Good accommodation for man and beast." This board was of the rottenest description, and in imminent danger of falling upon the head of the unwary customer beneath. Nearly all the windows were broken, and the doors and frames were fast decaying for want of paint, while what little paint-work there was had been burnt and blistered by the heat beyond recognition. In fact, the whole building was warped and twisted from the same cause, for the whole strength of the sun fell directly upon it, there being no shade whatsoever from morning till night.

A verandah was erected in the front of the place, which consisted of about half a dozen rough tree stems, supporting a sloping iron roof, and rough boards for flooring, many of which had decayed and fallen in, leaving a nasty hole to catch the foot of the intoxicated customer.

An old barrel turned on its side, at one end of the verandah, did duty as a kennel for a savage mongrel dog on a chain, who did not disguise his animosity to us. On the right hand side of the building a tin shed was erected, which went by the name of "The Deadhouse," where the gentle customer was deposited to sleep off the drunken frenzy that always succeeds a too liberal imbibing of the vile concoction that passes for whisky at these hells.

Even as we arrived terrific yells and cursings emanated from this shed, telling only too well the state of its occupant. A man, evidently a station hand, reclined in a drunken stupor upon a bench on the verandah, while another supported himself against one of the tree stems that did duty as a pillar. His face bore signs of a recent bout, for it was ashen grey, and the eyes were sunken and bloodshot to the last degree. Altogether it was a beastly sight, but yet one that we had grown accustomed to see at these places, and if it had not been that Moira was lying ill here, we should have thought little of it. As it was, I felt eager to go up and kick the drunken brutes away, and take the proprietor by the neck and give him the soundest hiding he had ever had in his life. My heart sank when I thought of what Moira might have to listen to in this abominable place. Many a time I have ridden by these grog shanties, and heard some poor devil howling and shrieking in delirium in the "deadhouse"; while the landlord calmly sits in the verandah and smokes his pipe, no doubt speculating as to how much he could rob the poor brute of from the cheque which he handed him when he arrived—perhaps the fruits of months of hard work at some neighbouring station.

These places are one of the curses of Australia, and a never-ceasing anxiety to the authorities, for they do an incalculable amount of harm; yet, notwithstanding the risks they run, these blackguards, by their nefarious doings, manage to secure huge profits and retire on a handsome competency.

When he heard us pull up before the entrance, the proprietor came out on the verandah, and regarded us with a curious expression on his surly countenance, the while he puffed clouds of foul smoke from the foulest of pipes.

I knew the fellow well. Many a time I had had cause to remonstrate forcibly with him, on account of his having given the black boys liquor, and on more than one occasion we had almost come to blows over the matter.

He was as bad a rascal as any in the district, and half the discontent and strikes among the station hands emanated from his fertile brain. He set up as a politician, but in fact he was merely an agitator, and a lazy and blackguard one at that.

However, on this occasion it behoved me to be very cautious in my dealings with the worthy, until I had ascertained what treatment he had meted out to Moira, for if he had behaved decently, then he should have sound compensation; but, on the other hand, if he had neglected her—well—I should break his neck.

In response to my "Good afternoon," he gave a surly grunt. I then dismounted and gave the horse into Snowball's charge, and stepped up on to the verandah.

"Snowball here tells me that you have been kind enough to take a lady in, who was injured in the Bush. That is so, is it not?"

"Yes, it is," he replied, while he blew his filthy smoke almost into my face, "and a tarnation nuisance she's been, I can tell you, shrieking and shouting, like a mad cow. Blest if I shan't lose my license if the police hear of it, for they'll be after thinkin' I'm allowing drunkeness on the premises."

At this moment a piercing yell came from the "deadhouse."

I looked at the rascal before me, but he didn't move a muscle.

"What's that then?" I asked meaningly.

"Oh, that's a dog I keeps there for protection."

I looked him fair in the eye, which meant that he was a liar as plain as a look could mean it. He couldn't face me after this; muttering something about fetching his missis, he went into the house.

I cooled my heels for a few minutes listening to the deep snoring of the purple—faced drunkard on the seat near me. Inside I could hear a muttered conversation taking place, evidently between the proprietor and his wife, and after a while she appeared, wiping her hands on the dirtiest of aprons.

She was a huge, raw-boned woman, with thin black hair combed tightly back over her skull, her eyes were jet black and protruded slightly, while one was ornamented with a blue and green bruise, and she had also lost one of her front teeth, both of which defects I put down to her lord and master. The sleeves of her bodice were tucked up, and her arms, though thin, were muscular as a man's. Altogether she looked an ugly customer to tackle, and I confess that I would much rather have discussed the subject with the husband than with the wife.

Yet, as it proved, there was a rough kindness about her that one would never have expected from her appearance. She told me how ill Moira had been, and that she had insisted on her being put to bed despite her husband's objection, whom she spoke of as a dirty dog before his face, at which he scowled menacingly, and I saw prospects of a big battle when we departed.

It appeared that Moira had been insensible for more than twenty hours from concussion of the brain, and that even now she was in a feeble state. I was taken in to see her, and was shocked at her appearance. She seemed pleased to see me, and softly pressed my hand when I told her that we had come to take her back to the Station.

It took about half an hour to get her ready for the journey back to Montalta, but it seemed hours before we were informed that all preparations were completed. We had her wrapped in blankets that we brought with us, and then Flaxman and I carried her as tenderly as we possibly could to the buggy, and laid her upon the mattress, and placed pillows under her head. When this was satisfactorily accomplished, and she was as comfortable as possible under the circumstances, I returned to the house. Without addressing the landlord, I enquired what sum would compensate them for the trouble they had been put to on Moira's account. Hereupon the man demanded twenty pounds, but the woman immediately shut him up, and ordered him from the room, and it was curious to note how meekly he obeyed her. When we were alone together I handed her ten pounds, and offered my thanks for the kindness she had shown to the injured girl.

"Don't thank me, sir," she said, as she took the money and placed it in a mysterious pocket. "I would not take anything at all, only things are so very bad one way and another. I was right down sorry, and my heart ached for the young lady, sir. I can tell you that it was just lucky Snowball came when he did, and she was brought here, for she'd have died in the scrub for a certainty. Although this ain't the place for the likes of her, yet it's a mighty sight better than lying in the Bush. She'll soon get well when she can have better food and rest."

"That we shall most certainly give her," I replied, making my way to the door, for I was very anxious to get off.

"Before you go, sir, I'd like to tell you something," she said, dropping her voice so that no one might overhear her words. "The young lady has been here before, it was some months ago. Bob, that's my dog of a husband, was powerful bad after a liquor bout, and gave me a murderous cruel blow over the head with an axe, which fair knocked me out. If he hadn't been in liquor he wouldn't have had the pluck to do it. Well, when I came to my senses I opens my eyes to find this young lady bathing my head and nursing me like an angel. Yes, in this black, dirty hole. A wicked place for a dog, let alone a human being. I've known better days myself, and I can tell you I was just struck dumb to see her pretty face a-bending over me."

"How did she come to be here?" I inquired eagerly.

"Why, she came with her husband, Flash Jim; he was killed in the Bush by lightning two or three days after he left here, and from all accounts it served him right, for I never in the whole of my natural came near such a dirty blackguard. Yet they tells me he was a gentleman born, and powerful rich once, and kept racehorses, down Melbourne way. But he weren't powerful rich here, for they'd neither of 'em got more than they stood up in."

"Was he cruel to her?"

"Cruel! Lord, man, he was a devil, especially in his cups. She told me, poor soul, that she expected he would kill her one day, and she his wife! Only a chit of a thing hardly out of the nursery."

"The brute! But can you tell me where they were going then?"

"Bob, that's my man, says they was agoing to meet a cove named Black, least—ways he was, and she had to go where he wanted, poor child. I don't know what the game was, but Black is a wrong 'un of the worst kind, and Flash Jim, well, he was as bad, so I've no doubt they'd got a nice piece of devilry on. In her illness she would call out, 'George, George, don't, don't let him come near me; he'll kill me, he'll kill me,' and I guessed that was about true, but who George is, Lord only knows."

I turned away to hide the emotion that these few words brought to me. Thank God, then, I was in her thoughts, if it was only in her delirium.

How I longed to be able to take her in my arms, and speak to her of my love, and tell her how much she was to me, that I could not live without her, and implore her to marry me. Somehow I had always expected that she would prove to be the wife of the man who was killed by lightning, but now that he was dead she was free, and I could make her life happy, affording some recompense for the misery and cruelty that she had so long been subjected to.

But I had to put these thoughts from me for the present. We must get her back to the Station, and make her well once more. Then—then—I could speak, but not before.

I held out my hand to the landlady, who took it in her hard one and shook it warmly, while I fancied I saw tears in her eyes.

"It's my hope, sir," she said, "that the young lady will soon be well again and safe from these rough brutes. God knows, she's seen enough of sorrow."

"Thank you, thank you," I replied, and went to the door. I quickly mounted my horse, and we set off, the landlady standing on the verandah watching us until we were out of sight.

We went back by the route which would prove easiest for the invalid, and it was quite dark before we arrived at the Station, to find the Doctor awaiting us with Braithwaite.

Moira was at once put to bed, and the Doctor attended her, while we waited with impatience for the result of his diagnosis.

In the meantime our meal was prepared, and, having changed our clothes, we sat down to it. We were just about to commence, when the Doctor entered the room and informed us that the patient had borne the journey satisfactorily and was going on well. More than that, he promised us that in less than a fortnight, with proper care and attention, she would be about again. The blows that O'Connor had given her had been serious, but, thanks to an excellent constitution, we might expect to see a complete recovery.

I was delighted to hear the report, and promised myself that I would see that everything possible was done to hasten this desirable result.

We were a pleasant little party to sit down to our substantial meal, and nothing was wanting to make it thoroughly enjoyable. Many and varied were the topics of conversation that we discussed, for both Braithwaite and the Doctor had been through queer experiences and each could tell a good yarn. So the time passed very pleasantly.

Having at last satisfied the pangs of hunger, we betook ourselves to the veranda, where we discussed all points in connection with the recent occurrences while smoking our pipes and sipping our grogs.

Braithwaite informed us that he had brought with him two homing pigeons that we were to keep handy, and on the first sight of Vandergrave, or any other of his crew, were to set free, and directly they returned to the police station the Superintendent would know that his services were required, and would set out forthwith.

This was a most satisfactory scheme, and I felt that I could now sleep easily in my bed, knowing that in the event of trouble arising I could communicate at once with the authorities.

As we sat in our easy chairs and smoked unceasingly, the full moon began to rise over the distant ranges and to flood the intervening landscape with its mellow light. How beautiful it made everything appear! There was something most exquisitely peaceful in looking at the long shadows cast by the trees and bushes across the well—cut lawns, and then away over the undulating plains, dotted here and there with gums standing out like grey ghosts, and, above all, the majestic moon hanging in the heavens, a ball of gold. All around us the flowers gave out their sweetest perfumes, and not a sound was heard.

As I watched there came over me a feeling of intense peace and thankfulness that all had turned out so well.

How little did I know that it was but the calm before the storm, how little did I reckon on the awful occurrences that were about to take place, deeds that would change the whole tenor of my existence, and leave an abiding sorrow never to be put out of my mind! However, at that time, I saw only peace and comfort before me.

I was aroused from my reverie by a prolonged snore from the Doctor, which warned me that the hour was late. Looking at my watch I found it was one o'clock, whereupon I roused myself and suggested bed.

As we were all agreeable, we turned in, and before long the entire place was wrapped in slumber.

CHAPTER XIV

THE BUSHMAN'S YARN.

During the next few days Moira made steady progress towards recovery, owing to the excellent nursing and unceasing attention lavished upon her by the overseer's wife. Nothing could equal the devotion shown to her gentle patient—with her night and day, waiting upon her hand and foot, attending to the slightest wish as soon as expressed. It was small wonder that the colour began to return once more to Moira's cheeks and the brightness to her eyes. In a week she was strong enough to be taken out on to the verandah, where she could enjoy the sunlight and obtain benefit from the fresh air, while we made every effort to interest and amuse her, for we knew it was most important that she should forget the episodes of the last few weeks.

I watched the signs of her returning health and strength with the sincerest pleasure. There was nothing in the world that I would not have done to promote her happiness and welfare. She had only to ask for anything, and I would have gone to the end of the earth to obtain it. For I was hopelessly and desperately in love with her. She was in my thoughts night and day, as I went about my work on the Station, or rode to the distant parts of the run; often, I confess, to my danger, for so engrossed did I become in my reveries that I narrowly escaped severe falls more than once owing to not watching where my horse was treading.

Everything connected with the Station prospered exceedingly. After the good rains that had fallen all looked so bright and hopeful, that we were led to fancy these halcyon days would last, and that we should never again be subjected to the unwelcome visits of O'Connor and his rascally friends. At this time we determined to send a large draft of store cattle down to the market, and I made arrangements with a former acquaintance, Dick Marsland, a drover, one of the best overlanders in Australia, to come up and take charge of them, and to deliver safely at the sale yards.

Pending his arrival, our time was fully occupied in riding to the different parts of the run, cutting out and bringing in the pick of the beasts, and the scene in the drafting yards was one of continual interest and excitement. The cattle proved quite up to our expectations; a finer lot no man could have wished to own. We were proud men as we sat on our horses, and noted the splendid bullocks that passed before us, for more than two-thirds had been bred upon the run, and it was pretty evident that we should obtain very substantial prices when they had been sold. Montalta had always earned a splendid reputation for the quality of its stock, and there was no doubt that the beasts now being sent would enhance this reputation still more.

When the lot had been brought in, we took one last look at them, and then turned our horses' heads to the Station, dog-tired, man and beast, as we had for days risen at sunrise and been in the saddle nearly all the time till sundown, and the task is far from an easy one.

We ordered a good supply of grog to be taken to the hands, for they one and all had worked like niggers and deserved their extra allowance. As for ourselves, we changed into comfortable togs, dined, and afterwards dropped asleep in our chairs on the verandah.

Next morning we began to head the cattle down to splendid grazing land by the creek, where they were to await the arrival of Marsland, who was expected at the camp in the evening.

I stood by the rails and counted the mob as they passed out, and found that they numbered over six hundred. There were some splendid young bullocks and heifers amongst them, too, in the prime of condition, and I felt delighted that I was able to hand over such a fine lot to Marsland's charge, who was as good a judge of cattle as I was myself, and perhaps better.

Dick turned up punctually as was his wont, and I sent a note down to the camp, inviting him to come up and have a smoke and chat over old times, in response to which he made his appearance during the evening, whereupon I placed him in a big chair in the verandah, gave him a cigar, and filled a noggin of grog for him, and then we began to talk of many things dear to us both.

Good old Dick! I can see him now, with his long grey beard, of which he was inordinately proud, passing it through his fingers continually, even when riding along, as if it were spun silk. He possessed a large hooked nose, and a pair of brown, twinkling eyes, over which bristled bushy grey eyebrows. His hair was white and thin, over a broad and high forehead. It was a very shrewd and honest face, and few men tried to take him in; if, however, they did, it was ten to one they came off second best. He was a thin, wiry man, standing about six foot two, and as strong as a lion, despite his fifty-eight years. I have never run across anyone equal to him on a horse. Ride! Why, he could ride anything on earth that ever went on four legs, Good, bad, or indifferent, mad or sane, they were all the same to him. And what a hand he was with cattle! It was a lesson to any man to watch him cutting out a half-mad bull in thick, scrubby country, or heading and turning beasts in rough, rocky districts. He generally had a gentle way with him, but when occasion required it, he could be a very devil. Altogether he was what he looked, a born Bushman, and anything he didn't know about the game wasn't worth learning.

He suggested that I should go with them for the first two days, as cattle generally travel badly at first out of their own country; so I arranged to take with me one of our own hands and Snowball, who was as good as an average two. So over our smokes and grogs we discussed the prospects of an early start on the morrow, and then passed to other topics.

After having talked of many old mutual friends, I asked him if in his travels about the country he had ever run across a man called Black.

"Black, Black?" he said. "Let me see, the only Black I can remember was a card that got into devilish hot water, in fact, was lagged once or twice for dirty work; you can't, of course, mean him. I think he was called 'The Captain,' but that was years after I first met him."

"Yes, that's the man," I answered, "the very one. What do you know of him? I'm particularly anxious to hear."

"Well," he said, "it's rather a curious story, that of my first meeting with the gentleman, for I reckon it as one of the episodes of my life. I'll tell you all about it, if you like."

I was quite agreeable, so I replenished his glass, and bade him set to work. The old chap took a puff at his pipe, and settled himself comfortably in his chair prepared to spin me a yarn. All Bushmen love to yarn, it's one of their greatest pleasures, and Dick Marsland was no exception. Many and many a time at the camp fire have I listened to the deep voice of the weather-beaten old drover, relating, in most dramatic tones, some thrilling story that he swore had happened to himself; while the burning logs threw up great lurid flames, weirdly illuminating the stems of the gum trees near at hand, intensifying the darkness beyond, and bringing into high relief the figures of the eager listeners who stood or reclined in the cheerful blaze. They were gruesome stories, too, some of them, yarns that made the hair stiffen on the scalp and cause a feeling of chill on the spine. Of course they mostly emanated from his fertile brain, but that did not matter to us; they were blood-curdling enough to make one jump at the sound of a breaking twig, kick the fire into a blaze, and throw on more wood to keep the darkness out.

So the old man shifted the tobacco in his pipe, made it draw to his satisfaction, took a pull at his grog, cleared his throat, and gave me the following story:

"It's nigh upon sixteen years ago now since I first set eyes on Black. I was asked by old Johnny Luscombe, who owned the place, to go to a station on the borders of the 'Never, Never Land;' about the worst part of Australia, I reckon. If I remember right it was called Baroomba. What for, Heaven only knows; I should have called it Hell, if I'd been asked to name it, on account of the dry heat of the hole. I remember the old man told me he had placed a manager in, and wanted me to go and see exactly how the land lay on his behalf, for he was in no way satisfied with the existing methods of the management. I was to report to him how I found things in general, and to give my opinion of the manager and of his ways. I didn't much like the job, but I wanted it badly at the time, and needs must when the devil drives, so I accepted Mr. Luscombe's offer; he had always been a good friend to me one way and another, and I felt that this job might lead to others, perhaps good ones, so I arranged to start forthwith. He told me that the manager's name was Black, and black he proved, as you will see when I have finished my yarn.

"After receiving a letter of introduction, I set off. I can recollect as if it were only yesterday my feelings when I began to travel over some of the most wretched country that it has ever been my lot to see. Arid plains of burnt up grass, poor even in the wet seasons, which, by the way, they don't get much of, but during the hot times scorched to a cinder, the earth really hot to walk on. Flat as your hand for miles and miles, then sand and spinnifex, spinnifex and sand, in deadly monotony, until you feel that you would give anything for a blade of green grass to look at. Hardly a tree to be seen, and what there is, stunted and almost dead by the heat, and deuced little animal life, but rock-wallaby and crows.

"By the time that I arrived within view of the iron shanties forming the Station I had fairly got the hump. Old Luscombe must have been a dashed fool to have bought the place at all; but, there, it wasn't my business to discuss the wisdom of my employer's investments, but I couldn't help wondering what induced him to touch such a dog's hole as this.

"I took a spell of rest in the shade of a rock, near by a stagnant water-hole, where I could get a view of the wretched place, for I didn't want to arrive there until sundown. When that time came I mounted and rode to the principal building, which was little more than a fair-sized wool-shed, and proved to be the manager's house. As I came near it, all the dogs upon the place began to bark, and there were plenty of them too, poor half-starved mongrels at best.

"As I sat on my horse and looked around in the fast declining light at the miserable hovels, expecting to see someone about, I got the hump worse than ever, and this desolation absolutely finished me off. Where on earth had I got to, I wondered; not a soul about, nothing alive but dogs. I felt that for two pins I could turn tail and make off again without waiting to interview my Black friend. Then I remembered that I was hard up and wanted the job, so I dismounted, tied up my horse, and went and rapped at the door with my whip handle. By and by a black boy came, and I inquired whether everyone was dead or asleep; if not, would he very kindly fetch the boss. So off he started to call Black, leaving me to cool my heels, metaphorically, on the doorstep in the stifling heat.

"I waited a goodish time until I heard someone coming through the house.

"It turned out to be Black, who was a good-looking chap enough, but with a nasty, cruel look in his eye, that I could not help remarking at once. He was evidently used to something better than this life, as I could easily see from his hands, which were clean and smooth, not those of a working-man, and there was little doubt that he was a gentleman born.

"He wanted to know my business, and I produced my letter of introduction from Luscombe, asking him to put me up for a day or two, as I was passing through the district. As he opened and read the letter I watched him very narrowly, and I could easily see that he was not best pleased with my call, but, of course, he expressed his pleasure at seeing me, the while he inwardly wished me at the devil. However, we shook hands, while he said he hoped that I would stay as long as I liked, and he would endeavour to make me comfortable, so far as the limited capabilities of the place would admit.

"When I informed him that my stay would probably be very brief, as I was making my way South, he brightened up pretty considerably, and suggested that I should turn my horse into what he was pleased to call the horse paddock. I agreed, and he showed me the place. We gave the beast some bush hay and a drink, then returned to the house, where he offered me a refresher, which I was glad enough to accept, for the heat had fairly parched me up, just as it did the grass.

"The living room into which he brought me was a bare, wretched place, just like the rest of the dog-kennel of a house, and the furniture, if you could call it so, consisted of four wooden chairs, a deal table, a broken looking-glass on the wall, and one or two coloured prints torn out of illustrated papers and nailed on to the walls; altogether it was a room calculated to make one a fit candidate for a mad house.

"The view, too, from the verandah was equally dreary, and one saw nothing but the arid, treeless waste of burnt-up plain, with the ranges showing purple on the horizon.

"Having brought my things with me, I asked him to let me have a clean-up, and he took me into a room where I was to sleep, which was furnished even more plainly than the other—a truckle bed with two blankets not over clean, a piece of broken looking-glass on the wall, a wooden box doing duty as a washstand, a tin basin, and a bucket of water completed the arrangements. However, I could rough it with anyone, so I didn't worry on that account. I had a wash aud felt more comfortable. When I arrived in the sitting-room, I found that he had prepared a meal of corned beef and bread, with tea, so we sat down and discussed it, and as I was pretty peckish I did justice to it. After the meal we went on the verandah and smoked our pipes, and he told me all about the Station, how the cattle died off, the general desolation and decay of the place, and how he had come to it full of hope, but soon lost even that, and now didn't care a d—what happened to him, whether he lived or died, it was all the same to him, for the desolate hole had given him the terrors. He told me that the former manager went mad, murdered his wife, and hanged himself in one of the rooms, and that his ghost wandered about the place and shrieked at night, setting all the dogs howling and moaning.

"As you know, I am not the sort of man that's easily frightened, and I took all this yarn as the outcome of a disordered brain, for I felt that the horrid monotony of the place had got upon his nerves.

"I told him that I was pretty tired and should like to turn in, and I therefore wished him good-night and went to my room.

"It took me a very short time to get between the blankets, and soon I was asleep, for I was dead beat after my ride.

"How long I had been in the land of dreams I cannot say, but suddenly I was awakened by finding myself sitting bolt upright in my bed, with that curiously un-canny sensation of tickling at the roots of the hair that is caused by physical terror. As I did so, a long piercing shriek rang out, and echoed away through the hot night air, followed immediately afterwards by howls and moans from all the dogs on the place; then died into silence with a wail of the most heartrending description. Despite the fact that I was streaming with perspiration from sheer funk, I got off the bed and felt my way to the window; of course, having no light to guide me, I found it difficult, but I was determined to try and account for these awe-inspiring screams.

"Just as I reached the window and was about to step out, there came another low wail, ending in a piercing shriek that turned my blood to water, and then more howls and moans from the dogs.

"This was too awful, I could bear it no longer; so, notwithstanding my bare feet, I sprang out into the verandah, bent on ascertaining the cause, but I reckoned without my host, for all I did was to tread upon a rotten board, and fall, catching my head on a projecting piece of wood and drop senseless to the ground, where I lay until dawn, when I came to, with a splitting headache and an immense lump on my unfortunate cranium as big and round as a cricket ball for a souvenir.

"I went back to bed again, and after a while fell into a troubled sleep. The sun was well up before I was roused by my host, who informed me that breakfast was ready, and having dressed I was soon sitting down to it.

"After he had inquired how I slept, I informed him that my rest had been dis-turbed by the terrible shrieks. He laughed, and replied, 'So you have heard them, too? By Jove! when I first came here they nearly upset my reason, but I've become used to them now.'

"'What's the cause of it?' I inquired anxiously. 'They sound as if a woman was being murdered.'

"'I thought I told you the place is haunted; the former manager is said to have strangled his wife and buried her beneath the floor of the place, and fancying afterwards that she was haunting him, he hanged himself in the room you sleep in, and it is said that she appears there to watch his body swinging from a hook in the ceiling. I've never seen either of them, and I don't suppose an idle tale will affect you in any way; we hear the shrieks plain enough, but that is all.'

"I sat and wondered at the gruesome story. There was absolutely no doubt whatever about the shrieks; but as to the appearances, they had yet to be realised."

"During the day he took me over the run to show me all the desolation, and I could plainly see it was impossible that anything could make the place pay; the dearth of water and herbage was enough to break a man's heart. What cattle and sheep existed on the place were of the poorest and most wretched description. Old Luscombe had far better shut the place and let it rot, I felt, and I intended to tell him so. When we returned to the Station from our ride, we had one or two drinks together, and I noticed that he helped himself from the bottle rather freely. Getting tired of this amusement, I asked to be allowed to look at the buildings, and he, I thought a little ungraciously, consented."

On looking about, I inquired what an isolated shed was for, and was informed that he kept it locked, as it contained oil and tar, and he was afraid of fire. This answer struck me as rather a lame one, seeing that there was deuced little care taken in other respects for the safety of the place; however, it did not appeal to me particularly at the time.

"As we were returning to the house, a dilapidated buggy appeared, drawn by a pair of the poorest old screws I ever set my eyes on, and driven by an innocent—looking slim lad of about twenty.

"As we came up to him I noticed that he was greatly surprised to see me walking with Black, and I was morally certain that Black was anxious to get him away, so that I should not get a chance of speaking to him.

"'Will you excuse me a few minutes, Mr. Marsland, I want to give my foreman a few instructions.'

"'Most certainly,' I answered. 'Pray don't let me interfere with your arrangements.'

"With that I strolled on to the verandah, leaving him speaking in low tones to the lad in the buggy.

"The youth glanced towards me once or twice, I thought, meaningly. However, Black got into the buggy, and they drove off together.

"About ten minutes afterwards, as I was sitting quietly smoking, I suddenly heard a shouting, and saw the youth running towards the house chasing a dog that was bolting for dear life. Stooping down, he picked up a stone and threw it, but it missed the cur and came towards me and rolled to within ten yards of the verandah. I noticed that it was a peculiarly white stone and, looking towards the youth, I saw him make a sign as if he were picking up another missile. I caught on at once, and nodded my head, whereupon he returned to the place that he had come from.

"After a while I walked down the verandah steps, and strolled about for a bit, kicking the stone nearer to the house, in case Black might be watching me. Pretending to be examining the woodwork, I picked up the article, and found it was a piece of paper wrapped around a stone. Then, making my way to the bedroom, I smoothed it out and read the following message: 'If you are the friend you seem to be, go to the locked shed to-night; but please be careful of Mr. Black. I run the greatest risk in sending you this message. Destroy this. He's a devil.'

"I struck a match and set alight to the paper, and then returned to the verandah and finished my pipe, trying to think out a scheme to obtain possession of the key of the shed, for I was fully determined to get at the bottom of this mystery.

"I had noticed before that Mr. Black possessed a great liking for whisky, and it struck me that I might induce the gentleman to take more than his usual allowance, and then, getting him off his guard, secure the key, and the rest would be comparatively plain sailing.

"When he returned to the house he was as affable as possible, and set before me the best spread that he could manage to get together. It was very evident that he was acting with a motive, and it behoved me therefore to be on my guard. When the meal was over, we took our chairs and went out on the verandah to smoke and chat, and it was not long before he suggested that it was a long time between drinks. Thereupon he produced the bottle, and pressed me to take some.

"So this was his little game. It almost made me laugh when I thought that we were both on the same lay, and it was evident that we were going to have a big fight. The whisky was tolerably good, or I should never have succeeded in doing what I did. I drank even with him for some time, until I could see that the spirit was beginning to tell upon him, for he was somewhat handicapped, in that he had certainly indulged rather freely before the meal.

"When I saw that it was possible to do so without his noticing the fact, I poured the whisky he gave me upon the ground and filled the tumbler with water, while I also managed to give him an addition of spirit to his glass. I afterwards proposed that we should go back into the sitting-room, which he agreed upon. So inside we went, and lighted two candles and stuck them in the necks of bottles. I removed my coat as it was hot, and suggested he should do the same, for I knew he carried his keys in the pocket of his coat. He fell in with this suggestion also, and threw the garment on to the floor.

"Then we continued our beastly occupation, and by the time he had partaken of half a dozen more drinks, deftly strengthened by myself, he had sunk into a drunken sleep over the table. Now, here was my opportunity. I rose, picked up his coat, and felt in the pocket, and there sure enough was a key, which appeared as if it would fit a padlock.

"I closed the window, filled a very strong drink for him, in case he desired one when he woke up, put one of the candles in my pocket, and left the room, locking the door after me and leaving him to sleep off the bout.

"It took me but a very short while to reach the isolated shed, and in a twinkling I had the key in the padlock, and was about to open the door, when it suddenly struck me that I had no sort of idea what the shed contained. As I did so I could plainly hear something moving inside. I tell you it wasn't the pleasantest thing in the darkness trying to get into that shed, with probably a madman ready to spring on to you. However, it was my duty to ascertain what it contained, and I was going right through with it. When I had got the door open, I struck a match, lit the candle, and stepped in, closing the door after me.

"To my astonishment I saw before me, lying on a heap of straw, a woman, pale and emaciated to a fearful degree, a thing of skin and bone only, for it was evident that she was being literally starved to death. It made my blood boil when I saw her and noted her poor, thin, sunken cheeks, and great black eyes gazing at me with the most unnatural brilliancy; her jet black hair, which was uncombed, fell around her face, which, in the candle light, gave her the most extraordinary appearance. Just like a skull with burning, glowing eyes.

"Altogether her appearance was such as would have caused alarm in the heart of the bravest man, and certainly touched the hardest of hearts.

"When she saw me enter, she tried to rise, but she was far too weak to do so. I therefore crossed over and knelt by the side of the poor creature, who shrank away from me in abject fear as if I were about to strike her.

"'Don't be afraid of me,' I said; 'I am your friend, and desire to help you.'

"'Who are you?' she almost whispered. 'I don't know you. Oh, if only I could trust you, but you may be deceiving me.'

"'I swear to you that I am not. My name is Marsland. I am a friend of Mr. Luscombe's. I don't exactly know what is going on here, but I had my suspicions, and have now confirmed them. I can easily see that Black is a greater scoundrel than I at first thought him. Now I'm going to help you to escape from him.'

"'No, no, there can be no escape, save by death, and that, please God, is near at hand now. The brutal cruelty of that man is beyond everything; my life has been one long hell of terror ever since I was fool enough to listen to his temptations. Oh, my God, my God, let me die, let me die!'

"Here the poor soul burst into a torrent of tears. I tried to comfort her by asking her if there was anything I could do for her. In a few minutes she ceased her tears, and implored me to help her in one thing, so that she might die in peace.

"'Black has threatened to kill me because I refused to make a will in his favour. I was fool enough to run away with him from England, leaving a good husband, and shortly after I arrived in Australia a child was born, a girl, the daughter of my husband.'

"'Black hated it, and refused to allow me to have it with me, and I was forced to leave her with some people in Adelaide, while he compelled me to come up with him to this horrible place, but not before I had managed, secretly through a firm of lawyers, to make my will in favour of my child, for I have money of my own.

"'When we were in Adelaide he had insured my life heavily, in his favour, and soon after we came up here I found out that he had discovered I had made a will, and ever since that I have received nothing but the most frightful cruelty from him, for he declares that he will kill me by inches if I don't give him the will. But I shall never do that, for I have hidden it, and if you want to do me the service that you say you do, I will bless you for ever if you will go and take it to Adelaide, to the lawyers who drew it, so that my child may get the benefit. Will you do this for me?'

"'Yes, I will,' I answered. 'You may rest assured of it. To-morrow morning I will start, and I shall go straight there, and afterwards return with friends to take you away and bring you and your child together, so you must keep your heart up and all will be well. In a week I shall be back again, and your troubles will be over. Now tell me the solicitors' names and where the will is hidden.'

"'You will find their names on the will, and also a letter to be sent to my husband in England, giving him the address of the people who took the child. The will I placed in a tin box, and put into a hollow gum tree close to the water-hole. The tree was struck by lightning, and I threw sand and stones over it so that none should find it. God bless you always for your goodness. I shall pray that you may reach Adelaide in safety.'

"I softly pressed her hand and told her to be of good cheer, and that I was now going to fetch her some food.

"I then returned to the house, and found Black still sleeping. I brought away some food and whisky, which I placed in hiding so that she might easily get it, and, after bidding her good-bye, returned to the house and put the key into Black's pocket again, and then tried to rouse him. After a long time I succeeded, eventually getting him to bed.

"Next morning I was out before sunrise and walked to the tree, where I found the tin box with certain papers wrapped therein. These I put into my pocket at once and threw the box away.

"I then returned to the Station and found Black getting up. He was a wreck, and I pretended to be.

"However, I ate a good breakfast, and told him I proposed getting away, and thanked him for his hospitality. Having obtained my horse, I wished him good-bye, and set out with a lighter heart than I came.

"Well, to cut a long story short, I went straight to Luscombe and told him everything, and afterwards we both journeyed to Adelaide, saw the lawyers, and deposited the will with them. Having finished this business, we visited the police, and with them went to the Station; but, unfortunately, Black saw us coming and got away, although he was chased for many miles into the scrub.

"We brought the poor lady back with us to Luscombe's Station, but unfortunately she died directly she got there. However, we took good care that Mr. Black didn't get the benefit of the insurance money.

"Now, that's the story concerning Black and my first meeting with him. But, I say, what has he to do with you?"

"Well, that's a long yarn, and I'll keep it for to-morrow night, Why! I say, it's eleven o'clock. Here, have another drink, and I'll see you to the camp. You know we rise at dawn."

With that I poured him out a nightcap, and we went together to the camp, when I wished him good-night and returned to bed.

CHAPTER XV

THE HOME-COMING!

I was up at daybreak next morning, and found my horse ready for me, with my swag strapped before the saddle and Snowball at his head. I drank a cup of tea, said good-bye to Flaxman, who had risen to see me start, mounted, and passed out at the slip-panels, where I was joined by the hand that was to accompany me, and followed by Snowball bringing up the rear on a rawboned, half-wild horse, which very few men would have cared to mount.

Soon we were at the camp, to find all busy, and the cook-man preparing the breakfast. It was a very picturesque scene, and one that is not easily forgotten. I saw before me the herd of splendid cattle, quietly grazing on the excellent herbage that grew abundantly by the creeks, watched over by statuesque figures of man and horse only dimly seen through the morning mists, each man with a stock whip balanced on his hip ready for any emergency; while nearer, a group at the fireside anxiously awaited the call to breakfast. Dick Marsland's tall figure I perceived standing apart from the others, superintending the general proceedings. All around stretched a green plain, dotted here and there with blue gums, just showing ghost-like through the mist.

I shouted a cheery good-morning to Dick as I came near, and he turned on hearing my call and walked forward with outstretched hand to bid me welcome. As I looked down at him I thought that I had never seen so striking a figure as he presented, with his red Crimea shirt and cord breeches and stout leather gaiters, and his broad—brimmed cabbage-tree hat pushed back on his head, while he eternally toyed with his beard, a typical Bushman from top to toe, wiry, alert, and keen, ready to face any difficulty, and possessed of a decisive action that told well the nature of his calling.

"Morning to you, Mr. Tregaskis," he cried, as we shook hands warmly. "You're one of the right sort. Get early to work is my motto. One can move cattle fifty times better before the sun is high."

"You're right there, Dick," I replied, as I dismounted and handed over my horse to Snowball. "I see you are well on with the breakfast."

"Yes, you're just in time. We'll get ahead with it now, and then we can think about making a move with the cattle, after we have sent on the ration cart. Now then, Billy, look alive, man; we shall be asking for dinner before you have given us our breakfast."

"All right, it's ready now," replied the cook-man as he began to help the savoury—smelling concoction. In a very short space we were all busy sampling the substantial and excellently cooked meal that was set before us. Having finished, blankets were rolled, "billy" cans and other utensils stowed away on the ration cart, the cook given his final instructions and sent off, so that a meal might be prepared when we arrived with the cattle at the next camp, the situation of which he was to choose for its general convenience and proximity to water.

This very necessary portion of the proceedings having been accomplished to Dick's satisfaction, everything was now ready for the start of the beasts. When we were mounted, Dick gave his orders as to the positions that we were to take up.

I was given the extreme right with my own man, while Dick took the left with one of his men, and two others acted as whippers-in, and Snowball, with another quick hand, was told off to act as galloper after stragglers and bolters.

Everything being finally fixed up, we tightened girths, and Marsland, riding into the mob, cut out a splendid bull as leader and headed him in the direction we wanted to travel; then the whole herd was put on the move, following the bull, who strode with his splendid head thrown well in the air, bellowing loudly as if to declare his exalted position.

We had all our work cut out to keep the lot going as we wanted them, and many a hard gallop was necessary to bring in breakers and stragglers, while the sound of the cracking of twenty-foot stock whips was continually in the air, and I can tell you that there was some pretty good execution done with them, too, for there wasn't a man amongst us that could not flick a blow-fly off a beast's back with the cracker, going pretty fast as well.

At noon we halted by a water-hole to give the animals a rest and drink, and take one ourselves, for the first few hours after starting are tiring with a strange mob of cattle.

Very little of interest occurred after we left the water-hole, but we eventually picked up the cook's camp and found a meal; then made ourselves comfortable for the night, but of course doing turn and turn about as guard over the cattle. After my two hours were done I was not sorry to roll myself in my blankets and fall asleep.

Next day I started off with them until the first rest, when it seemed that we were not necessary any longer, as the beasts had settled down to travel. I therefore said good-bye to Dick, and received his promise to let me hear of his safe arrival with the mob. I was just about to mount my horse when he came near and said:—

"By the way, Mr. Tregaskis, I don't think I told you the night before last the name of the poor, wretched lady your friend Black desired to make capital out of. I couldn't recall it at the time I was spinning the yarn, but it came back to me in a flash to-day. The name on the will was Mary Flaxman, and the letter she wrote was to her husband, Robert Flaxman; the solicitors were to deliver it. Curious, wasn't it?"

I staggered back from my horse's side as if I'd received a blow. Marsland saw my intense surprise, for he continued—

"The coincidence is too strange for there to be no connection. Your partner's name is Robert, isn't it?"

"Yes, and, by Jove, that in a manner is a clue to our now being troubled by Black. Stay, do you ever remember hearing the name of Mrs. Flaxman's daughter?"

"Yes, I remember it well, because I considered it a very sweet name and suited to the pretty child. 'Moira' it was."

"'Moira?' Ah! how very strange. Did you ever hear what happened to her afterwards?"

"Yes, I believe—mind you, it's only hear-say, I'm not certain of it—that she married a chap with money named Jim Pendragon. They lived in Melbourne for about a year, then moved away."

"What sort of a man was he?"

"Well, they used to call him Flash Jay Pen; I always had my suspicions that he was a cardsharper and a cheat, but p'raps I'd better not say so, however; that's what I have been told."

"Thanks for the information, old chap. You don't know the interesting things that you have told me; when I see you again I will give you a yarn that will surprise you. Good-bye."

"Good-bye," he shouted as he watched me ride off to join Snowball and the hand. Well, well, what a wonderful world it is, I thought to myself; just fancy that a few words spoken by this queer old drover should throw the true light upon this mystery!

Now I could appreciate Flaxman's motive in not showing me Moira's letter after our most unfortunate quarrel, and also his remarks during our ride back to the Station from the township, when he declared that with Moira's coming to Montalta his peace of mind had gone for ever; doubtless he saw a likeness in her to her mother, for, now I came to think of it, I could remember him gazing at her often, very earnestly, which fact I, in my unreasoning jealousy, had set down to his love for her. Ah! fool that I was, it was all made plain to me now, and I cursed myself again and again for my blind folly and contemptible selfishness; I swore that in word and deed, for the future, I would try to make it up to him.

But how true is the saying that "Man proposes, and Heaven disposes." Even now as I sit here writing this story I feel that had I always acted in a better spirit to my friend the course of events might have been changed, and much of the pain that my conduct caused us both would have been saved, and I, on my side, would have had less to reproach myself with.

It was a long ride back to the Station, and darkness had begun to fall when we saw its roofs. In my mind's eye I pictured Moira on the verandah waiting and wondering if I should return that night, I thought of the pleasant dinner table with its cheerful surroundings and merry conversation, how she would ask me to tell her all that had occurred, from the moment that we started until I reached home, for she took the very greatest interest in all that concerned the Station and desired to acquaint herself with even the slightest details of its management. Again, I thought of the delightful evening in the drawing-room afterwards, how she would sit down at the piano and play my favourite "Nocturne," of Chopin, the "Eleven o'clock Nocturne," that would send me to my bed more in love with her than ever. These were the thoughts that passed through my mind as we trotted along on our tired horses in the gathering darkness.

As the hand lived at the distant home-stead, I bade him good-night, after requesting him to come to the Station next morning for orders, whereupon he turned his horse in the direction of his home, and Snowball and I made for the paddock together.

At the slip-panels I gave him my tired beast, with instructions that he was to give him an extra feed and then come to the house for his "grub."

With that I made my way across the lawn and round towards the verandah, and I remember wondering why it was that I could not see the lights from any of the rooms shining over the grass, for by now it was quite dark.

Perhaps they had closed the curtains, as it was slightly cold; or, maybe, they were sitting waiting for me on the verandah. I coo-eed, but there came no answering cry, nothing but the weird echo of my own, that rang round the place like a Banshee's shriek.

Then there stole over me a sensation of intense fear that chilled me to the marrow. Good God! what if Black and his gang had been there while I was away, and… No, no, I would not allow myself to think of anything so awful. I felt in my hip—pocket for the revolver that I always carried now in case of emergency. Finding that it was properly loaded, I slowly mounted the verandah steps, but I could not see anything at all in the gloom. I felt in my pocket for my match-box, but only to discover that I had used every one; however, I knew where I could put my hand on some.

I stood quite still, opposite the spot where I was certain the dining-room door should be, and listened intently for any sound that would tell of the existence of my people, but none came, only the thud, thud of my beating heart, which seemed to echo in my very brain.

No one but those who have been through experiences of this terrible nature can realise the sense of abject terror that laid hold of me. Here I was, returning to my home in expectation of receiving the warmest of welcomes, but only to find darkness, silence, and perhaps death…no, I could not, I would not believe it. There must be some accountable reason for the absence of my friends. Perhaps they had gone for a ride and lamed one of their horses, or perhaps they had lost their way and would turn up shortly. Yes, a thousand trivial things might have happened; but, stay, where were the servants, surely they were about somewhere.

Anyway, I must pull myself together and not act like a poor-spirited and frightened child. I should find myself laughing at my fears very soon, when my people appeared.

Trying to bolster up my courage with these hopes, which I almost knew to be false, I took a few steps into the room. Suddenly my foot struck something heavy, and I pitched headlong over it, and fell prone; as I tried to raise myself my hand came in contact with the thing, and to my intense horror I felt the face of a dead man, cold and set. I remember giving vent to the most terrific yell, that went echoing away into the pall of darkness outside, intensified by the hollow roof of the verandah, until it died away somewhere in the blackness of the garden, with a wail like a demented soul.

Even now I go through it all again in my sleep, and wake in terror, and I suppose it will haunt me as long as I live.

In less time than it takes to tell, I was out of that room, across the verandah, and down into the garden, shaking like an aspen. Many minutes passed before I could pull myself together sufficiently to make up my mind once again to go near that form, lying so cold and still up there in the house. But it was evident a most terrible tragedy had been enacted only a few hours since, and, horrible as it was I felt compelled to find out without further delay who the dead man was, for a great dread was in my heart and I feared to learn to what further extent the crime had been perpetrated. I made my way in the darkness towards the horse-paddock, where I knew that I should find Snowball and a lantern. Any human being, even a black boy, would prove an agreeable companion under existing circumstances.

As I went along in the dark, stumbling like a drunken man over the flower beds and borders, I saw Snowball coming towards me with his light; I called out to him in a hollow voice, which, I fear, he could hardly recognise as mine; I saw him stop dead. My appearance, I suppose, must have scared him a bit, for he hesitated as if he meant bolting. But when I addressed him again he was satisfied that I was not a spook, although I must have looked like one, for I expect I was as pale as death.

"Snowball," I said, "while we've been away something awful has happened; there is a dead man here. Give me the lantern!"

He handed me the light, and together we began to walk towards the house. For a minute or two neither of us spoke a word, we were too much engrossed: he, in apparently studying the lamplit ground, and I, in trying to grasp the mystery of the tragic events that were now passing.

Evidently something of a very extraordinary nature must have struck Snowball's ever alert brain, for he suddenly stopped dead and pointed to the ground, at the same time calling my attention to certain marks on the turf in his peculiar language.

"See here, boss, all along hoofs brown hoss, him long hoss, ridden by Connor. Snowball 'member, some well."

Sure enough there were the hoof marks of a big horse, such as the boy tried to describe. We carefully followed them along and found that they became mixed up with others as they neared the place. It was evident that the riders approached the house from different points, doubtless with the intention of rushing it.

Leaving these evidences to be examined more closely by daylight, we went up the verandah steps and proceeded into the house. But I confess it took a great deal to make me muster up sufficient pluck to face the ordeal of entering that dark and silent room where lay the figure of the dead man. But at last, pulling myself together, I crept into the dining-room and made straight towards the figure that I saw lying prone upon the floor.

Bringing the lantern close up to the face so that I might see if I could recognise the features, to my horror I at once saw that it was the face of Flaxman. He lay there with his eyes wide open, staring up at the ceiling. Shot through the chest, he had fallen backwards with his right arm flung straight out and the fingers still grasping a heavy revolver. I placed my trembling hand upon his heart, in the hope that I should still find it beating; but, alas! no, the poor fellow was stone dead. Oh! the bitterness of that moment! Never as long as I live in this world shall I be able to put it out of my mind. I almost went mad. I flung myself upon the body and took the cold hand in mine and rubbed it, trying to bring back warmth and life, while in piteous words I implored him to speak to me. But no—only silence. Dead! My

God! I could not realise it—gone from me for ever. What should I do? It was too awful, too bitterly cruel, to think that this kindly, loving companion should meet his end in this manner without being able to say one word of farewell to anyone, alone, and unhelped.

No words of mine can adequately convey the anguish of mind that I suffered then. He was the very best friend that I ever had, and to lose him in this terrible way was a blow from which I should never recover. What would I not have given to have been able to recall him, if only to hear him speak one word to me again, just to watch the kindly smile that we all loved so well, and to feel the true warm grip of his hand in the old familiar friendship. But no, death, cruel, cold death had him in his clutches, and we had spoken our last in this life, given the last handshake, and looked for the last time into one another's eyes. God rest his soul, and forgive me for my past offences to him. To my dying day I shall recall the words he spoke when we were returning from the township, that he would never live to see the wonderful view again. After all he was right. There was some definite warning in his mind that the end was drawing near, and now his words had become accomplished facts.

How the tragedy happened we had yet to discover. I was too much affected to concentrate my attention on discovery for a long while; but at last, roused by Snowball, I pulled the tablecloth off the table and covered the body with it; then I went back into the hall and out on to the verandah, and, turning to the right, I made towards the place where I knew the pigeon basket stood, for I wished to see if the birds had been released. Yes, the basket was empty and the birds gone; that was a certain amount of relief to my mind, for now I might expect the police at any moment, although I had no knowledge of when they had received the warning.

Snowball followed wherever I went like a shadow, for he was determined not to lose me for one minute. As we turned away to walk back to the hall, his quick eye saw something, for he gripped my arm and whispered, "Look alonger," at the same time pointing to an object that lay huddled up in a heap at the French windows leading into the dining-room; it was so indistinct and undefined that from where we stood we could make nothing of it. Without a moment's hesitation I strode towards it, and in the light of the lantern I discovered that it was the figure of Moira, who was quite insensible; her heart was faintly beating, and I cried to Snowball to help me to carry her at once to her room. We placed her on the bed, and I went off to fetch some brandy. I then determined to send off to the homestead for the overseer and his wife, and with that end in view I tackled Snowball.

"Snowball," I cried, "I'll give you five pounds if you'll start off at once and fetch the overseer and his wife here to me, and the other hands too. Miss Moira is very ill, and I know that you want her to get well again. Now, will you do it for me?"

Poor Snowball, nothing loth, acquiesced immediately. I daresay he was only too pleased to get away from the death-stricken place.

I went with him to the verandah steps, and saw him set off into the darkness. I was about to return to the house, when I heard a voice in the distance cry out, "Now then, hands up, whoever you are."

Whereupon I feared that Snowball had fallen into an ambush. I waited at the verandah railings with my revolver ready, peering into the darkness to see if I could make out the approach of any figure, for I was in just the mood to kill any man who showed fight. My heart was full of the desire for vengeance against the miscreant who perpetrated the cruel murder of my friend, and it would have gone hard indeed with Black if I had happened upon him then. Suddenly I heard the tramping of feet nearing the house, and a voice called out, that I immediately recognised as Braithwaite's—

"Tregaskis, are you there, old chap? Show a light. What's up?"

I can tell you I was never more relieved in my life than when I heard him speak. What a comfort it was to think that he had turned up so soon. I called out in response to say that I was on the verandah, and I snatched up the lantern, and very soon four figures came into the light, Braithwaite and two troopers, one on each side of Snowball, who appeared in terror of his life.

"We've taken a black boy here, who declares that you sent him with a message to the homestead, that you are in sad trouble, and that all the hands are to come. Is that so?"

"Yes, indeed, it's Snowball, so you can let him get off at once. It's a case of life and death to Miss Pendragon now."

"What on earth do you mean? What's happened? Nothing serious, I hope?"

"Come up here and see. We have only just returned from starting a mob of cattle and arrived at nightfall to find the place in darkness and, as I thought, deserted, but on making a search I have been horrified to find Flaxman dead on the dining-room floor and Miss Pendragon in a state of collapse."

"Good God, you don't mean it! Here, you men, let that boy go. Snowball, you set off to the homestead at once with your message. Hyde, tell the Doctor and inspector to come up here immediately."

Snowball, released, made off into the darkness, while the trooper addressed as Hyde went on his errand, and Braithwaite came with me into the house, leaving the other trooper on the verandah. I led the way into the dining-room and showed him the dead man lying there, and the good chap was as much affected as I had been.

"This is most awful," he said. "A shocking business. Poor old Flaxman! I never thought that he would come to such an end. I wonder how it all happened? Perhaps you had better get some more lights, as we shall have to examine carefully everything in the room. I suppose you have not moved anything?"

"No, my dear man; I can tell you I received far too great a shock to think of anything. I shall never get the memory of this night out of my mind."

"I fear not," he replied, gazing down at the body. "A tragedy of this kind is quite enough to haunt a man for the rest of his life. And Flaxman, too, was one of the best in the world. It's too terrible to think about. Ah! Doctor, here you are. There has been a most awful time of it going on here. Look, this is poor old Flaxman."

"Good heavens! you don't say so," answered the Doctor, who had just come into the room. "Is he dead? Let me see."

With that he bent over the body and carefully examined it.

"Yes, I fear so," he said. "Shot through the heart. I expect I am right in saying that he has been dead quite three hours, now. But the only consolation that we have is that death must have been almost instantaneous. Poor old Flaxman. What an end. How did it occur?"

"We don't know yet," I replied. "I have been away starting a mob of store cattle and returned to the Station with Snowball just as darkness set in. I left my horse at the paddock and came up here alone, and was very much surprised to find the place in darkness, and on entering this room I fell over the body of my dear friend. I can tell you it has been such a shock to me as I shall never get over. However, fearing worse troubles, I nerved myself to search about, and found Miss Pendragon lying insensible outside the French windows of the dining-room, and I want you, Doctor, to go and see her immediately, for I fear she is in for a recurrence of her late illness. I hope that before long the overseer's wife will be here to nurse her."

"All right, I'll go to her at once," he replied, and straightway departed.

Braithwaite and the Inspector then went with me very carefully through the house and outbuildings. In the woodshed we found the two Chinese servants hiding in terror of their lives. They were brought out, and made to tell us all that had occurred to them. It appeared that late in the afternoon they heard angry voices on the verandah, and, cautiously looking out, they saw two men with pistols standing there, while another sat upon a horse at the foot of the steps and held two others. This was quite enough for them, and they made the best haste they could to the shelter of the woodshed, where they hid, in no peace of mind, however, for the sounds of shots and screams came to their terrified ears, and they feared every moment that the men would make their appearance and drag them out and murder them. We asked for a description, and from what we gathered there was little doubt but that Black and O'Connor were the assailants.

Having conveyed them back to the house, and somewhat allayed their fears, we ordered the preparation of a meal, and in the mean-time the overseer and his wife arrived in the buggy, convoyed by the hands.

It was to their general astonishment and grief that they learned of the terrible episodes that had taken place during the last few hours, and sincere and genuine were the expressions of sorrow and regret, for poor old Flaxman was a general favourite, beloved by every hand and jackaroo on the Station.

I gave orders that the whole place was to be gone over and carefully searched with lanterns, in case there should be any clue discovered that might guide us in the elucidation of the details of the murder; not that we wanted any further knowledge to tell us who the criminals were.

It only remained for us now to convey the body of my friend from the dining—room to his room, which we did very reverently, and laid him on the bed and covered him with a sheet; then passed out and locked the door.

Meanwhile, the rooms had been set in order and a meal laid for us, which we sat down to. Although I was in no mood to eat, I forced myself to do so, as I knew that it would do me good after the long ride that I had done, not to mention the troubles that I had gone through since.

The Doctor came in to take some food, and while doing so he informed us that Moira was now in a most critical condition, and that, at the time, he could only hold out the very slightest hope of her recovery. I knew he must think very badly of the state of his patient if he was forced to take this gloomy view of her condition. He must have seen how very much I was affected by what he told us, for he promised that he would leave nothing undone to restore her to health, but that we must be prepared for the worst.

My state of mind when I realised what he meant was too sorrowful for words. I was utterly cast down and wretched. The loss of my best friend was bad enough, but the thought that I might most probably lose Moira was a blow that utterly unnerved me. So miserable was I that I felt everything was against me. My God, what if she did die! There would be nothing left for me to live for, all the charm and pleasure in life would be gone with her. I was in such a nervous and wretched state of mind that the Doctor insisted on my going to bed, and came and himself administered a sleeping draught, in the hope that when the morning arrived I should be better and ready to start with the others to endeavour to trace the murderers to their hiding—place.

With sleep came peace, and the next thing that I knew was the sensation of being shaken by Braithwaite at dawn.

CHAPTER XVI

AFTER THE STORM, PEACE.

It did not take me long to jump out of bed, and get through my toilet. On arriving in the dining-room, I found breakfast awaiting us, and the Doctor sitting down to it. I told him that I had slept well after the draught he had given me, then eagerly enquired how Moira was.

He looked at me with a sly smile, as if he suspected that I was in love with her, and then informed me that she was, if anything, a shade better—certainly no worse. He also told me that he did not intend leaving his patient until he had satisfied himself that there was a great and lasting improvement in her condition, and further, that I might go away perfectly easy in my mind, knowing that she was in good hands, so delighted was he with the attention and unswerving devotion that the overseer's wife paid to the poor girl.

I thanked him again and again for all his kindness, and told him how very much happier I felt in my mind, now that I knew so much was being done for her. He replied by jokingly telling me that if I wished to complete the cure that he had begun, it would be necessary for me to return pretty quickly, or I should find that he would be standing in my shoes, so deeply was he interested in Moira. I felt myself blushing like a school-girl, as I looked at him. I held out my hand to say good-bye, and he warmly shook it, wishing me a successful journey, and a speedy return.

Having stowed away a plentiful supply of sandwiches in my pocket, against the time of famine, I mounted my horse and rode off to join Braithwaite and the Superintendent at the slip-rails.

Our object was to follow the tracks of the precious rascals, until we could ascertain the position of their hiding place; then, should the opportunity occur, endeavour to surround and take them.

Braithwaite, the Superintendent, three troopers, and myself constituted the expedition, with Snowball as tracker, and no cleverer one existed than he. No bent twig, broken branch, hoof-print, or other Bush mark ever escaped his vigilant eye. He could tell to the hour what length of time had passed since a mob of cattle had gone over ground by the state of their tracks; and moreover, he could faithfully inform one whether a horse was tired or not, by the mark of its hoof. Such is the wonderful gift possessed by the Australian aborigine, that he can find his way by instinct through the very thickest scrub, and follow an almost imperceptible trail with certainty, where the best white man living is nonplussed. The Bush is an open book to him, which he reads as he runs, by sign and symbol; and it is an extremely rare occurrence to find him making any mistakes.

As we had very earnest business to transact this time, it behoved us to move with the greatest caution, knowing as we did, that we were about to deal with very desperate men, to whom the shedding of blood was of little or no account, so long as they were able to resist being taken; but it was a thousand to one that if we were successful in locating them, before we could effect a capture, we should have to be prepared for a stiff fight.

It was, therefore, necessary to be ready for any emergency, so, before starting, I slipped a heavy revolver and plenty of cartridges into my pocket, for I was determined that Black and the other rascal should not escape me, whatever else happened. My poor friend's death was on their hands, and I had sworn to avenge it before I took any rest. The feeling upon me now was one of an overwhelming desire to get within touch of the scoundrels, to come to close quarters, so that we might settle accounts once and for all. I had made up my mind to bring Black to book, or to die in the attempt, and was in a feverish state of anxiety to be off on the mission.

One of the troopers was told off to lead a pack horse, laden with a good supply of provisions, in case it was necessary for us to encamp, while each man carried food for his beast, as we might have to enter districts where there would be difficulty in obtaining sufficient grass for them.

The first thing to be done before setting out was to examine carefully the imprints of the hoofs; then, having satisfied ourselves that there were three horses, we started, and began to track them across our best pastures, and then away into the scrub, following Snowball, who trotted along before us, gazing on the ground to right and left with the keenest scrutiny, missing nothing.

It was not long before we began to get into the sandy district, where the imprints were extremely easy to follow, for we could plainly see that they had been riding abreast. But we were at a loss to understand why it was that they did not try to cover their tracks, as, up to the present, the work was simplicity itself. However, we were destined to find that we were not to have everything plain sailing and agreeable.

For hours we followed the patient Snowball, who spoke no word to anyone, but kept his eyes fixed earnestly upon the ground. At length we began to leave the plains and to ascend into the Ranges, coming across large rocks and stones, where the going was extremely difficult and trying. The sand had given place to small stones, and the prints of the hoofs were almost impossible to distinguish. Many and many a time we were at a loss to see any whatever.

At last, Snowball had to confess that we were without evidence of the path that they had taken. So we halted and held a council of war, when it was decided to take a rest and get some food, as by this time we were very hungry; whereupon we hobbled our horses and left them to forage for what grass they could find, while we set ourselves down to our improvised meal.

I questioned Snowball as to what he thought of the prospect of our coming up with them, but the only reply I could get out of him was, "On, up. On, up." So it was pretty evident that he considered they were making for the highest point in the Ranges. Having satisfied the pangs of hunger, we lit our pipes, and watched the black endeavouring to find further traces to follow. He carefully examined every stone, right and left, and at last seemed interested in a mark that he saw upon a white, smooth rock, that no one but himself would ever have noticed. When I perceived that he had discovered what looked like a clue, I went over, and was told that he was quite sure one of the riders had touched this rock with his boot as he passed by, and sure enough, this one led to others that we came across as we moved further on.

Having satisfied ourselves that we were not mistaken, I returned to Braith-waite and informed him what Snowball had discovered. He then gave orders that we should mount. In a very few minutes we were again following the black, who was more careful than ever to note any apparent clue that might guide us. Soon we reached a fairly level plateau of sand, and here we discovered the tracks to be very distinct: so much so, that it must have dawned upon the riders that they might easily be followed, for they now separated, and took different directions, riding to three points at the distant edge of the plateau; but fortunately for us, and unfortunately for them, our guide was aware of a peculiarity in the shape of the hoof of O'Connor's horse, and as we knew that the rascal was in the habit of finding his places of refuge in the Ranges, it was well worth our while to follow him, for the others would most probably go to his hiding-place eventually. With that end in view, Snowball began to search for the hoof mark that he required; and, sure enough, we found that it led to a very narrow and difficult path, while each of the others passed to easy and broad ones. However, we felt that we were now on the right track. It was a very toilsome and trying path to follow: up and up we went, round great boulders and sharp corners; ground over which, under any other circumstances, we should never have thought of taking a horse.

Before long we arrived at a very great height, and we began to feel the difference in the temperature: the air had become keen and chilly, and our thin clothes did not afford us sufficient warmth. However, the good must be taken with the bad, and it was no use thinking of luxury, although I must confess, I could have done with a good, warm coat.

The path had by this time become so narrow that not only had we to go in single file, but the walls of rock touched our legs on either side as we proceeded on our way; and in many cases, it was the tightest of fits to get through at all. Higher and higher we went, until I began to wonder if we should come out right at the summit. Now straight before us we saw the track leading directly upwards. It was little more than a narrow cleft in the rock, caused, most likely, by the action of tremendous torrents of rain, that had found their way in this manner to the plains for centuries, and had thereby worn this immensely long passage.

As we toiled upward, we could look above us and see the rocky walls towering over fifty feet high on each side, with a thin line of blue sky above, and little or no light below to guide us. It looked as if the passage was endless, but at last I distinguished a point of light, that seemed to come from the left, near the ground; and this, no doubt, was an opening to the world once more.

All the time that we were in this cutting, there was a bitter cold wind tearing down the narrow, funnel-like passage, that chilled one to the bone, and numbed the very marrow. It was an extremely trying time, and I was most anxious to get to the end of it. My teeth were chattering in my head like so many castanets, while my hands were absolutely numbed with cold, so that I could hardly continue to hold the reins. At last I was forced to dismount and lead my horse, as I could stand it no longer, and my example was followed by the others who, no doubt, were suffering quite as badly as I was, although my body, and that of my horse, must have kept a little of the bitter blast from them.

Over the rough stones we stumbled, dragging our poor, tired beasts after us, and I never remember a more difficult or arduous task; it seemed as if we were never to reach that streak of light which, like a will o' the wisp, appeared to move further and further away the quicker we travelled. Snowball kept bravely on in front, guiding us with unflagging energy, never relaxing his scrutiny for one minute; I could not help admiring the marvellous patience and hardiness that kept him going, where we, mounted men, were almost done.

At length, after exhausting efforts, we approached near enough to make out that the shaft of light came from a turn in the passage, and soon we were rewarded for our toils and tribulations by seeing the end of the cleft only a short distance in front.

I hurried forward, and emerged upon a flat plateau, covered with short, mountain grass almost like peat, where we revelled in the warm rays of the declining sun, which after the chill of the last portion of our ride was comfort itself.

The plateau was about one hundred and fifty feet long, by some fifty feet broad, bounded on three sides by towering cliffs of rock, quite perpendicular. On the remaining side there was a precipice of the most awe-inspiring nature. I tied my horse to a jagged rock, and then proceeded to look over the edge, and nothing could equal the solemn grandeur of the scene that met my astonished gaze.

The precipice fell away sheer, hundreds and hundreds of feet, and my brain reeled at the awful depth of blackness far below me. A few cruel-looking, jagged rocks jutted out here and there, as if they were set for the purpose of impaling the unfortunate human being who had the ill luck to tumble over the edge. Directly in front of me, about three hundred yards distant, rose another wall of black rock, towering hundreds of feet into the air, stabbing the sky with a keen, serrated edge; while the whole valley or gorge was shrouded in the deepest purple shadow, except away to the left, where a glorious glimpse of plain lay bathed in sunlight far down beneath us; and it was truly one of the grandest, and yet most dreadful views that I had ever looked upon.

Braithwaite joined me, and for a long time we gazed in profound silence. Suddenly there came up from the depths of the grim blackness of the silent gorge a rush of wind that tore howling and shrieking along, just as if ten thousand furies were at war; and then it passed off into the distance, and we were left again to the silence of the mountain, except for the whirr of the wings of an immense eagle, that flew up, disturbed by the rush of wind, and soared away into the sky.

I looked around, when silence came once more, to the scared faces of the men who had joined us to gaze at the view, and I don't think I ever saw anything like the expressions thereon. I am quite ready to confess, too, that never had I experienced such a feeling of absolute awe, as was impressed upon me by this tremendous episode.

"By gad! Tregaskis," said Braithwaite, as he stepped back three or four paces and gazed around, "It's just like the entrance to Dante's Inferno. I cannot bear to think what would happen if one of us were to fall over."

"No, it's too gruesome to think about," I answered; "but, I say, I wonder where this place leads to. Look at Snowball! He surely doesn't expect us to take our horses round there. By Jove! I don't believe they'd ever do it."

We both turned and watched the black, who had passed along to the right, and close to the precipice edge. Presently, he disappeared round the corner of the immense cliff, and was lost to view.

Braithwaite agreed with me that it would be most hazardous and foolhardy to attempt to take horses round a cliff such as that, with a track less than six feet wide to pass along, and a sheer drop of thousands of feet. If one should happen to fall! It made my blood run cold to think of it. So we agreed to camp there for the night. Leaving the men to endeavour to find something to make a fire with, I accompanied Braithwaite to see what he made of the pathway, and to have a talk with Snowball. We passed to the corner, and found that the track did not widen out at all, and was worn quite smooth by the rains of ages.

After passing the rock, we found Snowball examining tracks, and we came upon fairly smooth land. Here the walls of rock began to decrease, until we were able to scramble over them, and see for a comparatively long distance ahead. It appeared evident that we were nearly at the summit of the Ranges. Suddenly it dawned upon Braithwaite that Black and O'Connor were endeavouring to get right over the mountains, and away on the other side, and the more we thought of it, the more certain this appeared to be.

Turning my gaze around, I called Braithwaite's attention to the sky, which now portended a severe storm. Great masses of lurid cloud were tearing up from the West, magnificently coloured by the declining sun, but wild and angry to an alarming degree; and it behoved us to hurry back to the plateau. Just as we arrived there, the light began to fade, and very soon it was dark. We found that the men, on searching about, had discovered a long, lofty cave, which would prove a most useful and warm resting-place for the night, as there was not the slightest doubt that we were in for a bad storm.

They had managed to dig up the turf, which was quite dry and tinder-like, and would burn excellently; so in the mouth of the cave we lit a fire, and very soon "billy" cans were in requisition, and tea was boiling.

We gave the horses their feed, and tied them out of harm's way at the back of the cave, where they would be warm, and not liable to stampede, with the possible chance of falling over the precipice if they did so.

It was a most extraordinary and weird scene that I looked upon, as I walked a short distance off. The fire, blazing away at the mouth of the cave, flung up great flames, which lit up the surrounding rocks and boulders into rugged relief, casting immense shadows of intense blackness on every side. When a figure passed in front of the fire, the shadow was tremendously magnified on the distant wall of rock. As I first caught a glimpse of it, I was astonished at the awful effect it produced. To add to the already weird and uncanny nature of the place, the wind began to rise, and there came the same fierce rushes of sound that we had experienced before sundown, the same shrieks and howls, most human and terrifying in their intensity, far down in the gorge below, which made everyone of us sit bolt upright to listen.

I could plainly see that we were in for an experience that was beyond anything I had ever known in my life.

We had agreed that two should take turns to watch for a couple of hours during the night, and as soon as our meal was finished, the Superintendent and one of the troopers took their carbines, and went to the mouth of the cave. The rest of us wrapped our blankets round us, and with our feet to the fire, endeavoured to get some sleep. It was a long while before this could be accomplished in my case, owing to the roar and shriek of the wind outside the cave. In fact, the most terrific storm was raging, and every now and then appalling peals of thunder crashed overhead, with the most brilliant forked lightning following, which added still more to the terrors of the night, while I could hear the rain lashing down in perfect torrents continuously.

At last my exhausted brain could act no longer, and I sank into a troubled sleep, only to dream of horrors and murders, until at last I felt myself violently shaken, and, starting up, found Braithwaite kneeling over me in the light of the fire, dripping with water from head to foot.

"Your turn, George, old man," he said; "and I wish you luck of it. By gad, it's hell out there. Look!"

I did look, and saw such a flash of lightning as I never believed could have occurred. It was immediately followed by the most tremendous peal of thunder, that shook the entire mountain to its base, and we could distinctly hear enormous rocks falling on all sides. It was the nearest approach to an earthquake that I ever knew. Then the rain came again in a deluge beyond words. It lashed down in furious cascades on all sides. Luckily, the men had been wise enough to pile the peat in the cave, or the fire would have been completely extinguished.

Calling the trooper who was to take his watch with mine, I told him to put more peat on, and as he complied with my request and the flames leapt up afresh, I looked out of the cave, and noticed that there was a perceptible sign of dawn coming up. As I gazed towards the cliff corner, to my astonishment I saw in the dim light a figure riding a terrified horse round the corner, right at the edge of the precipice. At first I thought it must have been imagination on my part. I could hardly believe my senses. I rubbed my eyes and looked again. Yes, there was absolutely no doubt about it. I called softly to Braithwaite, who was standing drying his clothes at the fireside, and he came over on hearing me.

"Look; can you see a man coming round the cliff there?" I whispered, pointing to the spot.

We both gazed with the utmost eagerness at the place, when suddenly another terrible flash of lightning came, followed instantly by a crash of thunder more awful than before, and to our horror we saw the horse rear straight up in the air. Right on the edge of the ghastly precipice horse and rider stood for a second or two, and then both fell back into the abyss. Never as long as I live shall I forget the heartrending shrieks that man and horse gave vent to, as they dropped thousands of feet down, to be dashed to pieces on the cruel rocks below.

Only a few seconds passed when another figure appeared, that we easily recognised as O'Connor; but he was wiser and led his horse. We saw him go to the edge of the chasm, and heard him cry out, "Black, Black"—but there came no answering voice, except the echo of his own.

Braithwaite called out to me to come on, and we both rushed to the place where he stood. He turned and saw us. In a second, he took a spring for the saddle, but his horse swerved round, and before we could utter a word, slipped on to his knees, throwing the rider completely over his head. The man still held the reins, and hung there with this flimsy rope alone between himself and eternity. The horse struggled and tried to regain its footing, but nothing could save it, and at last it overbalanced, and both disappeared. I covered my face with my hands to shut out the horrible sight, but the cry the wretch gave as he felt himself falling into the abyss, will ring in my brain as long as I live.

Never shall I be able to banish this awful tragedy from my mind. Bad as these men were, it was a most terrible end, even for them: so sudden and unexpected, not one moment given them for repentance—hurled into eternity in the twinkling of an eye! To me, this was most harrowing; even the feeling that poor Flaxman was avenged had passed away, and only the sincerest sorrow remained.

Nothing could be done now but to return to the cave and await the day. Sitting around the fire, in hushed and awed tones, we discussed the tragedy, while we listened to the storm outside, that was slowly passing away, just as if it had completed its work and earned its rest. All the while I thought of those poor wretched creatures lying dead and mangled upon the rocks below in that deep and black chasm. God forgive them for their sins, which they had so awfully expiated!

At last it was quite daylight, and we went out to find the world bathed in sunlight, and a blue sky above us. Surely, a good omen of halcyon days to come! While breakfast was being prepared, Braithwaite accompanied me to the corner where the accident happened, and we could see the awful folly of the deed. They must have been in great straits to have attempted such a thing. We shall never know the cause of their return, but, no doubt, the thunder-storm had cast down some natural bridge which they had expected to pass over. However, it was certain that we should never again be troubled by Black or O'Connor in this life. We did not concern ourselves about the other man. Whoever he was, no doubt he got off scot-free.

We peered over the edge of the precipice, but could see nothing; most likely they struck rocks at once, and then bounded off and fell far below to a spot hidden from our view. We therefore returned once more to the cave, and found breakfast ready. Having eaten, we started to descend to the plains. The return was almost as difficult as the climb up, but so very anxious was I to get back to the Station with the greatest speed, that I did not notice it.

When we reached the lowlands, Braithwaite suggested that the Superintendent and troopers with Snowball as guide, should endeavour to enter the gorge, to see if the bodies could be discovered and identified; and to that end they set out, while we went on to Montalta.

In due course, we saw the familiar roofs of the place before us, and I can assure you, I was very thankful to dismount at the horse-paddock, and walk up to the verandah with my friend. Tears forced themselves into my eyes as I looked at the place, so peaceful and pretty, nestling in its wealth of foliage, for it reminded me so keenly of the dear companion lying dead upon his bed within, waiting to be taken to his final resting place.

The Doctor sat on the verandah smoking his pipe, and he rose to welcome us. I immediately enquired for Moira, and was delighted to hear that she was making the best of progress. I was told that I must get someone to take her away to the sea for a month or two, where she could recover her health and strength, for within a week she would be in a state of convalescence, and fit to travel. This was indeed good news, and I immediately despatched a letter to our old friend, Mrs. Dawson, the good lady who had been the innocent cause of my quarrel with Flaxman. I told her all the terrible events that had happened at the Station, and asked her whether she would arrange to go with Moira for two months' holiday? If so, would she come to me at once?

Later on the Superintendent returned, with the information that Snowball had led them to the gorge, where they had discovered the bodies of the men and horses, fearfully mangled, at the foot of the precipice, and after they had been identified, they were buried.

The next few days were spent in going through the legal formalities made necessary by the nature of Flaxman's death; but at last we were given permission to bury him. A grave had been prepared close to those that contained the remains of the late owner's wife and son. My heart was full of the most intense grief when I laid my dear friend and companion at rest for his long sleep, and never since have I been able to shake off the feeling of void that his passing away has caused me. Now that I have everything else in the world that man can wish for, I still want him back, and yet there is a comfort in the thought that we parted good friends. God rest his soul!

After the funeral, it was necessary for me to go through poor Flaxman's papers, and in his desk I discovered a will, leaving everything he possessed equally between Moira and myself; and I also found that I was appointed executor. By this will, we inherited an estate in England jointly, as well as his share of the Stations in Australia.

There were also two letters, both sealed and addressed, one to Moira and one to myself, and the latter I proceeded to open and read:—

"My very dear friend,

"Something is warning me that my days are numbered. Soon, God knows best when, I shall be gone from you for ever. I know, dear friend, that this will cause you pain when you read it, but the knowledge of my great friendship for you, and yours for me, will, I hope, comfort you in your sorrow.

"It is incumbent upon me to tell you something of my life's history, and I hope that you will therefore bear with me for a while.

"Many years ago, I married a girl whom I loved beyond expression. For one short year I was extremely happy, until an enemy crept into my wife's heart, and, God forgive her! she left me for him.

"I do not complain now, since the Almighty has worked out the end as He has appointed, and His ways are always the best, although we poor instruments of His Divine Will seem often to see in them nothing but disaster.

"I could not bring myself to divorce her, but tried to live alone at my place in Cornwall, and to endeavour to forget her, but that I found was quite impossible. I stood it for five years, and began to think that the wound was healing, until I received a letter, forwarded by a firm of solicitors in Adelaide, and written by my poor wife, informing me that she had a daughter who was my child, and imploring me to protect and love it, and to forgive her the wrong she had done me, for which she was now paying so dearly; giving me at the same time an address in Adelaide where the child was to be found.

"I hastened with all speed to Australia, and to the address given in Adelaide, only to find that the child had been taken away one year before by a man who stated that he was the father. Heartbroken at my want of success, I called on the solicitors, who showed me a will they had received but had been unable to prove, as there was no one to prove it, the child having mysteriously disappeared. For years I searched high and low without finding any clue; but at last, utterly worn out, I took a position at Mr. Wilberforce's Station, Carrandara. Then I met you, and up to the time of Moira's coming, have known what real happiness means.

"Then you brought Moira. I don't blame you for that, but acknowledge that it was the working of God's mysterious ways.

"I saw, directly I met her, a wonderful likeness to my wife; and yet I hardly dared to think that such a coincidence could be true.

"I learnt to love her, feeling all the while that she was my own daughter; but I fear that I did not realise how others would take this affection. One day she told me that she was pained to see her presence at Montalta was causing bitterness between us two friends, and that there was nothing left but for her to go. I tried to dissuade her, and told her that it would all come right, and that, if she went away again, it would break my heart. God knows, I meant it, too. Oh! how I longed to tell her who I really was, to be able to protect and guard her as a father should. But I dared not. I had to substantiate it first.

"The next day she went away, and you remember what occurred— our one quarrel. She wrote us each a letter, but made me promise not to shew you mine until she had been gone a month.

"I enclose it now, and you will understand when you read it. I shall be dead. George, she is my daughter. Something tells me that I shall prove it before I die.

"Marry her, George, and make her happy. Love her for my sake, and for her own.

"God bless and protect you, dear friend, always, and give you every happiness you desire. "Yours in death."

"ROBERT FLAXMAN."

When I finished this letter, I sat dazed; my head swam. The poor fellow, so true, so kind and loving—what his suffering must have been, God alone knows! How true his words all were. No doubt, God did let him find out the truth, at the brink of the grave, when the brute Black came face to face with the man that he betrayed so long ago, and shot him dead.

I opened Moira's letter to him, and read—

"My dear Mr. Flaxman,—

"My heart tells me that I must go away. For weeks I have noticed that both you and Mr. Tregaskis are strained in your behaviour towards one another; and I cannot help seeing that it is on my account.

"I am not worthy to be here. If you only knew the depths of degradation that I have been forced into, both by my father and my husband, you would turn me away, although I feel sure you would pity me.

"But I am tortured to think that harm may come to you both by reason of my presence. For weeks I have been watched here by a scoundrel, who threatens if I do not give him a letter which is in my possession, and which implicates my husband and my father in a terrible crime, he will take steps to burn the place down, and I know only too well that he will keep his word.

"My heart is near to breaking point now, as I write, for here is the only place where I have known what happiness and respect mean. To lose two such true and noble friends cuts me to the heart, but it is best for all.

"Don't shew this letter to Mr. Tregaskis, I ask you on your word of honour, until I have been gone a month; I want him, more than anyone, to think well of

"Yours.

"MOIRA PENDRAGON."

I rose from my chair as I finished the letter, and paced the room in an agony of mind. How it brought all back to me again! That miserable, wretched business, my jealous brutality, my ungovernable and impetuous temper. What a fool I had been! What a contemptible cur! God knows that I was being bitterly punished for it now, but not more than I deserved.

I felt that the only possible return I could make was to endeavour to try and cause Moira's life to be happy as long as I lived.

I took up the letter addressed to her, and after having locked up the will in my desk, I passed out on to the verandah, where she was sitting in a deep chair with a book on her knee.

"Moira," I said softly, and took a seat close to her, "I want to speak to you, on business matters."

She looked up at me with a smile which spread like a ray of sunlight over her thin, pale face. Her dark-rimmed, sad eyes told of the unutterably horrible time that she had passed through, and I promised myself inwardly that I must change all this at once.

"Well, what is it?" she replied, closing her book.

I felt very nervous when I realised what I had to say to the poor girl, for in her present delicate state of health, I knew that I must be extremely careful; but the matter had to be gone through, and the sooner it was over and done with, the better.

"I've just been through poor Flaxman's papers, and have found his will; in it I see that we are appointed his joint heirs."

"We?" she said slowly; "I don't quite understand you."

"What I mean is, that he leaves everything to us both, jointly—Moira Pendragon and George Tregaskis."

"I—I really don't understand," she reiterated, "he surely cannot leave me anything; I was nothing whatever to him."

"Don't you be so sure of that, my dear girl," I replied. "I don't want to distress you, but I think that it is only right to let you know that I have found, with his will, this letter, written by Flaxman before his death;" and I handed over my letter, which she read in silence. When she came to the end she turned scarlet, but I went on—

"Now, I happen to be able to verify all this, if it is necessary, but I think you had better read a letter that he has left for you."

I gave her the note addressed to her in Flaxman's handwriting. When she had finished this, she burst into tears. It read—

"My dearest Moira,—

"I, who am dead, yet speak. The good God has told me that you are my child. Your poor mother, who was more to me than words can express, left me for another, but I have forgiven her. You are mine: I know this is true. George Tregaskis loves you; marry him, and he will tell you all.

"From your loving father.

"ROBERT FLAXMAN."

"Oh! George," she cried, as I finished the letter, "somehow I know it's true. I can never rid my mind of the horror of seeing my true father facing that terrible man in the dining-room; I heard what was said before the shot was fired that killed him. Oh! my God, my God, it's too awful."

"Moira, Moira, my darling," I cried, as I flung myself on my knees before her, and took her thin white hand in mine. "I love you, I always have, ever since we first met, and I want you to learn to love me, so that I may make you happy always."

"Oh! don't, don't," she replied. "You cannot tell, you do not know what you are saying. I am not worthy of your love. If you only knew the true story of my life, you would—"

"Moira, I don't want to know anything at all; all I want is you, yourself. I know enough to make me register a solemn vow to give you for the rest of your life as much happiness as ever I can. Will you marry me, and make me happy?"

What she eventually said in reply is sacred to me, and is not for the reader's ears. It is sufficient to say, I went about my work afterwards a bright and cheerful man, where only a few hours since I was a gloomy and miserable one. The reader can, no doubt, gather what caused this change.

As for Moira—well—when Mrs. Dawson arrived three days later, she did not appear to think that there was any cause for alarm in Moira's condition. However, I packed them both off to the sea, with instructions that certain preparations were to be made forthwith.

When they had departed, I set about finding a purchaser for Montalta, for I had determined to sell it, lock, stock, and barrel. It was not long before I found one willing to give a good price, and having completed the purchase, I joined Moira, and our wedding took place, with Mrs. Dawson as sole witness.

After a short honeymoon, we started for England, to take up our abode in Flaxman's ancestral Cornish home, where I can see the blue sea and the ships passing, some of them on their way to Australia. It seems years since the occurrence of the events that constitute the foregoing tale, but in reality it is only just two years ago.

To say that I am happy is to put it too mildly. With such a wife as Moira, who could be anything else? I can see her now, as I sit here writing; she is walking in the garden carrying something, of which she seems inordinately proud. It's name is Robert Flaxman Tregaskis, and I pray to God that he will turn out as good and worthy a man as was my partner Flaxman.